Where a Wave
Meets the Shore

Where a Wave Meets the Shore

Kathryn Guare (signature)

KATHRYN GUARE

KILTUMPER
CLOSE
PRESS

Kiltumper Close Press
Montpelier, VT
kiltumperclose.com

ISBN-10: 0-9911893-3-7

ISBN-13: 978-0-9911893-3-5

There was no part in Ireland I did not travel,
From the rivers to the tops of the mountains,
To the edge of Lough Greine whose mouth is hidden
And I saw no beauty but was behind hers.

- Antoine Ó Raifteirí
18th century Irish poet

1

Ireland, Dingle Peninsula, 1952

*O*n *the day he met Brigid O'Sullivan, he caught her by surprise. That was hard to do, but Tom McBride wouldn't realize that until later, when he knew her better. On that afternoon—a brilliant one, the sky bluer than the Virgin's holy robe—he knew only that he'd happened upon the most beautiful girl he'd seen in all his twenty-two years, and that he'd frightened the life out of her.*

In fairness, though, she'd startled him as well. He hadn't expected to see anyone half so lovely when he'd set out on the water that day, ferrying a government officer over to the Great Blasket Island. The fellow had been at Regan's the night before, arriving just as that evening's session was getting underway...

In the low-ceilinged pub, it seemed half the town had gathered, in the way crowds often form—responding to one man's opinion that grows to a rumor before swelling to the firm expectation of a mighty night. Regan himself was sweating behind the bar, serving out pints as fast as the barman could pull them. There was hardly the width of a floorboard left to stand on, but until a few minutes earlier, the space next to the door had remained empty, protected by an invisible boundary that few would dare cross. It was the musicians' corner, and if you sat in it you'd better be planning to give out a tune.

Tom was planning exactly that as he squeezed in between the regulars and pressed his back against the unforgiving oak bench. He'd already lifted the fiddle to his shoulder when the stranger entered, a pudgy, round-faced man, punched through the door by a dose of the wind that had been blowing off Dingle Harbor all day.

The cold gust followed him in, but had no chance against the air inside, which had grown tropical with the collective breath and bluster of a packed house. It took a final swipe as it retreated, lifting the feathery hair on the man's head until it stood out like the ruff of an orange tabby. Tom lowered the fiddle and stared.

"Will you look at yer jackeen in the suit." His uncle Patsy's gravel-edged voice rose to a squeak, as if an exotic zoo animal had stepped into the pub and asked for a pint. "That's a Dublin man, and no mistake. I'll wager a week's catch he's one of de Valera's boys."

Along with every man present, Tom reflexively tensed as he eyed the middle-aged stranger. He was clearly from the city, but it was hard to see how Patsy had connected him with their *Taoiseach*—the prime minister, Eamon de Valera.

"What's he want with us?" Tom asked.

Patsy snorted. "What do they ever want? Our money and our tears."

In this instance, the stranger wanted neither. He confirmed Patsy's intuition, but he wasn't there to trouble any of them. He was from the Irish Land Commission, and his business was with the islanders on the Great Blasket, which he intended to visit the next day. Tonight he was no government officer. He was Dan O'Brien from Tralee and he was there for the craic.

Dan was fond of music and stout in equal parts, and after several pints of the latter he proclaimed himself a dab hand with a pair of spoons. The musicians allowed him to sit in, providing he bought them a round and stopped trying to speak to them in Irish. Although game in the attempt, the Dubliner had only a schoolboy's grasp of the language, and their ears couldn't bear the unholy mess he made of it.

By the end of the evening they'd adopted him as one of their own. Nursing a final pint while the barman stacked chairs around them and wearily called "Time, please," they took turns quizzing him about his plans.

"You'll get no boat to the Blasket tomorrow if this wind keeps up, and that's a solid fact." Dennis O'Connell pulled a powerful sniff up through his prodigious nose, indicating no opposing view was worth considering. Patsy gave Tom a private wink.

"Who have you lined up to take you across?" Tom asked.

Fixing an eye on his own private horizon, Dan took a pull from his glass before answering.

"Nobody."

Patsy hooted. "Nobody, is it? Sure you've done well, Dan.

'Nobody' is a fine sailor. You'll be safe as houses with him."

The remark prompted a unified roar of laughter, but Dan only shrugged. "I thought perhaps one of you lads might take an interest. The landlady where I'm staying told me this pub is crawling with fishermen."

"I'd say you've left it too late," Patsy said. "The fishermen are after crawling home to their beds, now."

"Except for you, Patsy."

All heads turned towards the piping voice of Donal "Tiny" Quinn, who sat wedged into a corner, pinned against the bench like a beetle under glass. At eighty-two, Tiny was still the best accordionist in all of Kerry, but now he pulled the cherry-red instrument around on a wagon, too small and too old to lift it on his own. For the pleasure of hearing him play, his friends were happy to hoist the thing onto his knees, but they sometimes forgot to remove it when the music stopped.

"Jaysus." Patsy rolled his eyes. "Tom, pull it off him before he's smothered."

Tom was a step ahead of the command, hurrying to the rescue and doing his best not to laugh. "Sorry, Tiny."

Ramping up the charm, de Valera's man from Dublin aimed a smile at his target that could have lit the dark side of the moon.

"You've a boat yourself then, Patsy."

"I do, Dan." Patsy lifted his own glass. After draining it, he stood and stretched, drawing himself to his full six feet. "And I've been ten days without a day off, so I'll not be putting a foot on it tomorrow, not even for a fine fellow like yourself, but Tom here will bring you over, so."

"I'll what, now?" Tom nearly dropped the accordion back onto Tiny's arthritic knees.

"He's only a farmer," Patsy continued, ignoring his nephew's yelp, "but he can manage a boat. He's been out on the sea with me often enough, from the time he could walk."

This was certainly true. Mixed in with the smell of silage and manure, Tom's earliest memories included the oily reek of his uncle's trawler – the first diesel-powered boat on the Dingle peninsula. With no interest in emigrating and limited options at home, his father's six brothers had divided themselves between two equally difficult livelihoods – three had decided to fish for a living while the others stayed in farming. Most were scattered across three counties now, from Kilrush to Skibbereen, but Tom's father had stayed in the area and settled on a farm above Ventry Harbor, and Patsy had remained as well.

"Go on, Tom." Patsy's voice trembled with laughter, enjoying his nephew's consternation. "Do you not want to help this poor man get to his meeting? The two of you will have a great day out on the water."

"Not if this wind keeps up … " Dennis started in again.

"Oh, you shut up now." Patsy waved him away, still grinning at his nephew.

Tom gave a noncommittal shrug, knowing the idea of a "day out on the water" would surely draw fire at home. Of his parents' four sons, Tom had been the only one to remain on the farm in Ventry, and while this came as a relief to his parents, both were skeptical – for different reasons – that he was cut out for the life of a farmer.

"He's a hard-working lad, but he hasn't the strength for it," his mother said to anyone who would listen. "It's because of the asthma. It's knocked him about since he was a baby."

"It's because he's a dreamer," his father insisted, often to the same audience. "The fiddle and the craic, that's all he cares about, but a fiddle won't hoe spuds or put his tea on the table, will it?"

Tom resented both arguments. He wasn't nearly as wheezy as when he was a boy, and although the time he spent with the fiddle was the best part of his day, he never picked it up before the work was done. He loved his parents, but at an early age he'd known his mother's anxious pessimism and his father's materialism and pride were nothing he wanted to emulate. His own cheerful temperament tracked closer to that of his uncle, who'd taught him to sail and fish, and to play the fiddle.

As Patsy well knew, Tom was always ready for a lark. He wouldn't mind bringing Dan over to the Blasket, but he wondered if it was worth the lecture he'd have to endure.

"I'm meant to be moving the cows into the back field tomorrow," he mumbled.

"Sure I'll be happy to go at your convenience." Dan turned his smile in Tom's direction. "I wouldn't dream of interfering with your work."

"I'm not sure how long I'll be."

"How's twelve o'clock, Tom? Will it suit you?" Dan was starting to sound more like a government man, hearing only the things that helped him and ignoring whatever didn't.

"I suppose twelve o'clock would be –"

"Grand, grand. We'll make it twelve, so. Now, where will I meet you?"

2

The following day, Dan O'Brien's breezy confidence was much diminished when he arrived at the pier. After apologizing for being an hour later than expected, he watched in alarm as Tom hopped from the landing into a small wooden dinghy tied next to it.

"I'd an idea of something a bit larger than this, Tom."

"Did you?" As he secured the outboard motor Tom squinted up at him, maintaining a neutral expression. "Well, we keep our boats fairly light and sporty out here in the west. I hope you aren't bothered by the odd shark? I thought maybe you'd sit in the prow and keep an eye out for them."

Already pale from the previous night's indulgence, Dan's face dropped a shade closer to transparency. Unable to keep a straight face, Tom lifted himself from the small boat into the fifty-foot trawler tied in front of it, and then—still laughing—he extended a helping hand up to his passenger.

"The dinghy is only for the last hundred yards, Dan. The Blasket has no deep-water pier."

When they pulled away, the sun was directly overhead, its

reflection on the water almost too bright to look at. The trawler scattered seagulls as it chugged along, with the dinghy trailing behind, slapping against the waves in its wake. As might be expected of someone carrying the title of land officer, Dan wasn't happy on the water, nor was he comfortably dressed for the occasion. Before they were even out of the harbor he'd become too warm in his brown tweed suit, and his matching brogues were already wet.

Sitting on a bench in the wheelhouse, he gripped the metal handrail next to him, lips pressed together in grim patience.

"About how long a journey would you say, Tom?"

"I'd say an hour and a half. Maybe less if it stays calm."

"Ah. It's a calm day, is it?" The boat bounced out of a shallow trough. Dan bounced with it and landed with a groan.

Standing at the wheel, far more comfortable in waterproof boots, a thin flannel shirt and twill pants, Tom gave him a nervous glance, and reached for the cooler near his feet. "I've a few bottles of red lemonade here, would you like one?"

"I would, Tom. Thank you." After several healthy slugs of the fizzy stuff, some of the color returned to Dan's cheeks and he seemed more fit for conversation. "We've a fine day for it, at any rate. It was lashing rain the last time I made this trip."

"You've been there before, then?" Tom shot him an amused scowl. "Who brought you over that time?"

"The government hired a ferry. On that occasion we were a great crowd of officials and dignitaries." Dan handed back the bottle of lemonade, two-thirds empty. "Have you been to the Great Blasket yourself, Tom?"

He shook his head. "I've seen every side of it from a boat, but I've never gone ashore."

"But you've a grasp of the island's history, of course."

"I do. Of course."

Of course, because, as Dan almost certainly knew, *Peig*, the autobiography of the Blasket's legendary storyteller Peig Sayers, was a required text for every secondary school student in the country. Tom's reading of it had given him an instinctive aversion to the place. He felt sorry for Peig's descendants, if any still existed; he couldn't remember how many had succumbed to disease or gone over the island's infamous cliffs.

The story of her life—gothic in its unrelenting hardship and written in a turgid style of Irish Gaelic—had won few fans, and much uncharitable commentary. Among his own mates, they'd speculated that Peig had lost so many relations because they'd run to the cliffs to get away from her.

He'd been left with an impression of the Great Blasket as a place of endless misfortune, filled with mournful, wizened people who believed in leprechauns and lived centuries behind the times. He'd never been inclined to pay it a visit, and thought it odd the Irish government would want to.

"Tell me about your meeting, then," he said, trying to distract his passenger from the motion of the boat as it headed into open water. "What sort of business do you have with the islanders?"

"Oh, it's a sad business, Tom." Dan sighed. "Heartbreaking, altogether."

"Sure it would have to be, wouldn't it?" Tom said drily. He adjusted course, moving farther away from the peninsula's rocky coast. "They've come to grief again, have they?"

"It will come soon enough. The Taioseach gets fairly romantic over notions of pastoral Ireland and the simple folk with their tales and traditions, but there's no future for the people out there anymore. Sooner or later, they'll have to come away, I'm afraid."

"Come away?" Startled, Tom dropped his hands from the wheel and turned to the land officer. "What, all of them, do you mean?"

"All of them, yes, but it's no great number. There's not more than a few dozen living there now, most with more years behind them than they have ahead. Most are ready to leave, I think. The younger generation have emigrated already – to London or America. They've hardly any women living there at all. The old men can't get out to fish anymore, and the supply of turf is running low. There's not a tree growing on the entire island, so they've nothing else to burn –"

"Sounds fairly desperate," Tom interrupted. Dan's litany was beginning to sound like a reading from the life of Peig. "But what's the Taoiseach, I mean 'the prime minister' got to do with it?"

Dan smiled. "You needn't translate that term, at least. I'm well familiar with it."

Before he could continue, a wave broke against the trawler's prow, sending a heavy spray of water against the wheelhouse window. He shifted, his tweeds catching and scraping against the splintered bench.

"Do you not need a hand clapped on to that wheel, Tom?" he pleaded. "Just the one, at least?"

He didn't, for the next few minutes anyway, but Tom humored him, wrapping his hand around a spoke of the mahogany wheel that his uncle kept polished to a high shine. "Go on, so."

"Well, it started five years ago, really. You remember the poor lad who died in '47?"

"I do. Sean Kearney." Tom grew more solemn. "Everyone around here remembers that."

It had happened at Christmas. They'd had dirty weather all over Ireland that month, but from Christmas Eve to the Epiphany, the storms never stopped. The wind tore the roof from a house in Ventry village, and the water breached the sea wall in Dingle, flooding the lower town. Usually there were evenings with the neighbors throughout the holidays, but nobody went visiting that year. Everyone stayed huddled inside, unaware of the tragedy unfolding on the Blasket.

Young Sean Kearney, only twenty-four years old, lay dying of meningitis, and with the radio phone knocked out and the mainland inaccessible, his family could only sit at his bedside, powerless to help him. He died before any boat could reach the island.

"Many in Dublin remember it as well," Dan said softly. "It was in the papers, and only a few months later the island was socked in again. They were out of food, but at least the radio was working. They wired a distress telegram straight to de Valera, begging him to send supplies. He got a boat over to them two days later, and made a visit to the island himself that summer—along with myself and others from the government—to see what could be done." Dan fell silent for a moment. "So *that's* what the Taioseach's got to do with it," he finally added.

Tom bobbed his head, acknowledging the tone of mild reproach. "And now he's sending you, to see what can be done."

"He is, but sure we all know what needs to happen. A sad business," Dan said again, and turned to face forward.

Tom followed his gaze. The Blasket was in view now, and he watched the island grow larger as they approached. It was beautiful, but also desolate and pitiless. No wonder they're ready to go, Tom thought. Why would they ever have wanted to stay?

⁓

Viewed from the nearest mainland village of Dunquin, much of the Great Blasket couldn't even be seen. It was a long, finger-shaped piece of land, with the tip pointing to America and the high ridge-line of its knuckle facing Ireland. Compared with the smaller islands farther out, it didn't appear very far away. On a clear day, anyone could look across at its white sand beach, and the little stone cottages sprinkled over a blanket of green, and think it looked a lovely spot to live.

Its looks were deceiving, though. Only after drawing near did it become clear the island might not be as benign as it appeared from a distance. It was actually three miles out in the North Atlantic, across a stretch of ocean that could turn treacherous in an instant.

The one and only village that looked so inviting from the mainland looked less so upon closer inspection. It sat on an acute, downhill slope several hundred feet above the shoreline. The rest of the island was even more steeply pitched, and all routes eventually ended with an abrupt drop into oblivion.

The high cliffs on every side were so sharp and vertical that it seemed as though the land had been sliced away with a surgeon's blade. At the base of the cliffs, the wind and sea pummeled the surrounding rocks, turning them into perilous, ragged shapes that no navigator in his right mind would approach, unless he was headed for the island's tiny harbor.

Tom kept a wary eye on the rocks as he steered the dinghy to the landing spot, which was no more than a stretch of uneven stone. A group of four men stood waiting for them, and he found it impossible to guess their ages. From their faces, patterned with lines and creases etched by fierce weather, he thought any one of them might be thirty-five or seventy.

The men had sized up Dan O'Brien before they even reached the shore. For a minute, they focused all attention on him, murmuring encouragements as they deftly lifted him from the boat and set him upright on a patch of dry rock that served as the island's pier. Far from feeling slighted, Tom was grateful. Getting Dan into the dinghy had been hair-raising enough. He'd been dreading the prospect of trying to get him out of it.

Unaided, he hopped from the dinghy himself, and as he dragged it onto the ramp, the eldest man (although Tom wasn't entirely certain of that) approached and offered a shy greeting.

"God save you," he said, in English.

"God and Mary save you," Tom replied in Irish, smiling at the man's surprise.

"You have some Irish?" his host marveled, continuing in that language.

"It's what we speak where I come from, sir. I'm not from Dublin. I'm only a farmer from the Gaeltacht. Ventry, over across the way."

The others received this news warmly, coming forward to

shake hands. They were dressed very much alike, in dark zippered sweaters, wool trousers and hobnailed boots, the only diversity in fashion being their hats. All had flat caps, but two wore them unfastened, and one wore his cocked at an angle.

As they continued talking, Tom was struck by the difference between his speech and theirs. He understood them perfectly, but the Blasket dialect sounded strange to his ears. It gave him an odd feeling. He had little patience for the superstitions and otherworldly legends some of his brethren loved so well, but listening to the courtly, antiquated form of Gaelic these men spoke, he felt as though he'd stumbled upon *Tir na nÓg*–the "Land of Youth"–and into the presence of long-dead ancestors.

Dan, who had very little Irish himself (and what little he had was painful to hear) was at a greater disadvantage. Tom saw he would need to facilitate, and that it would be a delicate business.

"Such a suit of clothes. I've never seen the like." The man with the angled cap, whose name was Petey, was gently teasing the Dublin man. "Did it come from America?"

"He's, ehm … admiring your suit," Tom said, answering Dan's questioning glance.

"You'd make a fine diplomat, Tom. I've no doubt he's having a laugh at it, and so he should. I haven't a clue why I'm wearing the bloody thing. Now, should we walk up? If you're ready?"

This last question Dan addressed to the men in tortured Irish with a bright smile, and Tom liked him all the better for it. Their hosts appeared to share his opinion. They laughed and nodded, then led them to the steep, slick crevice in the hillside that would bring them up to the village.

On the way, they passed the island's small armada of fishing vessels, which Dan admired. Already panting from the climb, he paused on the hill and made a point of inspecting the boats more closely.

"These are fine currachs."

"*Naomhóg*," one of the men gently corrected.

"Nah-vogue? A holy …" Confused, Dan looked at Tom, who nodded a confirmation.

"Right. 'Little holy one' is the closest translation, I suppose. It's a currach most everywhere else, but in Kerry we call it a naomhóg."

The boats were upside down, carefully perched on sturdy wooden stands, and as they started climbing again, Tom caught a whiff of the tar covering their canvassed hulls. They lay glossy black, like the skins of seals, growing hot in the afternoon sun. Petey ran his hand over one of them as they passed.

"As good as any motorboat. Light and fast." He winked at Tom. "We'll set a good price if you're wanting to take one home with you."

Tom laughed. "I've no need for a naomhóg, but I'll pass the word. Do you build them to sell?"

Petey briefly squinted, as if in pain, but then shrugged. "*Och*, no. We built them for ourselves, but each needs four strong men on a rough sea. We've enough for only two crews, now."

He continued walking, but Tom stopped and turned to look again at the boats lining each side of the path. There were at least a dozen.

3

When he caught up with the others at the top, he saw the village was divided into two parts. The first group of houses were arranged on the slope near the path they'd just climbed, and a second cluster sat higher up and a bit to the north, giving the entire hillside a terraced appearance.

Almost all were simple dwellings of stone and mortar, each pressed into its own hollow, some so low they looked half-buried. Several were in ruins, roofless and crumbling, and among those with their roofs intact, many appeared deserted. The homes still occupied were easily identified. Thick streams of smoke poured from their chimneys, infusing a loamy scent of peat into the air's seaside tang.

Most of the houses had a uniform appearance, built with the doors facing south and their gables pointing at the mainland, but higher up, above all of them, a line of two-story whitewashed structures boldly faced the sea. They looked out of place in the landscape, as though they'd been built some place else and dropped from the air onto the island.

It was clear one of them had been chosen as the venue for

the meeting. A group of men had gathered outside it, some standing near the side wall, others sitting on their heels in the grass next to it, smoking pipes. Looking up at them, Tom wasn't sure what was expected of him. He hoped it wouldn't include trying to translate every Irish expression of hardship into English for the Land Commission's chosen man.

The matter got settled when the welcome committee took another break from the hike out of concern for Dan, whose round face was red and shining with perspiration. Mopping it with his handkerchief, he noticed Tom's uncertainty and appeared to read his mind.

"I can see you're worried, wondering what sort of holy show I'll be making of myself."

"I suppose you'll need help with the Irish..."

"It's all right, Tom." Dan put a reassuring hand on his shoulder. "They've English enough amongst the lot of them. Go on, enjoy yourself, and the sunshine. I expect we'll have finished in two hours, or so."

"Enjoy myself," Tom muttered, reviewing his choices after the group had moved on again. There weren't many to consider. He was on a hill, and he could either go up, down or across. He picked the last option, moving north along one of the village paths.

The place looked deserted already, with most of the community gathered inside for the meeting. At some distance above him, he did see one elderly man sitting on a stone wall who nodded and lifted his hand in a slow salute. Tom returned it, and felt the man's eyes on the back of his head until the path dropped below a hump of grassland and put him out of sight.

He ended up on the White Strand. The long stretch of beach was the most visible landmark to be seen from the mainland, and it was the one spot on the island where the ground was completely flat. It was low tide and the waves were tame, collapsing in languid plumes of foam on the sand. The day had become hot, and the water looked enticing. Rolling up his sleeves he walked down to the surf and splashed some water on his arms, then retreated back up the beach, where huge strips of rock extended from the cliffs. Stretching over the sand like the claws of a giant paw, they created a series of shaded inlets that Tom thought worth a closer look.

He scrambled over broken bits of stone as he explored each cove, until he rounded the edge of one outcrop and stumbled against a small dark rock that appeared to be alive.

The rock shot up from the ground and spun about, shouting something cryptic in its garbled rock language. Except that it wasn't a rock, of course. It was a young woman.

At first, all Tom could see was a flying black shawl swirling around a lithe figure, but when the commotion settled he stood facing a pair of dark, flashing eyes framed by waving black hair. He stared, struck dumb and entirely senseless.

Dathúil. Beautiful. *Dathúil.*

He went on a few more times, swinging between Irish and English, but reciting the words inside his own head, thank God. At last, he saw that while he'd been gawking – silently, senselessly – she'd been saying something out loud with great force, but now the fire in her eyes abated a bit.

"Can you not hear me?" she asked, sounding curious. "Are you not able to speak?"

"I am. I can," Tom stuttered. "I'm just … surprised."

"Surprised are you?" Two spots of pink blossomed over her cheeks. "And what about me? Sitting here nicely, and you sneaking up from behind only to fall on top of me?"

"I wasn't, I didn't—" Frustrated by his incoherence, Tom stopped and took a breath. "I'm very sorry to have frightened you. I didn't mean it."

"Well? What did you mean?"

"Nothing. Sure I was only having a walk. I came around this bit of cliff, and I thought you were a rock."

"Thought I was a rock!" she exclaimed.

"Well, you were on the ground, weren't you?"

Her eyes softened into amusement. "And what about yourself, then? Did you come out from under a rock? Or up out of the sea?"

He smiled, and pointed back at the mainland. "I came out from that rock. My name is Tom McBride. I live in Ventry. Do you live here on the Blasket?"

She looked around and then back at him, spreading her hands. "Where else would I live?"

"It's only I was told there were hardly any women on the island."

"Hardly any. It isn't the same as none."

"Right. Will I shut up now?"

"I hope not. You've only just learned to talk."

Tom burst into laughter, and after watching him for a few seconds, the corners of her mouth tilted into a small smile.

"Since it's settled you're not a rock, will you tell me your name?" he asked.

"Brigid O'Sullivan." She held out her hand to him. Once in his own, soft and warm, Tom wanted to keep it there for a good long time, but he reluctantly let it go.

"And what is it you were doing there on the ground, Brigid O'Sullivan?"

She opened her other hand to reveal a sea green cockleshell lying in her palm. He took it from her, examining it more closely. "This one's empty."

"It wasn't for the eating, I took it." She plucked it back. "This one wanted to be somewhere else."

"Ah. It told you so, did it?"

Brigid dropped the shell into a pocket of the apron she was wearing over a dark dress, both of which seemed quite damp. After giving him a flat stare, she turned her back and started up the beach.

"I'll shift out of your way, now. Enjoy your walk."

"Wait. Don't go." Tom skipped a few paces ahead and turned, walking backward so he could keep looking at her. "I'm here for two more hours at least, and bored rigid. Will you not stay and talk?"

She came to an abrupt stop. "You came out with the man from Dublin."

From the look on her face, Tom instantly knew the view she'd take of any connection with the Land Commission. Quicker than Peter before the cock's crow, he abandoned everything to do with the genial Dan O'Brien without a twinge of regret.

"I don't know him, really. Not at all. He needed a boat so I brought him over, but he's nothing to do with me. It's not even my boat. It's my uncle's. I'm a farmer."

Lips pursed, Brigid studied the ground, moving a pebble around in the sand with one bare toe. "It's not a lot of time, but I suppose in two hours I could show you something of the island. If you'd like to see it."

"I would. Very much." Tom suddenly wanted to see every inch of the island, from top to bottom. He wanted to take it in from all sides, this fine cut gem he'd looked at for years and dismissed without knowing its worth. The Great Blasket. The name itself had become like a poem, or a piece of music rolling through his head. Sweet, and lovely.

〜

Brigid walked him past the fields that covered the slope above the beach, describing how the islanders grew their crops, and then led him higher up the hillside, tracing a path that eventually ended at the north-western edge of the island. At a spot where the land thinned to a slivered peninsula above a rocky strand, she sat down on the grass with her feet tucked under her dress.

Weighing his choices between how close he wanted to get to her and the distance she probably thought was proper, Tom opted to split the difference. He sat at her feet with his arms on his knees, and looked out at the ocean.

To their right, he could see a flock of sheep grazing over the pancake-flat island of Beginnish, and to their left the lopsided pyramid shape of little Tearaght stood against the horizon. Straight ahead of them lay the island of Inishtooskert.

"It's supposed to look like a sleeping giant, but it's a bit like a fish from this angle, isn't it?" Tom said, which reminded him of something else. "Would you believe it, my uncle Patsy and I saw a sperm whale in this very spot a few years ago.

We were out here one afternoon pulling lobster pots. Big as an island herself, so she was."

"Ah, I'd love to see one," Brigid said. "As often as I've sat with my face to the sea, I never have. You had great luck that day."

Tom laughed. "We never thought so. Sure the thing was no more than thirty feet away; we were afraid of our lives. It was just the other side of that little rock out there, the skinny one."

"*An nathair*," Brigid murmured. The snake.

"You have a name for all the rocks, then?"

Brigid gave Tom a sharp look to see if he was teasing her again, but he wasn't. He'd learned that lesson quick enough. Reassured the question was sincere, she relaxed.

"I suppose we do, really. Every rock and every cove. It's a bit like naming streets in the town."

"Have you always lived on the Blasket?"

"No, but I was born here. Before I was a year old my mother and I moved out to Kenmare. I spent every summer here with my aunt and uncle, and when I was nine years of age my mother died. I came in to the island for good, then." After a slight hesitation, she added, "I had no other relations."

"What about your father?" Tom asked.

"I hadn't any father." Seeing his startled confusion, Brigid's face tightened. "I think you know what I mean."

"Oh. Right. Sorry." He turned his face away to hide his surprise. He knew plenty of people his age who'd lost a mother or father or both, but didn't think he'd ever met anyone whose parents hadn't married. It shocked him how casually she'd revealed it, without any shame or fear. As he took in the extraordinary piece of information, Brigid stirred and started to rise.

"I expect that's all you're needing to hear about me, so. We'll go back now, will we?"

"No." Tom reached up to grab her hand. She raised an eyebrow, but didn't pull away. He tugged gently at her fingers. "Sit yourself down, Brigid O'Sullivan. I need your entire life story."

After talking for quite a while they noticed it was getting late, and started back to the village. By then, Tom had learned she'd just turned twenty, that she'd never graduated school but was taught by teachers who came to the island occasionally, that she had a small house in the lower village where she kept a cow and some chickens. He knew all about her aunt and uncle and the neighbors, and the places on the island where she liked to walk.

From some of her more solemn conversation, he also knew she was devout in a way that puzzled him. Tom took in religion automatically, something akin to the daily dose of cod liver oil meant to keep his asthma at bay. He was used to an inflexible ritual performed within four walls, but Brigid had altogether discarded the idea of walls. Maybe because the community had no formal church with a daily Mass, she seemed to regard the entire island as a church. He didn't understand, and he didn't care. Tom just wanted to see her again.

"Will I come see you again?" He tried to make the question sound carefree, even though he felt his whole life hung on her answer.

"You can please yourself." Hands in the pockets of her apron, she kept her eyes on the path. Tom thought he saw a hint of color steal over her face. He took it as encouragement, whether she meant it or not.

He looked ahead, and in the distance saw Dan standing on the path to the slipway with a small group of men. Tom realized he was keeping them waiting.

"There's your fellow from Dublin, I suppose," Brigid said, an edge in her voice. "He wants his boatman."

Tom swore under his breath and turned to her. "I'm sorry, I have to hurry."

"I'd say you'd better. The Taoiseach and all the government are waiting to hear his news."

"But not you." He took one more long look at her. "You didn't want to go to the meeting."

"I'll hear all about it, soon enough." She swung her hands in her pockets and darted a glance at him. "Go on, now, Tom McBride. Maybe I'll see you again some time."

He walked quickly down the path to the waiting group of men, making apologies in two languages.

Dan waved them off with a smile. "With the lovely company you've been keeping, I'm surprised to see you at all."

At the bottom of the slipway, they said their farewells, and Dan gave a little speech in Irish about the Blasket and all the good things the islanders could offer to Ireland and the wider world. It was heartfelt and fairly done, which made Tom think it had been well rehearsed ahead of time.

When the dinghy pulled alongside the trawler, there was a harrowing moment when the land officer's off-balance pirouette nearly knocked Tom into the ocean, but they managed to get safely aboard. Once he'd secured the dinghy, they sat side by side on the roof of the hold, recovering, and eating the remains of their lunch.

"So?" Tom asked. "What's the verdict?"

"None today. Slow and steady, Tom. That's the only way. You can't pull a civilization up by its roots all in an afternoon."

"Fair enough."

Dan took a long drink from their last bottle of red lemonade. "I'll need another meeting." He passed the bottle.

Tom accepted it. "Makes sense."

"It would be good to have the transport settled ahead of time." Still facing the island, the land officer smiled. "I wonder, could you be persuaded, Tom?"

"I could, Dan." Tom scanned the beach, trying to see whether any of the rocks were moving. "Sure it's no bother at all."

4
∂

From a shadowed corner outside her house Brigid watched the dinghy pull up to the trawler and saw the man from Dublin stand and reach for the side of it.

"Look at the state of him," she muttered. "Like a great brown bear. Fit to burst out of that silly suit."

She gave a low cry when he stumbled back. Arms flailing, he blundered against Tom, who'd jumped up to catch him but instead was immediately knocked out of the boat. Tom somehow caught the boat rail with one hand to keep from tumbling into the sea entirely, and she held her breath while he hung there for a few seconds with the ocean dragging at his legs. Then, he latched the other hand onto the rail, and in one swinging movement lifted himself over the side, light and nimble.

They were nice hands, she thought. Rough and calloused, but gentle. He'd taken hers as though cupping a bird's egg.

Tom was pulling his passenger aboard now, and she saw him laughing helplessly as the bigger man flopped onto the deck and into a puddle of water. Smiling, Brigid turned and went inside. In front of the niche next to the hearth, she took the cockleshell from her pocket and placed it among the others on the shelf. They made a collage of color—pastel pinks, yellows and browns, and now one green one. There was a small bird's nest on the mantlepiece as well, and a collection of pebbles at one end, arranged in a circle.

"Rubbish," her aunt Lis often teased her. "I'll come through one day and sweep the lot into a bucket, just see if I don't."

She didn't mind a little teasing from Lis. She'd been a mother to her for more years now than the one who'd given birth to her. Brigid's own mother had been born on the Blasket but had always pined for a life on the mainland, with all its shops and fine houses. She got her wish, but was back on the island before long, carrying Brigid inside her. Within a year she was restless and they were off again, to Kenmare this time. Her mother could tell everyone in the new town her husband was dead, but it didn't help much, and many didn't believe it, anyway.

"My life is nothing but a penance," she often complained, and to Brigid it seemed accurate. Frail, overworked, bitter and disappointed, her mother had been a ghost for years before she died. It was a relief to escape to the Blasket every summer, and a liberation to return for good.

After sweeping the hearth and adding a few bricks of turf to bring up the fire for making tea, she peeked out the window at the house across the way to see if her aunt and uncle had returned. The package she'd seen earlier on the doorstep hadn't been moved, which meant no one was home yet.

Lis and Sean lived in the cottage that also served as the post office, and Brigid had lived there as well, for many years.

She knew she'd be welcome there still, but when she turned eighteen she'd wanted a house of her own.

"You'll be going for something grand in Dunquin, I suppose," Sean had groaned. "A house painted blue, with curtains and flower pots."

Brigid had swatted him with a tea towel. "There are plenty of houses standing empty right where I am."

They were pleased she wanted to stay—their own two sons had emigrated to America already—but she knew they worried about her as well, wondering where a husband would be found, when the youngest man on the island was thirty years older than her and seemed happy to go on as he was, without any wife. Brigid was no more interested in him than he was in her, and she had her mother's life as a cautionary tale against unsuitable matches. She too, was happy to go on as she was, which was one of the many things the community found strange about her.

There hadn't been much discussion about her father when she was growing up. Lis and Sean had never met him, and her mother had been tight-lipped. Brigid only knew he was a Portuguese fisherman, this from an off-hand comment her mother made once about why her skin turned brown in the sun, instead of burning and peeling like good, full-blooded Irish skin.

There was talk on the island, and in Dunquin, that her father was a selkie, a seal-man who'd stayed on land just long enough to get her mother pregnant before putting on his sleek skin and diving back into the sea. Usually, the story was only told for a laugh. The community was generally tolerant, but a small minority, simple and ignorant, took in the tale as fact, and were afraid of her.

After swinging the kettle over the fire to heat, Brigid took a pail from the corner and went out to the byre next to her house, where she knew Starlight would be waiting. Every afternoon, on her own, the cow would come in from the field and return to the byre to be milked. The small pattern of white on her otherwise black forehead made for instant recognition, and as she made her way along the path, the villagers would greet her as they would any other neighbor.

When Brigid returned to the house, her pail full, she saw the package left outside the post office was gone. Lis and Sean had returned from the meeting up the hill. She knew why the Dublin man had come, and what he wanted to talk about, and she wanted no part of it. She'd refused to attend the meeting, but couldn't help being curious about the outcome.

She filled a jar with milk for her aunt and uncle, and remembering the kettle, went to pull it off the fire. Straightening from the hearth, she looked at the shelf next to it and ran a finger lightly over the newest shell in her collection. Yes. They were lovely hands, really.

⌒

When she came through the door, her aunt was standing by the table, examining the letters that were due to go in the next naomhóg headed to Dunquin. It was pure nosiness, Brigid knew. Such a tiny pile of envelopes hardly needed sorting.

"I suppose you've not had your tea yet," Lis said, without shifting her eyes from the letters. Although taller than Brigid and rail-thin, her aunt never thought she ate enough. Braced for a serving of exasperation, she shook her head.

Lis clucked impatiently. "You can't live on air, Brigid. One day, you'll fall over dead of starvation, and then what will you do?"

"Not a great deal, I'm thinking." Brigid bit the inside of her cheek and looked solemn, but her aunt wasn't fooled.

"Oh, laugh away. But it's a sin not to eat when the food is plentiful. Heaven knows, it's been scarce often enough." She swept the mail from the table and nodded at the cupboard against the wall. "Get down the plates, and one for yourself. Mind you lay the cloth first. There's a nice bit of salted mackerel after soaking in fresh water all day. It will need three to get it down."

Dutifully, Brigid took out the piece of fine linen with delicate, crocheted edge work and spread it over the rough wooden table. The cloth had been a wedding gift and was a source of great pride to her aunt. She set the table and placed the jar of milk on it, and then sat watching Lis prepare the fish.

"Will you tell me, now?" Brigid asked, quietly. "What's the news?"

Lis tucked a loose strand of her gray hair back into the bun at the nape of her neck. "Nothing to tell, really," she said, after a short silence.

"Go on, now. You were up the hill for hours, all of you. You weren't there to look at each other. What did your man from Dublin have to say for himself?"

"He didn't say a lot. Truly," Lis added, turning to meet Brigid's glare. She came and sat down across from her. "He listened, though. Mr. Dan O'Brien wanted to hear us talk, about the life here and the changes that have come and what we all thought about it. He got more than his fill, I'd say, but didn't complain. He's a kind man, I think. Respectful."

"Kind, is he?" Brigid sniffed. "And what will they do for us, Mr. Dan O'Brien and the Taoiseach? Was he kind enough to tell you that?"

"I think they may be waiting to hear what we want."

"Waiting to hear us say we'll abandon our homes. That our way of living can be packed in a suitcase and put on a boat. That all our history and traditions don't mean so very much after all, and the government needn't trouble itself over any of that. All the music and—"

"Easy now, child."

Brigid jumped as her uncle Sean's gnarled hands settled on her shoulders. Caught up in her own emotions, she hadn't heard him come in, and was startled for the second time that day. She looked up into his weathered face. His cap, which never left his head except at meal times, was pulled low over his eyes.

"No one's going anywhere yet," he said, giving her arms a reassuring squeeze.

"No, not yet," she whispered.

∼

There was music at the King's House in the upper village that night. The island no longer had a king, and it had never been more than an honorary title, but the house of the last man to hold it continued to carry the name long after he'd died. His daughter Mary, affectionately known as the Princess, still lived there, and she was the closest thing the Blasket had to an innkeeper. Any notable overnight visitors to the island usually stayed with her.

She was a small, delicate-featured woman with snow-white hair and a ready smile. Full of quiet good humor, she loved entertaining, and hosted an evening every June, a few days after the men had finished the annual round-up and shearing of the sheep.

Mary was standing in the yard with her nieces who were over from Dunquin for a visit. As soon as she saw Brigid approach, following Lis and Sean, she drew her aside, a spark of mischief in her eyes.

"Maras said he sat on the wall this afternoon to take in the fine day, and didn't he see a golden-haired lad walk all alone through the village? And when the lad walked back again, didn't he have you at his side and a smile on his face?"

"It was only the fellow who drove the boat over for Mr. Dan O'Brien," Brigid said. "He'll have no need to come this way again, I'm sure."

She tossed the words out lightly enough, but felt a tickling flutter in her stomach. In spite of Tom McBride's promise of a second visit, it seemed unlikely she'd ever see him again, but that hadn't kept her from thinking about his golden hair herself. It was more reddish gold, she thought, remembering the sunlit shine of it on his arms, and the gleaming strand that fell just above his light blue eyes.

"Well, we'll just have to wait and see, won't we?" Mary said.

"You can wait on him, Mary, if it pleases you." Brigid shrugged. "It makes no difference to me."

She walked on into the house, where a few lamps had been lit to add brightness to the room. The light was bathed in a haze of smoke as the men enjoyed their pipes, and along with the pungence of the tobacco, a musky smell of damp wool hung in the air. Mary had several new bundles stored in the next room, some for spinning and some for selling.

The room had been cleared, its hard dirt floor swept clean and sanded, and the chairs moved to the sides to make room for dancing. From the amused looks turned in her direction as she entered, Brigid could guess she'd been a topic of conversation, but that was nothing new.

Her aunt and uncle had been stingy with any news about that afternoon's meeting, but Brigid knew she could get it out of someone here. She looked around for Petey, knowing he'd be her easiest mark. He was over fifty but still had a youthful air, and he was a great talker. Her uncle often said he'd tell a secret to no one except the next man he saw.

She found him by the hearth, sat beside him, and asked for a small glass of stout. Petey handed it over, his eyes stretched in feigned shock.

"What's come over you, Brigid? We don't often see you out in the evening like this." The men around him chimed in with their own surprise.

"Next, you'll stand up for a set dance," Padraig said. "We'll be clobbered with amazement."

"I've danced before," Brigid said, taking a sip of stout. "You act as though you'd never seen it."

"Not often enough." Old Maras, Petey's uncle, had taken the seat next to her. He patted her knee, and his lips, just visible beneath a drooping white mustache, twitched into a smile. "But maybe that lad you walked out with today has put the air under your feet."

Instead of putting him off, Brigid saw this as an opportune opening. "I wouldn't say that, but I was happy to show him a bit of hospitality, with every man on the island hidden away for hours. And what have you come away with, after all that blather?"

"You'd know yourself if you'd joined us," Padraig scolded.

"But, sure didn't the birds tell you all about it, Brigid?" Petey said, "whilst you were down there with them, picking at the seaweed?"

"Don't mind them," Maras said as the other two roared with laughter. "I'd say they're drunk already. I didn't go to the meeting myself, but I'm told the government offered to help us."

"How? What will they do for us?" Brigid felt a faint stir of hope.

"I'll tell you what they'll do." Petey paused for dramatic effect, and filled his glass again. "Evacuation. Dan O'Brien said the government has finally agreed to organize it for us."

"That's not helping us." Her spirits deflated again. "I'd say that sounds more like giving up on us."

"Call it what you like," Petey said.

The dancing had started, accompanied by two fiddles and a low flute. The four dancers twirled each other around the room and their feet slid lightly over the floor, adding a rhythmic counterpoint to the music.

Brigid watched, and felt as though she were seeing the scene from above. The island lay in darkness, mist-shrouded and silent, but in one small house the windows were lit, the music poured out, and the heat from all its collected humanity rose into the night. Anyone who came close enough could see it. They were still here. The island was still alive.

"And did you offer no ideas of your own?" she said to Petey, when the dance had finished. "A plan for helping us stay, instead of helping us leave? I'm sure I could have thought of one. I'm sure I could still."

"Ah, will you ever stop, Brigid?" Lowering his glass, Petey stared at the floor, and then looked at her, his face sad. "I suppose you can't help it, but you're a strange lass, and you know it. You're away to the hills most of the time, but even you know evacuation is what some here have been begging from the government for years. The Taoiseach's heard enough from us, and he certainly wants no plan of yours. Anyway, nothing's settled yet." He rose from the chair. "He's only asked us to think about it."

Brigid watched him walk away and suddenly wanted to cry, because she knew he was right.

She'd already seen it, the way she sometimes did see such things. They were like dreams, although she was usually wide awake. They seemed half inside her head and half in front of her eyes. In this one, Brigid had seen the island deserted, its houses in ruins and the wind whistling through them. She'd seen the worn paths of the village erased by wild grass and heather, with only the faintest imprint left to show where feet and hooves had tramped for a hundred years or more. She'd stared at a scene she'd looked at all her life, scanning the hills to find flocks of sheep and a few wild donkeys, but nothing else. Not a cow or a pig, not a crop in the field. Not a single living person.

"This will happen," a voice had whispered. Maybe it was her own, she couldn't be sure, but Brigid knew it spoke the truth. The day was coming when no man, woman or child would call the Great Blasket home.

But the voice had not said when, and that was the reprieve she'd been clinging to, the hope she hadn't surrendered.

The voice had not said "soon."

5

When they arrived back at the city pier the sun had descended into it's long summer twilight, pulling most of the day's heat down with it. Since he was headed back to Dublin the following day, Dan suggested a parting round at Regan's, but Tom reluctantly declined. He'd promised to be home for evening tea and they'd returned later than expected. With the boat still to clean before he could make a start, he was already on borrowed time.

After catching a ride as far as Ventry, he continued home on foot. While walking, Tom carefully reconstructed every detail he could remember about Brigid O'Sullivan, from her flashing dark eyes down to the prints of her small feet on the sand. Lost in thought, he passed through the village and was on the coastal road that ran the length of the peninsula when the rain began. He walked the rest of the way in a cold downpour, but hardly noticed it.

He only came to his senses after crossing the familiar, invisible boundary that marked the beginning of his family's land. Its acreage began at the top of a wide slope and continued all the way down to the shoreline. Having already blindly walked by it, Tom retraced his steps to the narrow tractor path leading to the house, and started up the hill with the sea at his back.

The farmhouse sat high on the hill facing the harbor, a handsome, 19th century building made of roughly dressed stone, and it was one of the few two-story homes in Ventry. As a young man, his father had worked for the estate owner, but then during the turbulent years of the government's land redistribution scheme he somehow acquired all of the estate's land—as well as the house and several non-adjacent peat bogs—in a transaction Tom had never quite understood.

From this opportunistic beginning, Seamus McBride had become a surprisingly successful businessman. In the face of a miserable Irish economy, he'd become a "thirty-cow man", making the McBride farm one of the biggest in the region, and earning him a seat on the local creamery committee. The only farm larger was closer to Tralee, but Seamus insisted it didn't count because only half of it was actually on the peninsula.

That was typical of his father. He always wanted to be the biggest and best. Like most farms, theirs took back nearly as much wealth as it gave, but in a country—and more immediately, a village—where few prospered, Seamus was thriving, and nobody resents an Irishman's good fortune more than his neighbors. In Ventry, he was tolerated but not well liked.

By contrast, everyone loved Tom. They made much of him in the village, unlike his father, who these days seemed to always find fault with his youngest son. Most of his praise was reserved for Tom's three older brothers. They'd inherited his business savvy, but had taken their talents abroad to Liverpool and started a building company. During visits home, one or another of them – Hugh, Garrett or Dillon – would invariably ask their little brother what in the world was he doing at all, hanging about the farm instead of coming over to join the business. Tom had asked himself the same thing more than once, but had always returned to the simplest answer: he loved it too much. The farm. The cows. The smell of hay and the feeling of dark, rich earth sifting through his fingers. The salt taste of the sea on his lips.

Tom could taste it now as he walked up through the pasture. He could hear it, too – the muffled roar of waves crashing against the rocks far behind him. He turned to look through the mist at the harbor, oblivious to the rain soaking through his shirt, thinking about the predictability of the tide and the things revealed when it retreated. Seaweed, and cockle-shells – and beautiful dark-haired women.

Approaching the house, he was within a few yards of the front door before realizing he'd gone the wrong way again. Seamus was always making "improvements" to the house. The most recent was a small room added at the rear, essentially a second kitchen, built to accommodate the fancy turf-burning range oven he'd purchased in Waterford. As a final elaborate touch, he'd built a stone patio into the hillside behind the new kitchen and once finished, had declared the back door was now the main entrance. Tom couldn't get used to it, and was grateful for a gathering fog that hid a detour through his mother's rose bushes.

Arriving at the correct entrance, he'd just put a hand on the knob when it dipped and pulled away from him. Before she even had the door open his mother was talking, and by the time her narrowed green eyes settled on him Eileen McBride was in full-throated protest.

"JesusMaryandGodforgiveme I'm after thinking that filthy boat sunk and you lying dead these past two hours and have you any idea what that's like at all, picturing your wee boy drowned at the bottom of the sea? No you haven't any idea, not anything like it."

"I'm sorry, Ma. I didn't think—"

"Of course you didn't think. You've a head full of music and little else, and MotherofGod is that what you've had on for clothes, out in this weather?"

Tom looked down at his rain-soaked shirt. "It was more than I needed, really. I was blistered with heat most of the day, out on the island."

"Were you, so? Isn't it well for you, having a fine day out on the island." Tom looked warily at his mother's smile, and found his skepticism justified when she began roaring again. "Are you going to stand out there all night or what are you doing? And the water running off you in sheets. Will you ever get inside, now. You'll die of exposure."

Tom didn't mention that he'd be glad to get out of the rain if she'd only move out of the doorway, but the point became moot when she yanked him through it. Once inside she blocked his passage—easy to do in the tiny, narrow kitchen. Whatever space not taken up by the new range oven was devoted to an enormous oak dresser with open shelves full of willow-patterned china and hanging teacups. It was his mother's prized possession, an heirloom she'd brought all the way from her family's home in Galway city.

She started in on his head with a tea towel; he accepted

the assault without struggling. He'd already caught a glimpse of his father in the next room, glaring at him. He was happy to linger, and bask for a few minutes in the aroma of baked bread wafting through the kitchen – though the loaf sitting on the counter had cooled long ago.

Eileen's wrath was also cooling, as he'd known it would. His brothers might collectively be the apple of his father's eye, but Tom was his mother's favorite, and she made no secret of the fact.

As a young woman, she'd been a red-haired, porcelain-skinned beauty, and she was still lovely, even though the years had added gray to the red and a few extra pounds to her frame. Tom knew he was the cause for more than a few of those gray hairs. He'd often been ill when he was a boy, and when his asthma got bad he would sometimes spend weeks at a time inside the house with his mother. She'd worried and petted and fussed over him then, and although he was hardly ever sick anymore, she'd never stopped.

"Now," Eileen said, letting the towel drop. She put a hand against his face and gave him a real smile this time, though a fretful one. "From the time you were a baby, often enough I thought God was that close to taking you from me. I thought he was after stealing the last breath out of your chest, and I sitting there begging him to let you draw another. Will I ever stop worrying, I wonder?"

"*Whisht*, Ma." Tom bent his head to kiss the top of hers. "I wish you would. It isn't good for either of us."

"Go in to him, now, while I wet the tea." She nodded at the doorway. "He won't say it, mind, but your father was just as worried. I had everything laid on the table, but when he came in he said 'we'll touch none of it 'til the boy is home.'"

Tom offered no reply to this. No doubt his mother viewed the gesture as one of prayerful sacrifice, but he had a different idea about his father's motive. In the doorway, he braced himself with a stoic sigh before passing through it.

⁓

The big, open space Tom still thought of as the "kitchen" was cozy and warm, thanks to Eileen's tireless battle against the seaside damp. Her bright, hand-loomed rugs absorbed any chill from the stone floor, and she always kept the fire burning. Until the arrival of the oven, she'd done all the cooking in the old fieldstone hearth that took up one whole wall, and tonight the bricks of turf were supplemented with a generous scoop of coal.

Tom gravitated to the glowing embers to dry off and stood with his back to it, facing his father. Seamus sat at the dining table placed against the opposite wall, his face hidden behind the broadsheet of the county newspaper.

Silence reigned, punctuated only by the pop and crackle of coal breaking apart in the fire. After allowing the stand off to continue for a solid minute, Tom ended it, irritated that he was again letting his father treat him like a schoolboy.

"Well, Dad."

The mild overture was all his father needed. Snapping the paper shut, he tossed it onto the table. "Is this any time to be coming home? It's two hours we're waiting, and your mother in bits."

"I've apologized to Ma already – for worrying her."

"But you won't to me?"

"I will, of course." Tom paused, and then added, "If I worried you."

The sarcasm wasn't lost on Seamus. There wasn't much that got by him, and no slight was too small to ignore.

Although below average in height, his father was broad-shouldered and solidly built, pleasant-looking rather than handsome, with sandy hair that had been thinning ever since Tom could remember. He had the swagger of a prize-fighter and the sociability of a consummate businessman—a boisterous laugh, a firm handshake. Seamus could be good company when he was in the right mood, but he had a short fuse. His temper could escalate from a simmer to a confla-gration in the space of an instant. Seeing some impending danger of this, Tom moderated his tone.

"It's only that we got a late start, and then I had to see to the boat and find a ride, so I was late getting back on the road."

"After stopping off in a pub, I'll wager."

"I stopped at no pubs," Tom shot back, glad he could refute the accusation with a clear conscience.

"Leave it, the pair of you." Eileen appeared from the kitchen, carrying a tray with sliced brown bread, cheese made from their own milk, and a large, steaming teapot. Placing these between a platter of cold ham and a magnificent looking apple cake, she waved Tom over. "It's not his fault. It was government business, after all, and your man came straight from de Valera. Tom could hardly order the fellow to be quick about his work and not make him late for tea."

Reminded of this indirect brush with the nation's leader, his father's mood softened, and Tom smiled at his mother's wink. That morning, when he'd explained his mission to bring Dan O'Brien to the Blasket, Eileen's response had been predictable—a recitation of all her usual fears for his safety—but his father's had not. Seamus had seemed oddly pleased by the news, and after only a few questions had agreed to cover Tom's afternoon chores.

"I hope Dev appreciates the favor," he'd said, offering even this complaint with a slight smile.

Having expected a lecture instead of absolution, Tom had been relieved but puzzled, until he understood that by granting the Taoiseach the use of his son for the day, Seamus had only heightened his own sense of self-importance.

Tom took his usual seat at the table and realized he was famished. He loaded his plate with helpings of everything, while keeping one eye on the cake he was planning to tackle next.

He described the Great Blasket to his parents in detail, and told them about Dan O'Brien's purpose in visiting, but he tiptoed up to the news that he'd agreed to take him there again, and was careful not to mention Brigid O'Sullivan at all. For the chance of seeing her again, he would bring Dan to the island whenever and however often he wished to go, but although he longed to talk about her, he knew it would invite a level of interrogation best avoided.

In advancing his argument for helping Dan, Tom took a lesson from his mother, sprinkling in references to Eamon de Valera, as though the man himself had asked personally for his help, but he found that hand had been played out, already. His father apparently considered a single incident quite enough to impress the neighbors. Further trips would be superfluous.

"And that's bold, I'd say," he huffed, "Offering free use of a trawler that doesn't belong to you."

"Patsy won't mind."

"Maybe Patsy won't, but I do." Seamus slapped his teacup on the table. "Let the government find someone else. There's other boats in the harbor, and men paid to bring them out. You're paid to farm."

"I'm paid, am I?" Tom said quietly. He kept his eyes on his plate, working through a large slice of cake.

"You cheeky little gobshite. You're paid in acres. Unless you don't want them. Tell me now if you don't."

"All right, Dad. I'm sorry."

"Tell me now." His father's voice rose to a shout.

Glancing at his mother, Tom felt the sting of her sad reproach. He sat back from the table, tiredly pushing his plate away.

It was a worn out script, the "inheritance" routine—his father's threat of withholding it, his own threat of rejecting it. They both knew it was pointless, toothless; but they were forever stumbling into this battle, like a hole in the ground neither could see until they'd fallen into it.

He'd long ago learned that surrender was the quickest path to relief. Apologies were like lullabies to his father; Tom had learned to make strategic use of them.

"I'm sorry, Dad. I didn't mean it. I'm sorry," he repeated. Once assured the words were having their usual effect, he continued, treading more carefully. "Sure look, I gave the man my word, and I want to keep it, but I know as well as you the work that needs to be done here. I'll let nothing drop, and you won't have to step in again. I promise you that."

Seamus frowned, but in peevish curiosity now – Tom had punctured his ballooning anger. "I don't know why you want to be mixed up in any business with those islanders and their strange ways. You should leave them to sort themselves out. I've seen them a few times in Dunquin. They're queer folk."

"There was nothing queer about the folk I met." Tom shrugged. "And their ways aren't really strange. It's only that they're the old ways."

Eileen dropped another slice of cake onto his plate, next to the one he was just finishing. "Not that it matters what I think, but I wish you wouldn't do it."

Having settled a truce on one front, Tom patiently began the process again. "It'll be fine, Ma."

"I never liked the idea of you being out in that boat. Especially if Patsy isn't with you. And the weather doing God knows what from one minute to the next."

"I'll be careful."

"If you don't drown, the sun will burn you to a cinder," she insisted, gathering up the dishes. "And all that air. It's too much for your lungs."

"Too much *air*?" Tom couldn't help laughing. "Is there more of it out on the sea, then? I'd no notion of it."

"Jaysus, Eileen." Seamus rolled his eyes, but a faint smile signaled the end of his resistance. "Patsy wouldn't trust him with the boat if he couldn't handle it." Reaching for his pipe, he glanced at Tom and hitched his chin at the doorway. "Go on, now. See how much air you can find in the barn. The cows are milked, but I've left it for you to clean up after them."

6

❧

The radio telephone linking the Great Blasket with Dunquin had been installed in the post office since 1947. It was powered by wind, but the technicians had not accounted for the gale force strength of it on the island. With more supply than it could handle, the battery charger frequently responded by revving itself into a paralytic frenzy and toppling over. When it did work, most calls went from the island to the mainland rather than the reverse. The brassy rattle of the phone was not often heard in the house, so when it erupted next to her elbow Brigid nearly jumped out of her skin.

"Sure it would need to be now, wouldn't it?" Leaning against the kitchen table, Lis swiped at the perspiration on her forehead. "See what it's about, Brigid. I'm in no mood for fiddling with that contraption."

She was in no state for it, either. In fact, after a single glance, anyone unfamiliar with their task might run from the doorway in pale terror. The coppery smell of blood hung heavy in the steam-filled air. Lis was wearing an apron covered in streaky splashes of it, and both her hands were plunged up to the elbows in an enormous bowl, massaging a thickening slurry of it. At her station across the room—a second, makeshift table made from a plank stretched between barrels—Brigid didn't look much better. She'd managed to avoid most of the blood, but her apron and dress were soaked in water, sweat, and other unmentionable liquids. Her hands were a greasy, slippery mess.

A pig had been butchered that morning. The men—in a gathering larger than was actually needed for the job—had done the deed, and after collecting the blood in a white enamel basin, they'd completed their role in the grim ritual by delivering it to the house. The women took over at that point, and the rest of the afternoon had been devoted to the messy production of black pudding.

The hierarchy in the division of labor was strict. Like everyone else, Lis had her own recipe and allowed no interference in the mixing in of oats, onion, suet, and spices. Brigid and Margaret were given the task of flushing and cleaning the casings, and little Liam was repeatedly sent to fetch water as a means of keeping him away from the red-hot fire. Everyone in the village referred to Margaret's six-year-old son simply as "the child", because he was the only one on the island, and as such he was spoiled and catered to as much as any royal princeling.

The full assembly of the island's women was complete when Mary arrived from the King's House. She had been tucked into a corner, where she sipped tea and offered commentary. All was proceeding smoothly until the phone—more fire alarm than jingling bell—brought them to an astonished halt.

Having never answered it before, Brigid hesitated but then quickly scrubbed her hands on a towel, anxious to stop the unholy racket. She lifted the receiver, and immediately could hear someone speaking.

"Ah, didn't I tell you? It's likely broken. You can try again in—"

"Yes? Hello? Who's on the line? This is the Blasket post office." Ignorant of the correct protocol, Brigid offered every greeting she could think of.

"There you are, so." The voice hummed, as if someone missing had just turned up. "It's Eva here. Is that Lis?"

"Oh hello, Eva. It's Brigid. Lis isn't able to talk just now. Is anything the matter?"

"Not at all, at all, love," Eva said. "But there's a fellow here who wants to speak to someone about setting a meeting. I'll just hand you over to him."

Brigid felt a warm flush sweep up the back of her neck, instinctively guessing who the "fellow" would be. Before she could speak or react at all, his voice was in her ear, easily recognized. She'd heard it on one day only, but over the past several weeks she'd often resurrected the sound of it in her head. Even the metallic echo of the transmission couldn't mask his warm, melodious tenor.

"Right. Hello, or ahoy. It's something like that, I suppose?" He sounded as uncertain as she was with telephone jargon. "It's Tom McBride here. I was over visiting earlier in the month. I brought a gentleman from the Irish Land Commission—"

"Yes, I remember; and didn't I watch him nearly thump you into the sea on the way home."

The intake of his breath wasn't audible, but she could sense it. After a pause, he spoke again. "Brigid?"

"Hello there, Tom McBride," she said, lightly. "How are you keeping?"

"You're the radio operator as well?" There was a smile in his voice now. "Is there nothing you can't do?"

She laughed. "It's the first time in my life I'm picking it up. I hardly know what end to speak to."

"Is it? Fancy my luck, then, ringing today." Another voice in the background–Eva again–said something Brigid didn't catch. "Oh, right. Sorry." Tom cleared his throat. "I'm calling on behalf of Mr. Dan O'Brien. He's after having a load of committee meetings in Dublin and he's sent a telegram, asking could I bring him in to the island again a week from Tuesday–if it's convenient."

"I don't know about convenience," Brigid said, unhappy with this turn in the conversation. "If it were left to me, I'm sure we'd do better without any more visits at all."

"Oh. I see. Ehm ... " Instead of adding anything else, he trailed into silence. Brigid cursed her foolish, self-righteous temper.

"Oh, that's not what I meant! Or at least not the way it sounded. I didn't mean you." She sighed. "I'm being churlish and you've not earned such treatment. I'm very sorry, Tom."

"No bother." He sounded relieved. "I understand how you feel."

She doubted he could, but left the comment unchallenged. "I'll let the others know you'll be coming in to see us. Tell Mr. O'Brien we'll be looking for you both a week from Tuesday."

"Grand. He'll be pleased, and ... I'm looking forward to seeing you again."

"You might come a bit earlier this time. And stay longer," she added, "To get the best part of the day."

The suggestion was brazen, maybe a little immodest, but this time the words carried precisely the meaning she intended, and Brigid didn't care how bold it sounded. Judging by the strength of his reaction, Tom didn't, either.

"I'll make sure of it," he said. "I'll roll Dan out of bed and onto the boat meself if I have to. I'd best ring off, now. Yer wan – Eva is it? – she's fairly anxious over the price of the call."

Brigid gently placed the receiver back in its cradle. Turning, she found the room reduced to a dead calm, and every eye in the household trained on her. On her cozy corner throne, Mary's eyes twinkled at her over the rim of her teacup.

∽

Tom knew he'd been doing it all a bit backwards, but could only hope his luck would hold. Over several weeks, the memory of his visit with Brigid O'Sullivan had not faded from his mind. If anything, it had grown sharper. As he went about his usual routine, he replayed every sight, sound and smell, every word she'd said to him and he to her, as though memorizing all of it for a future competition he couldn't bear to lose. He was a racehorse in harness, anxious to get underway, and Dan O'Brien's telegram had sent him through the starting gate without a great deal of sense or forethought.

First, he'd fired off an immediate, affirmative reply to the land officer before remembering the people involved in the meeting might like to be consulted. Then, after getting confirmation from the island – and happily, from Brigid herself – it struck him that he hadn't given any thought to getting his farm work covered in his absence. Nor had he secured the use of the trawler, or even prepared Patsy for the possibility he'd be asking for it.

Nervous that he might have overplayed a "fortune favors the bold" attitude, he didn't raise the topic with his uncle until well into their regular Thursday session at Regan's—when it was his turn to get the next round.

He needn't have worried. Tom had no trouble getting the use of the boat, but Patsy showed a livelier interest in the details than his father had, and—even more disconcerting—a sharper intuition than his mother.

"He's paying you something, is he?" Patsy asked, when Tom returned from the bar.

"I didn't ask him to," he admitted. He carefully balanced the creamy pints on his tray while passing the first of them to his uncle. "But, if it's the diesel that's worrying you—"

Patsy waved him off. "I wasn't thinking of the diesel. I'm wondering why you want to do it."

"To be helpful, I suppose, and because I enjoyed myself the last time."

"Go on outta' that. It can't be only for the great pleasure of Dan O'Brien's company."

Tom sat on the bench next to him and placed his own pint on the floor between his feet. Picking up his fiddle, he frowned at it, fingers fidgeting over the tuning pegs.

"And what if it was? You're sounding like Seamus, now. Maybe once in a while, I'd like to do something for the pleasure that's in it, and not be forever brooding over how it looks on a ledger."

"Hmm." Taking a sip from his glass, Patsy regarded him with patient amusement. "Speaking of your father, what's he think about it?"

"Little enough," Tom said. He laid the fiddle across his lap, but kept his head down, squirming under his uncle's steady gaze. "He thinks the islanders are a backward pack of hard cases and I should be steering clear of them."

"No surprise there, I suppose," Patsy said.

He lifted his head and risked a peek. "What do you think about them?"

Patsy wiped the back of one hand over his lip, looking unusually serious. "I guess I don't think about them much at all. Nor do any of us. I expect it's partly why they've come to be in the state they're in, fading away and nobody paying attention. I'd say they're probably proud, hard-working folk like the rest of us, only poorer—and that's saying something, right enough. They've had hard lives. If the government means to help, they'll likely be happy to get away from the place."

"Not all of them, I think," Tom murmured, and immediately wished he could learn to keep his mouth shut.

"Oh? Well, maybe not."

To his relief, Patsy appeared to lose interest in the subject. He turned to join an argument about a tune called The Lark on the Strand, and whether it was or wasn't identical to the Kesh Jig. Tom thought he was in the clear, but as they finished their pints and prepared to begin another set, his uncle swiveled back to give him a wicked grin.

"Tell me, now. Does Eileen know you've gone sweet on a Blasket girl?"

Tom nearly dropped his glass on the floor. "What gives you

the idea there's any girl involved?" His face was a mask of curious interest, but he knew his flaming cheeks were giving him away. With a shout of laughter, his uncle clapped him on the back, so powerfully it rattled his teeth.

"When a man takes to the sea for no good reason, boyo, there's always a girl involved."

∼

The next thing that broke his way came so easily Tom almost couldn't believe in it, but since fate had tossed it in his path, in the shape of his friend Jamesie Gallagher, he decided to trust it.

Jamesie was from a family with too little land and too many sons. He'd worked occasionally for the McBrides and had a job in the creamery, and most nights he also pulled pints at The Swallowtail in Ventry village. To round out his busy life, he was courting a woman who worked at a sweet shop in Dingle, but was finding his progress stalled for lack of free time.

Once Tom had confessed his own predicament, it was easy for them to see the advantage in pooling resources. Jamesie agreed to cover Tom's farm work on Tuesday, and the following Saturday night Tom would fill in for him at the pub.

"It doesn't have to be just the one time, Tommy," Jamesie said while pumping his hand, his pink face beaming. "We could go on with it, helping each other, like."

Tom smiled. "I've only met her once, Jamesie. I'm not sure she even likes me."

"Bollocks," his friend said. "Sure why wouldn't she? Everyone else does."

At this point he thought the last hurdle had been cleared, but on Monday evening, Tom stood in the barn's open doorway, glumly looking out at a wind-driven rain. It drummed a hollow into the barnyard until the bare earth disappeared beneath a muddy lake, and beyond that it fell in vicious diagonal sheets across the fields. Farther out, past the shoreline, he could see sprays of wild, white-horse waves shooting up from the ocean.

It would be madness to try navigating the Blasket's rock-infested harbor in such weather. It looked as if the one detail he couldn't control might make all the others useless, but by the following morning the outlook had improved. The rain softened to an intermittent mist, and although it took most of the morning, the wind shifted at last, and the ocean settled.

Dan O'Brien thought it had not settled nearly enough. When Tom arrived at Malloy's Guest House in Dingle, he had a stiff job convincing the land officer otherwise. He had an even harder time cajoling him away from Mrs. Malloy's cozy fire and her boiled beef dinner. By the time they left the pier it was only a few minutes earlier than the last time, but the fact they were underway at all was cause for celebration.

After a smooth run out of the harbor and along the peninsula, Tom changed heading, easing the trawler through choppy water as they moved away from the coast. He looked to see how his passenger was weathering the ride. Unlike the first trip, Dan appeared less inclined to paint the deck, but from his worried frown Tom saw he needed diversion.

"That's a fine pair of boots, Dan," he said, nodding his approval at them. "You've a good eye for quality, I'd say."

They were spotless and pristine – Tom could almost smell

the newness off them – but otherwise the boots were an exact copy of his own. Dan had also not repeated his mistake with the rest of his wardrobe. Instead of a business suit, he wore a sweater and sturdy canvas trousers.

He leaned forward and looked down, admiring his own footgear. "I ordered them the very night I got home. They look well on me, I think."

"Indeed, they do," Tom said. "You look altogether more suited to the purpose."

"As do you." Dan angled his head in appraisal-. "That's quite a smart-looking jacket, and I see you've given yourself a good, close shave. Have you had the hair cut as well?"

Self-consciously, Tom fingered the zipper of the black, waxed jacket. It was a Christmas gift from his brother Hugh. He gave Dan a sheepish grin. "A haircut? No. I only combed it. Come here, now," he said, shifting the conversation. "How did your meetings in Dublin come along? Have you any good news for the Blasket folk?"

Dan looked thoughtful. "I do have news. I hope they'll think it's good."

Facing him, Tom leaned back against the side of the wheel-house and crossed his arms. "And?" he prompted. "You're being fairly close with it."

Dan shook his head. "I won't speak about it yet, Tom. I think *they* should hear it before anyone else does. You're not offended, I hope?"

"Of course not." Tom studied him for a long moment before turning back to the wheel. "Whatever the news is, they're lucky to have a man like yourself bringing it to them."

7

Brigid had convinced herself he wouldn't come. All night long, a storm had raged and hurled itself against the walls of her cottage. By morning it had all stopped. Without the shrieking wind, the island felt enchanted, bathed in a deep, mist-filled hush; but the sky was the color of ash, the air still had the smell of rain in it, and she saw it was impossible, and that she was foolish to think of having any sort of relationship with someone from the mainland. There would only be disappointment in it.

But then, the boat was motoring towards the island, and Brigid had to pretend she was the last person to notice it, when in fact she'd seen the first faint speck appear on the horizon. She tensed as the two figures again engaged in the delicate work of settling into the dinghy, then saw it push away from the trawler. She watched as – a little farther down-hill – Petey led a few men past her house, clomping along the path in their studded boots like an honor guard, disappearing into the crevice that led down to the slipway.

Although still too far away to see in much detail, Brigid

squinted at Tom's face, trying to see if it looked anything like the idealized image she'd been carrying in her head. She wasn't disappointed; if anything he was more handsome than she remembered. She shifted her eyes to the beefy man in the front of the boat who sat very straight, gripping both sides of the dinghy as Tom steered them to shore. Dan O'Brien. She'd nearly forgotten about him altogether.

What should she do, now? The phone conversation had been too short to talk about a meeting place. She considered following the men down to the shore and quickly dismissed the idea. She'd look ridiculous and they would certainly laugh at her. Should she go to the beach, where they met before? He might not think to look for her there. He might think to find her with the others in the upper village, waiting for the man from Dublin to tell them their fate.

Frozen in indecision, she did nothing. The dinghy disappeared beneath the cliffs and she stood in front of her cottage, waiting. Soon enough, the small party emerged from the crevice. Making the turn at the top, they rejoined the path that led through the lower village, with Tom bringing up the rear and keeping an eye on Dan, who was puffing like a bellows.

As they reached the bend in front of her cottage, Tom glanced up, saw her, and came to an abrupt stop. He let Dan plod on ahead of him, not taking his eyes from her. His expression was one of delighted admiration, and Brigid knew she had never in her life seen anyone look at her like that.

Noticing he'd lost his companion, Dan looked around for Tom and then up at her. He stopped as well, and after catching her attention he smiled and made a chivalrous bow. There was nothing mocking or derisive about it. It was a warm, full-hearted smile, and for a few seconds Brigid saw a brilliant white aura shimmering behind him—like a shadow, but its exact opposite.

It didn't happen often, but when it did it was one of the few manifestations she experienced that didn't confuse her. She knew what she was looking at. The only word she could attach to it was *anam*, "soul". It was more complicated than that, but she didn't think she could ever describe it. In this case it meant a choice was lost to her, now. She could no longer despise the man from Dublin; Dan O'Brien had too much goodness in him.

"Hello there."

"Oh!" Flustered, Brigid whirled to face Tom, who had bounded up the hill and now stood beside her. She stumbled and he reached for her arm.

"Not again," he said. "I wasn't sneaking this time. Sure I was in plain sight, the whole way."

"No, of course you weren't sneaking, I was just…" She fumbled for words, but couldn't find them. There was no way of explaining what had distracted her, nor did she want to. Not yet, anyway.

"I'm sorry we couldn't come any earlier. The wind was fierce, and then Dan wouldn't leave without his dinner. It was a struggle getting him here at all. Anyway," he said, his eyes shining, "I'm happy to see you, Brigid O'Sullivan."

Brigid started to reply with something flippant, but found she was tired of that charade. "Yes," she said, smiling. "I'm happy to see you as well, Tom McBride."

Since there wasn't enough time for a wider tour of the island, Brigid suggested she could instead show him the village.

They began at her house, and a visit with Starlight, who was in the byre, lazily munching from a bale of hay.

"She hasn't set a hoof outside all day," Brigid said. "She doesn't trust the weather."

"Who can blame her?" Tom circled the cow, looking with an experienced eye before running a hand over her back. "You're a real beauty aren't you?" he murmured. Mildly interested, Starlight sniffed at him, and then nuzzled her velvety nose against his palm.

"She likes you," Brigid said.

"Looks like it." Tom grinned. "Thanks be to God. What's my next test?"

She smiled. "One is enough for today. Will we have a bit of a walk, now?"

Passing the post office, they met Lis and Sean, who were on their way to the meeting with the land officer. Alarmed by her aunt's delighted expression at the sight of them, Brigid tried to restrain her by starting a formal introduction, but Lis was too quick.

"Is this Tom McBride, now? Well, it's grand meeting you, and it's lovely you're here again. We're after hearing so much from Brigid about your first visit. She's told us all about you."

Brigid sputtered, thinking such a bald-faced lie deserved a challenge, but after a glance at Tom she thought better of it. He shook hands with Sean and made polite conversation, while Lis continued her exultations.

"Ah, he has a gorgeous turn with the Irish, doesn't he? It fairly comes out of him like music, so it does."

Tom blushed all the way up to his forehead. Of the two of them, Brigid wondered whose face was redder. Even Sean could see they'd had enough, and came to the rescue at last.

"I expect they're wanting us up the hill," he said.

"I suppose they are," Lis said. "I won't try to change your mind this time, Brigid. We'll give you all the news when it's finished." She tore her eyes away from Tom, and to Brigid telegraphed a transparent "get on with it" directive. They watched in silence as her aunt and uncle ascended the path, then Tom turned to her, suppressing a smile.

"They seem nice."

With the village to themselves now, they wandered along the network of rocky paths between the houses, not minding which direction they took. Brigid couldn't remember when she'd last talked so much. She lived in solitude much of the time, and felt constrained when she did join in social occasions. Everyone around her talked easily, endlessly, and she had trouble keeping up with them, but Tom had a knack for drawing conversation out of her. He was like a miner probing a forgotten seam, convinced it had more to offer. Brigid discovered she did, and from his avid attention she saw Tom was taking in all of it.

She wanted him to talk as well, though, because Lis was right. He spoke with a soft, supple cadence—the words fluid, but finely cut. Truly, like a clear music, with every note heard. She could tell how much he loved music from the way he spoke about his fiddle. She could also tell he loved his work from the way he spoke about his land, especially in describing the fields and the potato varieties grown in them. There was an Orla field, a Rooster field, and even a Pink field.

"Kerrs Pinks, of course," he said. "The one near the shoreline we call the Oyster Field, because the gulls litter the place with shells. There's one way at the top of the hill called the Rock Garden, for obvious reasons. It's a brilliant view but fairly useless otherwise. I think you'd like it, though."

"So, let me see, I want to be sure to understand this." Brigid darted a mischievous glance at him. "You have particular names for all the fields?"

Laughing, Tom hung his head. "We do, just like your rocks and coves." He tipped an imaginary cap, and momentarily broke into English. "Clever lass. Fair play to you."

"It wasn't fair of me, really." Brigid smiled. "We've names for all our own fields as well."

They eventually found themselves in the upper village and stopped climbing. The community had once more gathered in the middle of the three newer houses at the very top. Brigid wanted to steer clear of all that, but she pointed to the house on the end closest to them.

"That was Peig's house, when she lived here." Brigid assumed he knew who she meant. It still seemed odd to think Peig Sayers had become such a celebrity, but there were people who wouldn't even know the Blasket Islands existed if not for her.

"Ah. Right. Peig." Tom's expression turned cautious as he examined the house.

"You read it, I imagine?" she said. "Her book?"

"I did manage to get it down, yes."

"You didn't care for it?"

"Ehm ... " He shrugged. "Sure look, I mean no disrespect to the poor woman, but she did you no favors with that book. I'd sooner have had a tooth pulled than chisel my way through the bloody thing. Well, what about you, then?" he added, seeing her feigned shock. "Have you read it?"

"Certainly."

"And thought it was brilliant?"

"Not really brilliant, but more like –" A half-choked snicker gave away the game. "More like torture. 'Twas a solid misery, trying to finish it." With a thump, Brigid sat down on a boulder next to the path. "*One foot in the grave*," she recited morosely, her voice quivering.

"*And the other on it's edge*." Tom's sing-song tone of gloom sent them both into a fit of laughter. When it subsided he sat down next to her and sighed. "Well, there you are. She'll be an affliction to students for years to come, but at least we're a united front."

"It's not fair, really," Brigid said, wiping her eyes with her apron. "Peig isn't like that at all, forever moaning and mithering. She lives in Dunquin, now. She moved out to the mainland the year after I came to live with Lis and Sean, but before that I was always in her house, listening to the stories. She had a deep, graveling voice like a man's, but she was always bright and cheerful. She was kind to me."

She closed her eyes, summoning the vision of evenings spent in the dim, smoky interior of Peig's house, and of the tiny woman in her chair by the hearth in her dark shawl, the rosary always wrapped in her hands. She'd seen that Brigid was unusual, but unlike others in the community, Peig acted as though the difference in her wasn't something to forgive or regret, but something to be grateful for, something to celebrate.

"You're a gift to the island," she'd once told Brigid. "You feel the spirit in it, and when the spirit feels you as well, there's less loneliness for both."

Brigid opened her eyes. "Something got lost, when they took all her tales and put them into a book. They've hardly any life at all, now, but they did when she was telling them. They were gorgeous stories, I promise you, they were."

"I believe you," he said. "Maybe those kinds of stories are like sheet music. They're meant to be listened to, instead of read." He looked at her. His face was close enough to count the long, silky lashes framing his eyes. "You've a lovely sounding laugh, Brigid. It's the first time I'm hearing it, and it goes down a treat."

"Oh." Whatever else she might have said dropped away when he leaned forward, hesitated, and then gave her a soft kiss on the cheek. "Oh," she said again.

Drawing back, Tom tilted his head, his smile uncertain. "Will I get a thrashing for that?"

"You won't, I think. Not from me, at least." Brigid stared down at her hands. The shivering thrill she'd felt from the simple brush of his lips against her skin was an entirely new experience. She took in a quick breath. "Will we just walk up to the well, for a sip of water? I'd say we could do with one."

She spoke without looking at him, not from shyness, but because he was so close that she could feel the heat of him, and she was struggling against the urge to take his face in her hands and press her lips to his.

8

The main well, near the top of the village, had been constructed around a stream that emerged from the side of a hill. Tom sat with Brigid on the rock wall next to it, listening to the water echo as it gurgled and dripped into a small shelter made from loose stones.

A few tin cups had been left on the wall for thirsty passersby, and he'd already filled his several times, conscious of having swallowed little else that day. Earlier at Mrs. Malloy's, he'd sat watching Dan murder a pound of beef, but had passed on the invitation to join him. Brigid had also offered him something when they first reached her cottage, but he'd politely declined that as well, thinking it an unnecessary distraction. He didn't want to eat, didn't need it. He could live on air. He could live on the sight of her.

As a result, Tom had been sustained for ten hours on the bit of buttered bread he'd grabbed on his way to the barn that morning. He thought a few pints of water might make up for the lack of nourishment, but had to admit it wasn't the real reason he felt lightheaded.

He was surprised he'd had the nerve to kiss her, although he'd thought about it more than once. In the course of their short acquaintance, Brigid had shown him her dry wit and fiery spirit, but beneath that lay something more reserved, contemplative even. Tom couldn't help feeling intimidated by her quiet self-possession – but her laughter had given him courage. The carefree sound of it somehow made her beauty more approachable.

There had been nothing volatile about the kiss itself, but when he'd leaned in, his breath had stirred up the scent of her skin, warm and flushed from the walk, and a strand of her hair lifted in the breeze and brushed against his lips. Touching her cheek Tom felt something change, but he didn't understand it right away.

Brigid's reaction was subdued. At first, she bowed her head and wouldn't look at him, but he saw a shy smile appear when they began climbing again. Sitting next to her by the well, he found himself again focused on a strand of her hair, this one damp with perspiration. His eyes traced its path, dark and curling against her neck, until it reached the base of her throat, and he could see the beat of her heart there, just visible beneath the satin-smooth skin. Tom watched its steady pulse, and felt the shifting thing inside him become an overwhelming desire – an arousal he couldn't prevent no matter how much water he threw down his throat.

"Such a terrific thirst," Brigid said, watching him drain another cup. "You'll have the well dry before you've finished."

"I might at that."

He smiled weakly, thinking she didn't know the half of it. She slid over to look at him more closely, a frown creasing her forehead. Tom didn't welcome the increased scrutiny at this particular moment. He leaned forward, arms on his knees, but he couldn't look away from her, and gradually he realized there was no hiding from Brigid.

"It's all right. I feel it, too."

She spoke so softly he nearly didn't hear the words. A second later he wondered if he'd imagined them, because she was on her feet, heading down the path.

"We'll go back now, and don't be telling me you won't take a bite of dinner before leaving. You're after going pale from hunger, and it's a long ride home."

Dazed, Tom watched her retreating back for a moment before he dared to stand up. He raised his eyes to the overcast sky, allowing a soft groan to escape as he straightened, and then followed her slowly, gathering self-control as he descended the hill.

Inside the cottage, Brigid invited him to sit at a table beneath the window and then didn't say another word while she prepared a meal for him. At first, Tom felt compelled to fill the silence. His naturally talkative disposition meant that he would often even yammer at the cows while milking them; but gradually he sensed Brigid's mood and reined in his tongue, realizing there was something in her peaceful serenity that needed his attention.

He watched as she raked the hearth, made tea, and put a few herbs into a simmering pot with a cut of bacon, some boiled potatoes and a few yellow turnips. Each task was like a ceremony concentrated in graceful movement, its solemnity lightened by her occasional smiling glance. He made a wider inspection of the cottage, which was small enough to take in without leaving his seat. Clean and brightened by whitewashed walls, it had an air of monastic simplicity. There was a sleeping alcove to the left of the hearth, with a bright checkered curtain drawn across it to screen the bed from view, and along the wall behind him was a pantry area. Its large dish cupboard was like the one in his own kitchen, but the colors and patterns of mismatched crockery made this one more festive.

There was only one exception to the room's uncluttered appearance. In a niche to the right of the hearth, a stone shelf beneath a plain metal cross held a crowded collection of odds and ends—pebbles, dried flowers and bird feathers, along with a rosary and a glass vial of holy water. He smiled at also seeing a pile of delicately tinted cockleshells in one corner.

All the items were arranged around a smooth, palm-sized stone deeply carved with Celtic spirals. Tom felt an impatient skepticism for such totems. The country already had a religion well-soaked in mystery. He saw no point in complicating it with knick-knacks and symbols that nobody really understood. Still, looking at the stone he couldn't help wondering what it meant to her. From her stool near the hearth, Brigid watched him with a wistful smile, and Tom wondered if she could sense his thoughts.

He grew more comfortable with the stillness, soothed by the atmosphere she'd created. Outside, the afternoon had become chilly, but the fire filled the room with a welcome heat, and the bubbling pot added its savory aroma.

The tranquil interlude lasted until Brigid placed the pot on the table and laughed as his rumbling stomach shattered the silence.

"Now," she said, taking a step back and spreading her hands in a commanding gesture. "Taste it."

"You'll have some as well," Tom insisted. "I can't eat it all by myself."

Her eyes gleamed. "Oh, I think you could, but I won't make you."

Sitting across from him, she took a small portion for herself but appeared more interested in watching him eat. He devoured it all—the meat, floury potatoes and buttery turnips all soaking in flavorful bacon juices—and Brigid made no secret of her amazement while successive servings disappeared from his plate.

"Has any of it reached bottom, yet?" she teased him. "Will I peel another round of spuds? I'd say we'll need a good few pounds to get the job done."

Giving her a sheepish grin, Tom put his fork down at last. "I was hungrier than I knew." He stopped her hand as she reached again for the serving spoon. "No, I'm well and truly stuffed, top to bottom. Thank you. I don't think anything ever tasted so good to me."

"I'm glad. You'll need your strength for dragging that big lumbering fella back into the boat with you. Will you have a smoke, now? My uncle left some tobacco here. Enough to fill one pipe at least."

He shook his head. "It's the only vice I've avoided."

"Good." Brigid nodded, rising from the table. "It's a nasty one. Uncle Sean says smoking helps digestion, but sure it sounds a load of rubbish to me."

Happy to have scored another point, Tom didn't qualify it by explaining his lack of choice in the matter. He sometimes had to quickly leave a pub when the smoke got too thick, and could only imagine the reaction if he tried sucking down an undiluted mouthful of the stuff.

"They'll be coming back, soon, but I expect we've time enough for one more cup." She refilled the teapot and brought it to the table, giving him a playful glance as she poured. "There will be no end of gossip if they catch you coming out of my house."

"Will there?" Tom was amused. "I didn't think you had enough women here for a good gossip."

"The men are worse than the women on this island." Brigid made a face, but then grew serious as she sat across from him again. "Tell me about the meeting. What news has Dan O'Brien brought with him?"

He tightened his grip on the cup, hearing the tension in her voice. It was a subject he'd been expecting earlier and by this time had hoped to escape.

"I don't know, actually."

"Go on, now." Suddenly angry, Brigid threw herself back in the chair. "After all the time spent with the man, you want me to believe you know nothing about his plans?"

Her eyes swept over his face and away, dismissively, and Tom felt as though she'd slapped it. "I'm asking you to believe the truth, which is that I honestly don't know. Dan wanted to talk with the people here before telling anyone else, but sure you'd know all about it by now, if you'd gone and listened to him. But, I'm glad you didn't," he hurried to add.

Brigid sighed, her shoulders slumping. "And why should I be snapping at you at all, when it's none of your fault? I can guess well enough what his plans are. He'll put us out of our homes and off this island without ever giving a moment's thought to a better idea."

"Do you have one?"

Brigid took a slow sip from her teacup before responding. "I do."

"What is it?" Genuinely curious, Tom leaned forward, resting his arms on the table.

"The government could give us a proper harbor." From the speed of her reply he could tell she'd given it a good deal of thought. "The only reason people want to leave is because we've been stranded before, and we've a fear for the day when that miserable radio phone won't work and we can't put a boat on the water—that we'll be forgotten entirely with none coming to help. If they'd build us a harbor with a decent pier, then we could dock diesel-powered boats like your own that go back and forth with no bother."

"Well, I'm not sure about 'no bother.' In some weather, there'd be no boat able to—"

"And with a good, sheltered harbor," she continued, ignoring him, "they could carry on with a bit of building. We could reopen the school and have our own shops as they do on Inishmor in the Aran islands, and then other people might like to live here again. It would make all the difference, don't you think?"

"It's certainly creative," Tom said.

The idea wasn't terrible—it had a sophisticated logic that impressed him—but it was almost certainly too sophisticated and he doubted the Irish government would finance any scheme for developing and re-populating the Blasket. The island was as different from Inishmor as a mountain from a hay field. This wasn't the time to be telling her and he wasn't about to try, but there was no need, really. His careful response hadn't fooled her.

"Oh, you're right," Brigid said, as though Tom had shared his doubts out loud. "I suppose they wouldn't do it, but it wouldn't have hurt to try. To have asked at least."

"Of course." Tom was willing to say anything that might take the sadness from her face. "There's never any harm in asking. Why didn't you?"

"I was stubborn and angry. I wanted nothing to do with Dan O'Brien, or any of the business that brought him to us, but it wouldn't have been any use, anyway. In this village I'm the one with queer notions, everyone knows it. I would have been laughed at. Oh leave it, so. " Sighing, she stood up and began collecting the dishes onto a tray.

Tom added his to the pile and then caught her hand as she reached for the teapot, giving it a light, reassuring squeeze. It was the only comfort he could think to offer that wouldn't be taken as overly bold. Brigid smiled, letting her hand rest in his for several seconds and removed it with a slow reluctance.

"We should be going out, now, I suppose. We can wait for them by the post office."

As they exited her house, Tom glanced up at the gray, congested sky and then at the ocean. It was threatening rain but he was relieved to see there was still only a light chop in the water. They walked along the path to a wall near the post office that provided an unobtrusive view of the houses at the top of the village. He insisted on spreading his coat on the damp rock for her to sit on, and Brigid insisted on sharing it. She moved a little closer when he joined her and Tom tested this unspoken permission by bracing an arm against the rock behind her back. When she shifted towards him again he tentatively circled it around her waist, and was content with the world and everything in it.

"Mr. Dan O'Brien." She spoke the name with more kindness than he'd heard before. "I should have paid more attention the first time he came in to see us. He's a good man. I see that, now."

"He is, Brigid," Tom said gently. "I think he'll do his best for you."

"I've missed my chance, though, haven't I? I could have talked to him, but now it's too late." Brigid turned her face to him, and tried to smile. "I may have wasted my opportunity, but at least I didn't waste the day."

Her brave attempt to shake off despair was too much for Tom. Already trying to control—or at least understand—a flood of bewildering emotions, he thought his heart might crack from the weight of something stronger than all of them.

"It's still worth a try. I'll tell Dan about your plan, if you like."

"Will you?" She pulled away to look at him, her face clearing in a surprised smile.

"Don't expect too much," Tom said. "Maybe he'll consider it, but it would need a fair bit of money. I'm happy to speak to him, but I've no idea what he'll say. It might not be any use."

"It doesn't matter what he says," Brigid said. "It matters that you offered, and didn't laugh at me."

She moved closer again, and he slipped his arm back around her—a natural, automatic movement that felt like something he'd been doing all his life. As though his arm had been formed for this purpose alone. He was all but certain

Dan would think the idea of a harbor project entirely unworkable, and was ashamed to realize he was counting on it.

"It mightn't be too bad, though, living on the mainland? I know it would be hard at first, but it can be wild and beautiful over there as well. Do you not think you could learn to like it?"

Brigid considered the question. "I don't think so. It isn't the place, really. It's me. For a start, I don't think I'd get on well with the people. Everyone here is used to me, now, but over there they would find my way of thinking peculiar. They wouldn't like it. Or me."

"What a load of bollocks." Tom put his hands on her shoulders, turning her to face him. "Why should you care what a lot of wee-brained eejits, think? There's nothing wrong with being different, Brigid. You're peculiar, sure, but only because you're better than most. You make peculiar seem like something brilliant."

At first it seemed as though his words had backfired. Brigid's eyes filled with tears, but then she smiled and brushed her fingers against his cheek.

"You're after becoming a fine heroic figure, Tom McBride."

Then she lifted her face and reached up to kiss him. Tom needed a few seconds to master his astonishment, but then gave the soft lips his full attention. They began with an exchange of light, tender caresses that quickly became more urgent. Still kissing her, Tom pulled her closer, feeling her fingers tightening on his shoulders as he cupped a hand to the back of her head, letting it slide along the silky waves of her hair. She pressed against him, but all too soon her lips slid away, and he felt the heat of her mouth against his ear.

"They're coming down, now." she whispered.

He followed her gaze and saw people had begun leaving the middle house at the top of the village. At this distance no voices could be heard, but their gestures were a pantomime of animated chatter. The meeting had ended, but Tom wasn't willing to give in just yet.

"Right so," he said, nuzzling her neck. She shivered, gasping a little, but then pulled away.

"They'll be here soon. They'll see. I have to go."

Tom surrendered to the inevitable, accepting a final, tender kiss, but he didn't really care who was coming, or how quickly, or what they might see. All he could think about was the taste of her mouth, of filling himself with the warmth of it, and of the cold ache settling into every muscle as she slipped from his grasp like a stream of clear water.

Brigid darted away, back to her cottage, and he turned just in time to catch a last glimpse of her dark-clad shape disappearing around the corner of the post office. A retreating shadow, trailing enchantment in its wake.

9

Waiting on the path, Tom stood watching the spectacle of Dan's approach. He strode down the hill, head bobbing amidst a crowd of islanders who moved him along like a leaf on the water. From the cautious pleasure in their faces and the land officer's broad smile, Tom assumed the meeting had gone well.

The group coming to see them safely off was larger this time, and included Brigid's aunt and uncle. Lis looked exasperated at finding Tom waiting alone. She drew him aside for a private word.

"She's run off on you, has she?"

"Only just," Tom said. "After showing me all around the place and filling me up with bacon and potatoes."

"Well, that's all right, then. Brigid's a fine little cook."

"She is, indeed."

Lis shot him an anxious look from the corner of her eye. "She gets her odd notions, I know. Feels the world differently, somehow. You mustn't mind it."

"I don't."

"And she's the kindest, most loving girl you'd ever like to meet. A solid treasure, so she is."

"I know." Tom smiled. "I need no convincing of that."

"Good." She gave his arm a brief squeeze. "Safe home, and we'll see you again soon, please God."

They embarked after several rounds of farewells, and climbed back onto the trawler with a merciful lack of excitement. Settled on the wheelhouse bench and looking more comfortable on it than he ever had previously, Dan confirmed the day had gone better than he'd dared to hope. Tom was too distracted to listen at first and needed several points repeated to him, but as the Land Commissioner patiently described the government's proposal he began listening more closely, and could see why the islanders would be pleased by it.

There were many complicated and emotional questions surrounding the evacuation of the Great Blasket, but in considering them Tom had always returned to the most obvious: evacuation to where? It would be easy enough organizing boats to carry the islanders and their belongings away from their homes, and God knows Ireland had mastered a talent for emigration, but these people were either too old to start fresh in a new country or they simply didn't want to—where would they go once their feet were planted on the mainland? They couldn't live on the pier.

The Land Commission had seen this as the central issue as well, and the plan Dan described was nearly as creative as a new harbor, but less expensive. The government would offer farming families in Dunquin an opportunity to re-locate to larger farms in Kildare and Meath, after which their Dunquin land would be made available to Blasket families.

"The Taoiseach approved the scheme last week," Dan said. "He's authorized me to advertise it in Dunquin and make offers for three houses, and we'll see how it goes. The best part is the islanders will keep the ownership of their houses on the Blasket. They can pasture sheep out here in summer and go back and forth as they like when the weather is fine."

Tom was surprised that a government commission could devise a plan so clever. It provided dignity and some sense of continuity for the islanders, and since the people of Dunquin would eventually be their neighbors, it seemed wise to engage that community as well, expanding the project's benefits.

"It sounds brilliant." Tom watched Dan's face closely as he added, "Who came up with the idea?"

"Ehm, well." The land officer's face turned crimson. "The members all contributed something to the plan."

"But you managed to keep them from sinking it?"

Dan laughed. "Myself and Dev. They could hardly say no to him."

He was in high spirits, and Tom didn't want to temper his happiness by mentioning Brigid's alternative. He thought her plan now even less likely to fall on fertile ground, but he intended to keep his promise, and he did so once they were back in Dingle, settled at Regan's with two foaming pints in front of them. With Jamesie covering his chores, Tom was in no hurry to get home this time.

He put forward the harbor suggestion as persuasively as he could, but was not surprised—or, to be honest, disappointed—when Dan eviscerated the idea. He was gentle about it, but had the reasoning and detailed statistics at his fingertips, and he concluded the rebuttal with a probing set of questions.

"Would you want to live on that island yourself, Tom?"

"Jaysus, are you joking me? Not if you built a bridge to it."

"But you care for the lass? I'd an idea you did, anyway. I could barely get your attention the whole ride back."

Tom knew where the conversation was heading. He slowly revolved his pint glass in the puddle of condensation forming beneath it.

"I'm fond of her, I suppose."

"So it would make things altogether easier if she came off the island, but here you are, trying on an idea that's against your own interests. Why's that, I wonder?"

"I made a promise."

"Ah. Right so. You made a promise." Dan signaled the barman, swirling a finger to indicate two more pints, and gave a low chuckle. "Fond of her. A bit more than that, I'd say."

Tom didn't respond, or take his eyes from the wet glass sliding under his fingertips. Of course it was more than that. He was in love with her; he knew that much already, but was afraid it might not be enough.

10

*C*he atmosphere was unsettled after Dan O'Brien's departure. Moods changed hourly, and Brigid felt every fluctuation in the level of nervousness, skepticism and sorrow. Everyone who'd attended the latest meeting had been impressed with the plan presented. In one stroke, it eliminated the biggest, most troubling obstacle to leaving the Blasket – the question of where they would live once the only homes they knew were left behind. Dan's offer was a development they never expected, and it seemed to change everything, but they'd never been a community to act in haste. A second meeting had been set for a week later, giving the islanders a chance to think about everything they'd heard and discuss it within their families.

Dan had left behind a rolled topographical map of the area around Dunquin, and it was passed like a holy relic from house to house. In each of them, men would spread and anchor the scroll with cracked, weathered hands, and then gaze down, pipes clicking against their teeth, studying their future.

Along with every other emotion she could feel among her neighbors, Brigid sensed an overall pulse of excitement. At first, she thought it unsustainable—the yearning for something new and adventurous—but once she understood it better, she knew her cause was hopeless. They weren't looking at the map as a route to adventure. In their hard, toiling lives they'd had their fill of that, already. They were looking at it as a path towards rest. How could she deny them that, especially when she felt so confused about her own future?

During her years in Kenmare, the sea had seemed so far away. From the dingy room her mother rented over Foley's pub, Brigid couldn't even see the long sliver of Kenmare Bay, growing thinner as it worked its way inland. She sometimes caught a hint of its swampy breath, though, and then would imagine herself stretched long and straight, slicing through the water with the seaweed sliding along her body, heading for the open sea and her beloved island.

For as long as she could remember, the Blasket had pulled her in, sewing her like a thread into its patchwork landscape, but now for the first time she'd felt its grip loosen ever so slightly, as though something had gently tugged at the stitching, testing its hold.

On the evening of the meeting, with a few hours to go before the community gathered, Brigid felt as agitated as she ever had in her life. None of the things that usually calmed and centered her were working. Having exhausted all other options, she burst through the door of the post office in desperation and threw herself into a chair.

Startled, Lis looked up from the sock she'd been darning. She set the sewing basket aside and rose, lightly touching

Brigid's shoulder as she passed.

"I'll put the kettle on, will I?"

Her aunt stirred the fire and swung the big iron kettle over a rising flame while Brigid fidgeted, fingering the piles of letters covering the table.

"What's this?" She pulled forward a thick book tucked inside a brown paper sleeve.

"It's a catalog from Sears and Roebuck." Lis threw a guilty-looking glance over her shoulder as she reached for the tea tin. "It arrived from Margaret's sister in America a few weeks ago. She brought it over this morning for me to look at."

Brigid pushed the book out of its sleeve and ran a hand over the cover. It was glossy and smooth, and brightly colored. The pages were tissue-thin and crammed with so many images it was difficult to focus on any of them. Whole pages full of socks and shoes, jewelry, automatic toasters and hair dryers, and of course page after page of men's and ladies' clothing. Lis brought over the tea tray and sat down at the table across from her.

"I thought we might do well to lay in a few new things to wear."

Brigid looked up from the catalog, hearing an odd note of strain in her voice. Her aunt's eyes ducked away, but she doggedly continued. "I don't mind how many times I darn a dress or patch a pair of trousers, but I won't have the folk of Dunquin sneering at the state of us, so I suppose we'll be needing something decent for the town, and for Mass on Sunday."

Lis took a quick gulp from her teacup, and then lowered it on to the saucer with a crack that echoed in the quiet cottage. She sniffed and rubbed a hand over her reddening nose, looking almost angry. "You'll be very welcome to come live with us over there. You know that."

A desolate, twisting pain engulfed Brigid. It felt as if someone was wringing her out like a rag. She began paging through the catalog again, brutally this time. The delicate sheets sounded like they were tearing as she turned them.

"So, we're coming to this, are we?" She glared down, barely seeing the pages as they flew past. "Going in for trinkets and rubbish and fashions that don't suit us."

"You don't know what may suit you unless you try it," Lis said. "You're a beautiful lass, Brigid. You'd look well in a new dress yourself."

"I'm happy as I am," Brigid snapped. "I've no need to paint myself up as something I'm not, only to impress a lot city gawkers who care no more for me than I do for them."

"City gawkers." Her aunt sighed. "You make it sound as though we're bound for London. There's none would mistake Dunquin for a city. And your lad's farm in Ventry?" she added. "That's a smaller place still."

Brigid stopped ripping through the catalog, but her eyes remained on it, as if she couldn't get enough of the marvels on offer. Lis picked up one of her hands, resting limply on the table, and wrapped it in both of her own.

"You mustn't think you're left without choice. Tom McBride seems a fine man, and I think he cares for you, but if you don't want him there's always a place for you with us."

Brigid nodded. Beneath her gaze a page illustrating handbags swam and shimmered, until a large tear dropped onto it, becoming an expanding circle of gray as the paper absorbed it.

"I do want him, Lis," she whispered, gripping her aunt's hand tightly. "But, I don't know if I can bear to leave this place. It breaks my heart just thinking of it."

"Your heart has good company. Sure aren't they breaking all over the island, tonight?" Lis ran a thumb over Brigid's face, smiling. "We'll keen and wail for a time, but then we'll move on, won't we? In the end, what does it matter which pile of stones you settle inside, if the fire is warm and the rooms filled with love?"

∼

The two halves of the village came together that evening in their assembly building, *An Dail*. Over the past hundred years it had seen countless gatherings – some joyful, others solemn – but until that night it had never hosted a meeting of such finite consequence. The tone was subdued, and there were no votes taken, because none were needed. Each family could choose its own course and timing, but the outcome was inevitable. Soon enough, they would all quietly relinquish what a century of Atlantic storms had not been able to rip from their grasp.

To begin the meeting, Sean cleared his throat to announce the decision he and Lis had reached. Brigid fought back tears, watching her shy uncle's fingers working against his knees, his eyes fixed on the paraffin lamp hanging from a beam overhead.

"We'll go, I think," he said, his voice hoarse but steady. "We'll get no better offer, and if the Taoiseach goes out at the next election it could be lost. I'd rather it be now than miss the chance altogether."

Around him, the men nodded and hung their heads, look-ing down at the ground between their boots. For a moment no one spoke. The only sound was the creak of the old wooden chairs they'd drawn into a circle, but Sean's words had loosened the tension. The room soon filled with quiet conversation, the low male voices peppered with occasional murmurs from the women. Brigid remained quiet and listened, knowing even this – the rolling, throaty notes giving the Blas-ket dialect its distinct character – would someday be lost. She let the sound wash over her, burning it into her mind like a tune she wanted to remember.

As often happened, the meeting gradually floated from its original purpose, the practical discussion of plans and logis-tics giving way to stories and reminiscence. It ended late, and when she left the building Brigid found Mary waiting for her.

"Come here to me, my girl. Help an old woman find her way home in the dark."

Brigid looked up at the brilliant moon shining on them like a spotlight, and smiled before taking her arm. She expected to be questioned about her own plans, but as they walked she discovered Mary had news of her own to share.

"I had a letter from Fiona today. She's going to be married in the spring."

"Married!" Brigid exclaimed. "You're serious?" Mary's niece had been widowed almost ten years earlier.

"No word of a lie," Mary said. "The fellow grew up in Annascaul and bought a farm just the other side of Slea Head. She met him at the cattle mart, and he asked her to a dance, and that was that."

"Please God she'll have great happiness, and none more

deserving of it. Give her my best, Mary."

"I'll do that, love. I will."

When they reached the King's House, Brigid accepted a blessing for God's protection through the night and then started back, but hearing Mary softly call to her, she turned to see the slight silhouette still framed in the doorway.

"Do you know what Fiona said to me in that letter, Brigid? That she'd been stuck for too long on endings, and never knew it was the very thing that kept something from beginning."

With that, Mary closed the door. Brigid stood staring at it, amused by the transparency of the message, but the words lingered in her mind. Still too restless to think about sleeping, she let the moonlight guide her down to the beach. Kicking off her shoes she sat in the sea grass, and looked across the water.

The distant shoreline was the same as always. Brigid could trace the dark outline of its hills from memory, but tonight she had a different view in her mind. Hidden behind the headlands of the peninsula, Ventry couldn't be seen from this angle, but that didn't matter. With the echo of Tom's voice reminding her of it, the vision came alive. She saw a bowl-shaped harbor with wide fields spread above it, and as each tidy parcel of land took shape before her eyes, she whispered its name.

11

It took Tom a bit of time to see the obstacles he faced as a long-distance suitor. At first, he could fix his mind on nothing beyond the fleeting thrill of Brigid's kiss. It wasn't his first, but there was certainly nothing in any previous encounters – all of them brief – that came close to matching it. He relived the experience in every waking moment, and in sleep, invented new ones of such vivid detail that he had trouble facing his parents at the breakfast table. All of it excited an impatience for more, which at last forced him to register the inconvenience of loving a woman who lived on an island.

He would happily navigate the windswept Blasket Sound every day to see her, but that idea was no more than a fantasy. Even occasional visits would be a challenge to organize now. Focused on finding houses for the islanders, Dan wouldn't visit again until spring. In the meantime, Tom felt his campaign for Brigid's affections hanging by a thread. He became desperate enough to appeal to Jamesie. His friend was not an especially deep or imaginative thinker, but he was Tom's only confidante, and he was stalwart.

He presented the dilemma to his friend one afternoon as they collected turf in one of the peat bogs Seamus had acquired. It was a few miles down the road from the farm, and they were in the section they leased to the Gallagher family. Shivering under a steady assault of rain, they picked their way through the pyramids of bricks they'd cut together that spring.

"Have you any ideas?" Tom asked Jamesie, who looked puzzled by the question.

"Did we not settle this already? Go see her whenever you like. I can get the work done at your place. No bother."

"It's not only a matter of getting the work done." Tom stepped around a small lagoon of ditch water. "What am I to tell the mother and father, at all? I've no good excuse for going now."

"They don't need to know that, do they?" Jamesie's lips curled in a mischievous grin, but Tom didn't return it.

"I won't tell lies to them."

"So then, tell the truth."

"I can't do that, either. Until I can be sure Brigid will have me, it's best they not know about her."

Jamesie sighed. "Sure you're a grown man, Tommy. You can court whoever you please. Can you not tell them as much?"

Embarrassed to admit he couldn't, and ashamed of the reason why, Tom made no answer. He was a grown man, right enough, but he was also the heir of a modern man of business with nineteenth-century sensibilities. Fixated on land and wealth, and forever angling to collect a bit more of both, his father's notions of courtship could be captured in a single, ancient word of Irish: *Spré*. Fortune, or—a translation more to the point—dowry. As far as Seamus was concerned, any family hoping to marry into the McBride farm should expect to put up a dowry appropriate to its size and stature. Judged by this standard, there could be no less suitable prospect than a penniless young woman who went about barefooted most of the time.

"It's best they not know about her," Tom repeated. Muttering the words under his breath, he bent to the next pile of turf.

Jamesie shrugged. "Fair enough. I suppose you should get started with the letters, then. To stop her forgetting you altogether."

"I suppose I should." Tom wondered if his deplorable writing skills and penmanship would hinder his cause instead of advancing it, but until he could think of something else, courtship by post seemed the only option.

He wrote the first letter in fear, since it required a confession of failure in advocating for Brigid's harbor idea, but her reply came quickly, full of gratitude and expressions of pleasure at hearing from him. With that as encouragement, Tom developed a habit for correspondence that verged on addiction. He began filing letters twice a week at the Dunquin post office. Once the pattern was established he usually found a letter waiting for him. Eva was always on hand to make the exchange, winking and smiling, and peeling an eye at Tom as if she wanted him for pudding.

Brigid's letters were reserved but affectionate, and sensibly organized. After reading them Tom loved simply to look at the careful handwriting, thinking of her cool, slim fingers as he ran his own over the ink.

By contrast, his letters were anything but organized, written in fits and starts, whenever he had time to pull the crumpled work in progress from his pocket. He'd pencil in a few smudged lines about his day, and round out the business with veiled declarations of love before jamming it all into an envelope. Often, he couldn't find time to slip away from the farm unnoticed, but Jamesie filled the breach, and in exchange for his personal courier services, Tom continued filling in at the Swallowtail in Ventry village.

The pub owner, Jarlath Fenton, was a merry, red-faced giant of a man. He was known as "The Wheel" for so often spouting on about the history of his name, which had something to do with a saint and a broken chariot wheel. Tom didn't fully grasp the details, but he found both The Wheel and the bartending duty a great bit of craic.

The room was long and narrow and the atmosphere unpretentious, with a red leather bench running the length of the wall opposite the bar. In the space between, a few tables and mismatched chairs were scattered over a formica-tiled floor. He liked moving around behind the sweeping, crescent-shaped bar, and was stationed there one evening when his father walked in with a few men from the creamery committee.

Tom nodded a greeting, his smile ironic. Despite frequent complaints about his son's fondness for them, Seamus liked the odd night out as well as anyone. Ignorant of the details, he also approved of the part-time pub duty. He seemed to think more exposure to the exchange of money would give Tom a greater appetite for it, as though half-crowns and shillings carried a virtuous germ that could be absorbed through contact.

Seeing him this evening, though, Seamus stopped in the doorway, and Tom understood the hesitation, even if his father didn't. In this place, the man had no authority. His son was in charge, with the discretion to provide a drink or refuse it, according to his own judgement. As their eyes met, the dynamic that usually existed between them subtly shifted. Tom allowed himself a moment of satisfaction, but rather than force the issue he poured out two fingers of Powers and slid the glass across to him.

Seamus accepted the whiskey with a grunt. "I suppose you'd be more happy this side of the counter, Tom, wouldn't you?" His father gave him a crooked grin, happy to have the order of the universe restored, and then joined his companions at the end of the bar.

The group settled in, staying longer and drinking far more than Tom expected. There was only an inch remaining in the bottle of Powers, and he was standing as far from Seamus as he could get, when The Wheel sidled up to him.

"On a tear tonight, isn't he? Yer oul' fella." His bright blue eyes were awash in laughter.

"Seems like it." Tom kept his attention on the glass he'd been polishing. He was trying to ignore his father's voice, which had grown progressively louder.

"He's a good few glasses inside of him, now."

"I know that, Jarlath. I do. Sure isn't it me that's after filling them these past two hours." He flicked a tense glance at the pub owner. "Is there something you're wanting me to do, now?"

"Easy, lad." Dropping the banter, he put a hand on Tom's shoulder. "The clock will do it for us. I'll be calling last orders in five minutes, and then we'll see –"

He trailed off as they watched Seamus climb unsteadily from his stool, rapping his knuckles on the bar and calling for attention.

"Jaysus," The Wheel muttered. "What's all this bollocks, then, Tom?"

"I haven't a notion, Jarlath. Fact."

It could be anything, at this stage. His father was rarely in such a state of inebriation. He was generally a sleepy, genial drunk, in contrast to his testy nature when sober, but there was a first time for everything. Tom stopped the obsessive polishing and set down the glass, afraid of shattering it with his rigid grip.

"All right, gentlemen, all right." Seamus held up his hands, bringing the room to order, but aside from the two he'd arrived with there were only a half-dozen customers left in the pub, all sitting at the bar, and his knock on the top of it had already captured their amused attention. Aside from a sprinkling of chuckles and low comments they'd fallen quiet.

"I've a few brief remarks." He spoke as though attending a dinner in his honor, with the assembled waiting on his speech. "A few brief remarks," he repeated, and paused again, swaying.

"Whatever it is, Seamus, you'd better get on, so. Your legs won't hold you much longer." His friend Kevin Vaughn, on a stool right in front of him, gave Tom a wink amidst the general laughter.

Tom mustered a weak smile, growing more nervous by the minute. The Wheel–ignoring customary regulations–quietly placed a pint of stout in front of him.

Seamus laughed along, then seemed to forget he'd been about to speak. He looked down at his glass, giving it a dreamy smile before suddenly coming to life again.

"I've taken a decision," he said, pitching his voice at a level meant to carry. "I'm bound for retirement, lads. It's thirty-odd years I'm working, and hardly a minute's rest. I've earned me bit of relaxation, and Eileen as well, God bless her. Come the spring, she'll be a woman of leisure, and mistress of a brand-new Salthill bungalow."

Having already sputtered on his Guinness at the word "retirement," Tom stared in shock at his father, who had surpassed the expectations of his audience. Seamus looked pleased by the interest he'd stirred up, and as the men peppered him with questions he sobered up a little, responding with exaggerated, good-humored patience.

"Well now, Jack, I've not bought the place as yet. We're to meet with the estate agent in two weeks and he'll be showing us around, so. No, sure we won't need anything too grand, Kevin. Nothing above a few acres for the house and grounds."

"A few acres, Tom," Kevin purred at him in a tone of false wonder. "And a cottage for the gamekeeper, I suppose?"

Tom could only shake his head. He had no words to offer regarding the as yet un-purchased bungalow or its surrounding amenities. He had no words, period. Salthill was a resort area in Galway City. His father was done with farming. His parents were moving to Galway. Here, in a pub, in front of their neighbors, this was the first he was hearing about any of it.

Kevin soon realized as much, as did the men lined up beside him at the bar. The pity in their eyes made him feel a fool, and all the while Seamus droned away, explaining that he'd promised Eileen they would move closer to her family when he retired.

"You'll stay at the farm I suppose, Tom?" one of the farmers asked. "You won't be deserting us for the seaside as well?"

It was a delicate, indirect phrasing of the inheritance question and before Tom could reply, Seamus hijacked it.

"Well ... " Drawled on a long breath, the word's sustained note of ambivalence hung in the air between them. "Am I not after sinking half the years of my life into the place? I'll want to be sure about the man who comes after me, won't I? We'll be staying up in Galway with Eileen's sister for six weeks. I'd say that's enough time to show me what he's made of, whether he has what it takes, you know."

The room took on an uncomfortable silence, and the men at the bar grew more interested in their glasses of stout. A line of cold sweat formed on Tom's forehead as he felt the color draining from his face. With stiff, fumbling fingers, he removed the long barman's apron, untangling himself from the strings circling his lean frame. The Wheel started towards him, looking nervous, but Tom waved him off.

"It's alright, Jarlath."

His father watched, his face already clouding in confusion and regret, but Tom ignored this. He directed an expressionless stare at him, then tossed the apron on the bar and walked out.

12

They didn't speak at all the next day. Tom was as angry as he'd ever been in his life, and made a point of staying away from his father, who for once appeared embarrassed by what he'd done. During the evening tea, they sat across from each other, avoiding eye contact and rejecting his mother's timid attempts at conversation. In the past, Eileen had been stern with them whenever he and Seamus locked horns, sometimes refusing to put food on the table unless they shook hands and made it up. This time she seemed daunted by Tom's cold fury, knowing some of it was directed at her.

"But, sure I didn't tell anyone, love," she'd protested, when he confronted her the morning after his father's boozy announcement. "I didn't think he'd ever go through with it, so what was the point?"

"He said it was a promise made to you long ago." Tom kept his head down, pulling on his barn boots near the kitchen door.

"So it was, but he's made promises before he never intended to keep."

"Well, it looks like he's keeping this one." He straightened and reached for the doorknob, still refusing to look at her. "You might have told me, Ma, as I'm not just 'anyone.' You might have said something to me, at least."

Closing the door behind him, Tom felt his anger turn to bewildered sadness. In his room that night, he piled all his emotions into a multi-page letter to Brigid, but once finished, he read it through and tore it up, ashamed of his self-pity. What were his troubles compared to hers? She had to endure the heartbreak of an entire village coming apart, a way of life being extinguished like a candle in a coal mine. She must be frightened and sad, but none of those feelings could be found in her even-tempered letters. He vowed not to burden her with his either, but he couldn't bring himself to produce something cheerful. Deprived of the happiness of writing to her, Tom went to bed, and after staring at the ceiling for several hours, fell into a dreamless sleep.

The following day, he spent a few hours working in the tool-shed. Built from the remains of a crumbling wall, it smelled of mold and wet rock and leather horse collars. Usually, he brought what he was working on out into the daylight, but on this morning the cramped space felt like a refuge. In the dim light, he stood at the workbench, sharpening the blades that would be used to plow up the maincrop in a few weeks. He was cautiously pressing a thumb against the steel, testing his work, when he heard a shifting of gravel behind him. Tom turned to see his father in the doorway. They looked at each other for several seconds before Seamus spoke.

"I need help in the calving shed."

"Doing what?"

"It wants cleaning."

Tom frowned. The shed was only used in winter, when it was too cold for a calf to be born in the fields.

"We'll not be needing it for months, yet."

"And won't it be whistle-clean when we do." Seamus was already turning away as he added, "Come on and help me."

Sighing, Tom put the whetstone back on the shelf and followed him.

The first phase of the work was clearing the floor of the previous winter's bedding. Without any further talk they fell into a rhythm, forking the straw onto a cart, and taking it in turns to dump the loads at the edge of the barnyard.

"Mind the dust," Seamus said, breaking their silence at last.

"I will, yeah." Tom hefted another stringy bundle onto the cart.

"It'll start you wheezing, and your Ma will crucify me for a finish."

"There isn't much dust. I'm fine."

His father moved to one of the back corners and became conversational. "I had a drop too many in the town the other night."

"Did you, so?"

After another long pause, Seamus tried again, defensive, now. "It's not the way I planned on sharing the news, Tom, I'll grant you that, but sure you bolt for the door with that damned fiddle as soon as you've the dinner ate, so where's the time to be talking to you at all? About anything?"

Tom jammed his pitchfork against a chunk of slate in the floor. His father jumped at the metallic clang and turned to see him with one arm balanced on the handle, stone faced.

"I'm here now. Talk away. What'll we discuss?"

Seamus hesitated, but then stood straighter—as he often did when trying to appear taller, as though height alone could command respect. He assumed a lofty tone. "The farm, of course. The business. You're expecting to carry on with it, I suppose?"

"I don't think I'm expecting anything at this point. I won't beg you for it."

"Who said anything about begging, for God's sake? I only want to know you're serious about it. It's the work of a lifetime, so it is. My legacy. I won't see it squandered."

"Who said anything about squandering?" Tom hissed. "Isn't it the work of my lifetime, as well? Didn't you have me out here the minute I could carry a pail of milk? And after leaving school, haven't I been out here every day since?"

"All right, all right." Seamus looked startled by the intensity of his rage.

"It isn't about the farm, and it isn't about your legacy. It's about you forever acting like I'm some gormless waster instead of your own feckin' son. Why's that, then? Am I such a weak substitute for the other three? Maybe you'd rather give the place to them instead, if you think so little of me?"

"That isn't true."

"Well why, then? Why make a show of me, in front of the whole town?"

Seamus tried holding his gaze, but then dropped his head, defeated. "I wasn't myself."

"You were, though, Dad," Tom said, quietly. "You were exactly yourself. And that's the trouble, isn't it?"

Without another word, they went back to work, turned

away from one another. Apart from the scrape of their forks and the rustle of straw there was no other sound in the shed. His anger spent, and none the wiser, Tom felt a dull ache drape itself around him.

∽

He couldn't get the answers he wanted from his father, but he got them at last from his uncle. On the day his parents left for Galway, Patsy rode along to see them off at the train station in Tralee. Tom could have easily driven the forty miles in their own car, but having something more stately in mind for their arrival in the market town, his father had hired a shining black Chrysler with white-wall tires. In front of the station, Patsy grumbled as he and Tom pulled innumerable cases from the trunk.

"Why are they going by train at all, when he could be driving this monster?"

"He thought the price too dear for more than a day's hire. I'm to have it back to the fellow in Dingle before sundown."

"Typical Seamus." Patsy laughed. "Sooner trust himself to the rattletrap Irish railway than part with an extra shilling."

Tom's smile was halfhearted. By now, he'd made peace with his mother, but relations with his father had remained awkward, and his uncharacteristic melancholy still hadn't lifted. When the train left, he stood watching it with Patsy, bathed in a coal-fired steam that settled into an oily taste at the back of his throat. He felt a queer emptiness spreading in his gut, and thought about others who'd felt it on the same platform, or on the docks, or even on the rocky shore of the tiny Blasket harbor—the people who'd watched sons and daughters disappear into a future that would not include them. It seemed a bizarre paradox, the parents leaving home. Sensing his mood and trying to shake him out of it, Patsy gave him a jab on the shoulder.

"Cheer up, for the love of God. It isn't Australia they're off to, is it? It's only bloody Galway."

"Right so." He gave a self-conscious laugh. "It's only that things seem different, somehow. Like I'm on the way to becoming an orphan."

"Rubbish. You're on your way to becoming a man, Tom." Patsy pulled him by the arm. "Come on, now. Let's get the best from this flash car before it turns to a pumpkin."

Driving through a drizzling rain, they took the long road home and stopped at a pub along the way. The place was deserted, and the cherubic landlady dusting the empty table-tops offered a warm welcome. After she'd placed two pints in front of them, along with ham sandwiches and a plate of hot chips, Patsy acknowledged that he'd heard about the scene at the Swallowtail.

"Don't mind it too much. He didn't mean anything. You'll do a fine job with the farm—you're doing it already, sure, and he knows that. He's told me himself, often enough."

Looking up from the chips he'd been picking at, Tom raised a skeptical eyebrow. "Fancy that. I've never heard as much from him. A bit odd, wouldn't you say?"

"I wouldn't, no." Patsy picked up one of the sandwiches and bit off half of it with one bite. He chewed slowly, his expression thoughtful. "Making money comes easy to Seamus, but nothing else does. He has to work at the rest of it. For all the posing and bluster, he's forever feeling the want of something, which drives him a bit mad, to be honest. Then, here's you. Happy as Larry, well-liked, and a knack for most things you put a hand to. He nearly resents that, somehow."

Patsy paused before continuing. His gaze slid from Tom to stare at a spot somewhere on the wall behind his shoulder, as if embarrassed by the intimacy of their conversation. "He cares for you, Tom, admires you even, though he'd never admit it, but I'd say he's jealous of you, as well. It's as simple as that, really."

"Jealous." Tom's lips twisted. "Go on and pull the other one, Patsy."

His uncle sat back, laughing. He waited for the landlady to deliver two fresh pints before continuing.

"Seamus was the youngest until I was born, of course – short and fat, and he got no end of slagging from the brothers. He was fairly delighted when I came along, thinking *he'd* have someone to slag now, and the brothers as well, but they never shifted off him, the poor sod. None of us could see the potential in him. Sure why would we? Nobody around the place ever had money, or any notion how to make it. We were pure blind to how smart and ambitious he was, but Eileen saw it, right enough. Jaysus, we couldn't believe it when he brought her home, couldn't imagine this lovely, English-speaking Galway girl wanting to marry the likes of him." Patsy picked up his glass, smiling and shaking his head. "An odd little success story, so they are. The pair of them."

"I wonder, why does she want to go to Galway, now?" Tom asked. "After all these years?"

"It's still her home." Patsy shrugged. "I think people don't ever get over missing their own native place, if they loved it. It's in their bones. It's who they are."

"I suppose that's true." Tom's thoughts again turned to Brigid. He wondered how it would feel to yearn for a home that no longer really existed. Distracted and moody, he'd not written a single line to her in the past two weeks, but she'd kept writing, and she'd been on his mind most of the time. It was a constant ache—the desire to see her, to talk with her about all the things he hadn't the skill for putting into a letter.

"I doubt they'll settle up there, you know," Patsy said. "Eileen will talk him around, so. For a finish it'll be only a little holiday bungalow. I'll wager they end up building a place in Ventry, right down the road from you." His uncle smiled at Tom's surprise. "Your Ma is stone mad about you, lad. Do you suppose she wants to be living away up in Galway while you're here? Your native place—that's all well and good, but it can't hold onto you if the one you love is somewhere else."

13

"*I*ve seen him, Brigid! At long last, the very man! Wasn't he standing right in front of me this afternoon, wanting to speak with you!"

Pleased as she was with the news, Brigid couldn't help wincing. It grated to think Eva Clifford had the inside track on her private business. She'd only met the woman once, during a shopping trip to Dunquin the previous year, but she could still remember the way the blonde ringlets all over her head bounced when she spoke. She could see them now, dancing and shivering with every exclamation. Brigid forced the uncharitable vision from her mind. Eva was doing her a kindness, and she was grateful for it.

She'd had no letter from Tom for over a month—six weeks, to be exact. On some level it felt foolish to be disappointed, since it had been a strange new experience to be waiting on the post at all. Until recently, no one had ever written to her before, and now here she was, moping over a lapse of six weeks. On the other hand, his letters had been as regular as the sunrise for the past few months, except when rough seas delayed the passage of the naomhógs. On some occasions she'd received two letters at once, which seemed as good as a Christmas stocking.

There weren't many things that could lift her spirits on the island these days, but Tom's letters did. They were bright and spontaneous and wandered all over the place. From the often ragged state of them it was clear he kept the pages close at hand, as though sharing each thought as it occurred to him. At some stage, the rambling observations would shift into particular expressions about his feelings for her. As she read those passages, Brigid imagined the same page she held in her hand being tucked inside his pocket, taking on his imprint, absorbing the warmth of him.

Then, without warning, the stream of letters ended – not a trickling off, but a full, dry stop. Brigid thought Eva and her Aunt Lis seemed almost as crestfallen as she was. She knew that whenever the radio phone was in use, the two of them were taking an extra minute to speculate and reproach Tom for his fickle behavior, but she didn't share their point of view. She had no information, no facts for interpreting the silence, but Brigid somehow knew it wasn't because his feelings had changed. She felt sure there was some other cause, and the possibilities worried her. Ignoring her aunt's gentle hints that she was being naive, she kept writing to him, trusting her own instincts to tell her when it was time to stop.

She'd been finishing one that very afternoon, when Lis had rapped on the door, calling her to the phone.

Eva was speaking now in a breathless rush of words. "Of course, wouldn't you know it, I couldn't make the call go through, but he's promised to come back tomorrow at one o'clock and we'll try again, so, and oh, he's just as handsome as ever, Brigid, but sure look, I don't mind saying I can't think what he's been up to at all, because he looked pale as paste, so he did, just pure knackered. He's fond of the music and the craic, isn't he? He's taking in a bit too much of it, maybe, but who am I to say?"

On the following afternoon, Brigid stood at the kitchen table in her aunt and uncle's cottage, ruining a batch of brown bread. First, she'd put in too much water, then she'd over-compensated, and now there didn't seem much hope for turning it into anything that even the pigs would eat. She was alone, since Sean was still out fishing, and Lis had tactfully removed herself to Margaret's house, telling Brigid to just come and fetch her when it was safe to return. Giving up on the mangled baking project, Brigid took a seat by the radio phone, praying it would work, and that she would have the patience to sit still if it didn't ring at one o'clock on the dot.

As it happened, the phone went off five minutes early. Just as before, the raucous noise of it momentarily stunned Brigid, but she recovered by the second ring and snatched up the receiver.

"Hello?"

"Hello to you as well, Brigid. Are you all right over there?"

She closed her eyes, feeling a surge of happiness at the light-hearted greeting. "My ears are playing tricks, I think. Can that possibly be Tom McBride, at all?"

He laughed. "I thought it worth the price of a call to let you know I'm living still." After a pause, he grew more serious. "I know I've been useless with the letters for a couple of weeks."

"It's more than six, now." Brigid silently scolded herself

for admitting she'd counted them. She heard Tom draw in a sharp breath.

"Dear God, is it that many? I didn't think—"

"Oh, maybe it isn't. It doesn't really matter, does it?" She affected a casual tone, as though his long silence was of little concern to her, as if it had not been like a stone settling on her heart.

"Of course it matters," he said, despondently. "There's hardly a minute in the day when I'm not thinking of you, but I still couldn't… what I mean is… oh, I don't know what I mean. I'm sorry, Brigid. Truly."

She'd intended to be cool with him a little longer, but the heavy weariness in his voice alarmed Brigid. "Never mind about it, Tom. Are you all right, though? Eva thought you seemed poorly yesterday. Have you been ill?"

"Did she say as much?" He brightened a bit, amused. "She thought I'd been having a good knees-up, I think. No, I've not been ill, only flittered. I've been cracking on, getting in the potatoes and trying to do a hundred other chores at the same time. September is the busiest time of year and the place is a bit shorthanded at the minute because things are … unsettled … at home. There's been a few things going on, and I couldn't come at the right words to get it all into a letter."

Brigid took a deep breath, and plunged ahead with the invitation she'd not yet had the courage to offer in writing. "Maybe you could tell me about it in person. The island is hosting a *céilí* at the end of the week. On Saturday. There are naomhógs bringing relations and friends over from Dunquin, and I'm told they have some room to spare—"

"I'll be there," Tom broke in.

"But, the boats won't return until the next morning, so if you're shorthanded with your work, and it puts you behind –"

"Brigid." His voice was low, urgent. "Haven't I been waiting months for the chance of seeing you again? I'll be there."

"Well, that's lovely, then," she said with perfect serenity, while her heart pounded at the tempo of a drumroll. "Lis and Sean will be delighted to put you up for the night, and we'll be wanting a tune from you as well, Tom, so mind you bring along your own fiddle."

They spoke for a few more minutes before ringing off, and then Brigid put the phone down and sat back to stare out the window. It was nearly an hour before she remembered Lis was waiting to be allowed home again.

～

It had taken the oldest man on the island to recognize a party might soften the edgy mood that had settled on the village. Since the meeting three months earlier, the idea of evacuation was no longer an abstract concept – it was an event with a scheduled timeframe. While some were eager to talk about and plan for it, others preferred to avoid the subject altogether. An awkwardness had begun creeping into relationships that had always been easy and casual, becoming a source of strain almost as great as the event itself.

When old Maras suggested hosting a céilí, the idea gained immediate traction, and a collective weight lifted. A festive night of music and dancing would give their sore hearts a rest, and the influx of visitors would add badly needed diversity to their conversation.

Brigid joined in the preparations with as much eagerness as any of her neighbors. She loved music and an occasional set dance, but she didn't often get swept up in the excitement of such celebrations. Her avid interest in this one took the islanders by surprise. She helped with the cleaning and sweeping—especially in the cottages where a woman's exacting standards had been too long absent. By the end of the week she had also baked three dozen scones, eight seed cakes, and three apple tarts. She'd hoped only Lis knew the truth behind her enthusiasm, but soon learned that everyone else had the guest list off by heart, and they knew it included the golden young hero who'd been Dan O'Brien's boatman. The general consensus was that their "queer little lass" might be in love, and they took her silence on the matter as confirmation.

Saturday morning arrived cool and damp but beautifully calm, with barely a ripple on the ocean. At first light, two crews departed the island, rowing out through a rising fog to Dunquin. Ostensibly, they went to escort the visiting boats and guide them into the Blasket's tiny harbor, but privately the men expressed more concern for the safe transport of liquid refreshments.

Later in the morning they returned amidst a small fleet of naomhógs, and by now the sun had burned through the mist, giving the day a warmth more common to late June than mid-September. Brigid was quick to join the villagers going down to welcome the guests, having spent the last two hours aimlessly moving things around in her cottage and searching the horizon.

The approaching boats were a fine sight, slicing into the rolling waves, sending arcs of water to either side of their high-tipped prows. When they drew close enough to distinguish passengers, she quickly singled out Tom. His hair shone like polished bronze in the sunlight. He was in the boat crewed by Petey and his two brothers, Mícheál and Martin. They formed the rearguard of the little armada, rounding up stragglers and correcting their navigation. Tom was in the stern facing the rowers, his arms resting protectively on two wooden kegs that were wedged in front of him.

They coasted into the harbor after the other boats had landed, and as the rowers stowed their oars, Petey looked over his shoulder, grinning at Brigid. "Never fear, lass. Here's your most valuable cargo, traveling with ourselves for safekeeping."

"It's these he's talking about." Tom braced a foot against the boat's gunwale as he hefted each keg into the arms of Petey's brothers. "In any storm, I'd be the first tossed over the side to save the whiskey and porter."

"It's more likely I'd pitch Mícheál out first," Petey said to Brigid in a low voice. "Your lad travels easy in a naomhóg—balances it like he was born in one. I wonder, can he stay long enough for a lobster run?"

"I expect he's work enough of his own without doing yours," Brigid said lightly, but she was secretly pleased. Petey was stingy with compliments.

She stood waiting in a hollow of the cliff wall while they pulled the boat from the water and flipped it onto a wooden stand. When the others started up the steep path, carrying the two kegs in a length of canvas, Tom walked over to her, a battered fiddle case in one hand and a rucksack over his shoulder.

"God save you." Brigid's throat was suddenly dry. The

greeting came out as a croak.

Tom smiled, and without speaking brushed his fingers lightly against hers. She shivered at their touch, which didn't escape his notice. After a glance up the path, he drew her further into the shadowed alcove. Only then did he give the traditional answer to her greeting, spoken between tender kisses.

"God ... and Mary ... save you."

~

They might have happily spent the entire day alone there in the shade of the cliff, wrapped in each other, with the lazy waves in the cove slapping against the rocks, but before long Petey called down from the top of the path, asking what had become of the pair of them. As if fighting the pull of gravity, Tom tore his lips from hers and called out a reassurance while grinning at her.

"Right. We're coming along immediately."

The interruption gave Brigid a chance to take a longer look at him. She saw all the things she'd been remembering so fondly for the last three months—the long lashes and glossy shine of his hair, the freckles sprinkled over sunburned cheeks, and above all, his earnest, openhearted gaze—but she also saw things that hadn't been there before. As Eva had already mentioned, Tom did look tired, but the difference was more than that. There was a tightness beneath the gleam in his eyes, a hint of strain at the corners of his mouth. The change was subtle, but to Brigid he looked a little more sharply drawn, a little less boyish.

She couldn't yet interpret the cause, but could sense something—like an image seen at a distance, an indiscernible shape. It was only pure instinct that prompted a question Brigid hadn't expected to ask.

"And your parents are keeping busy, I suppose? They're well?"

From his surprised reaction, Brigid saw she'd struck a nerve. Tom dropped his hands from her waist and gave a short laugh.

"In fine fettle, as far as I know, but I can't be sure because they're not at home. They've been staying in Galway for over a month now. It's where my mother was born, and ... Well." He made a wry face. "It's a long story. I'll tell you about it, but maybe not just yet?"

"All right, then. Not just yet." Brigid put a hand against his face, and felt the tension draining away. Satisfied, she bent to pick up his fiddle and started up the path. "They'll come looking if we don't show ourselves soon. Come here now, and listen while I tell you about this party of ours."

As they made their way up to the village, Brigid described the schedule. The music would begin in the evening. Before that there would be a dinner in the homes that were hosting visitors. The largest would be at the King's House. Mary was entertaining her niece Fiona and her betrothed, as well as three other nephews who had come all the way from Tralee. They were known to be brilliant dancers. Mary had also insisted on including old Maras, knowing he wasn't likely to put up a dinner worthy of the occasion for his visiting sister-in-law and her two daughters. Lis and Sean were hosting Tom, of course, and since they had no close relations left in Ireland, they'd invited a former Blasket couple who'd moved out to the mainland a few years earlier.

The dinners at each house were set for five o'clock. Until then, there would be visiting among the households with cups of tea and plates of scones, and perhaps a few small nips from the whiskey keg. Brigid had no intention of participating in this part of the day's agenda.

"We're the talk of the island already," she explained to Tom. They were meandering along a path through the lower village. "Parading from house to house will only be making their work easier, and now they've a bigger audience for all their carry-on. You can be sure that after every visit, we'd leave them all wittering away, inventing stories."

"Hmm. Maybe they would." After this noncommittal reply, Tom stopped and faced her, cocking his head to one side.

She glanced down at herself, and then looked behind her, puzzled as to what he was staring at. "What is it?"

"Do you mind it so much, Brigid? What people are thinking or saying about us?"

"Oh. Well."

The truth was that she wasn't bothered at all about the gossip, but about the idea of spending precious hours drinking tea in dim, crowded rooms when all she wanted was to be alone with him. Feeling caught in a web of her own invention, Brigid blushed.

"I don't suppose I do. Not really. Only I thought we could make better use of the time." Seeing the suggestive lift of his eyebrows she swatted his arm. "A picnic, Tom. It's a picnic I'm thinking of. You've seen so little of the island, and almost none of my favorite spots. There's plenty of time for it today, if you'd like to see them."

"*If* I'd like to see them?" His eyes narrowed. "You've the

sandwiches packed already, I'm guessing."

"I do."

"Well, why are we foostering about, then? Let's get on to these favorite spots. I'm not leaving the place 'till I've set eyes on every blade of grass you've ever smiled at."

14

*H*er picnic basket was a creel with a wide linen strap, ordinarily used to carry bricks of peat. Brigid had filled it with bacon sandwiches and lemonade, along with some scones and sliced seed cake, and had covered it all with a large wool blanket. Carrying the basket on his back as they walked uphill, Tom caught an occasional whiff of the bits of turf still buried amongst its rushes—a familiar, dark scent, somehow both bitter and sweet.

He wasn't surprised to learn that all of Brigid's favorite spots were in remote locations, and as luck would have it, the most important was on the back side of An Cró Mór, the highest point on the island. Scaling the modest summit was a small price to pay for being alone with her, well away from her nosy neighbors, but after six straight weeks of backbreaking work, Tom hardly needed the exercise.

Seamus had known exactly what he was doing with the timing of his Galway sabbatical. The implicit challenge of leaving during the farm's busiest season couldn't have been more transparent, nor could his parting words have expressed a greater presumption of disappointment.

"The place will survive, I suppose," he'd said before climbing aboard the train. "Try not to let it all settle into a porridge."

Knowing he'd get no satisfaction from clearing a bar set so low, Tom had fixed his mind on proving himself capable of managing all aspects of his father's so-called "legacy." He'd set himself a punishing schedule, dividing his days between the barn and the potato harvest, then, after fumbling together a meal he was often too tired to eat, he'd spend several hours in the room he'd always avoided—his father's office. It was a converted store room off the kitchen—small, dark and frigid—and he would stay in it until after midnight, deciphering balance sheets and other arcane bits of paper by the light of a guttering lamp.

Tom hadn't slept for more than four hours at a time in weeks. He might have been better off having the picnic blanket spread no farther than Brigid's front stoop, but his weariness had disappeared as soon as he saw her standing on the shore, and every time she touched him a burst of adrenalin shot along his nerves.

She took his arm now as they approached the coast at the northern end of the island. They were well above the village now, and the view was dramatic. Walking the lanes amongst the cottages, the steep pitch of the hillside was less noticeable, but looking at it from this angle gave Tom the sense that he was scrambling over the face of a lumpy, grass-covered pyramid. Brigid directed him to look at a point in the water off shore.

"There. Do you see her?"

At first Tom could make out nothing, but then saw a snout

emerge above the water line, followed by the long, glistening shape of a bottlenose dolphin.

"I wrote to you about her, do you remember?" Brigid said. "It was April when I first saw her, and I've seen her nearly every day since. I feel as though she finds me wherever I am."

"I do remember. Of course. How do you know she's female? Or that you're seeing the same one?"

"How do I know?" She sniffed. "Sure, can I not see her with my two eyes? We know each other well enough, I'd say."

"Do you, now?" Tom had cupped his hands over his eyes for a better view. He lowered them and squinted at her. "And? There's more to this story than was in the letter, I'm thinking."

"I suppose there is." Her haughty expression became more bashful. "There's a little cove on the White Strand where I go into the water sometimes. The seals come to visit, and she does as well. That's what I'd been doing, that day you found me there. I'd only just finished getting my clothes back on."

Tom smiled. "I wondered why they were wet." He took her hand as they started walking again. "Swimming with the seals and dolphins. I don't half understand you, Brigid O'Sullivan, I'll admit that much, but I'm learning. I've a long way to go, but I promise you I'm learning."

The route they followed along the northern coast was a level greenway carved into the steep hillside and wrapped around the island like a ribbon. Whatever doubts Tom harbored about the dolphin, he saw it kept pace with them, swimming along the coastline in graceful arcs. At one point, their progress was delayed by an impassive herd of black-faced ewes blocking the path, but the dolphin circled back, as if waiting for them. Tom had to admit it was unusual.

When they reached a point where the path curved sharply inland, Brigid paused in the middle of the bend, and as if on cue, the dolphin shot up in a breathtaking vertical leap. After a flick of the tail, it dove back into a rising swell and disappeared. While Tom stood gaping, Brigid nodded and swung back to the path.

"That's as far as she goes," she said, walking past him.

The tour she conducted followed no discernible pattern, and included frequent detours. Crossing spongy patches of furze, they searched out rock formations that interested her and puzzled Tom—and of course they all had names. Sometimes she moved uncomfortably close to the cliff's edge, to hear the particular music of the ocean sluicing through the caves beneath them.

Just below the lower of the Blasket's two main peaks, they came to the remains of an ancient fort, perched on the lip of the cliff. Brigid walked beyond the main footprint of the ruins to a small hollow, and sat on the steep hillside. She patted the ground, not taking her eyes from a jumble of rocks just below her. To Tom's eyes, they didn't seem to be shaped like anything. He slid the basket from his shoulders and went to sit next to her. The wind was stronger at this end of the island, the gusts booming in his ears like muffled explosions, but when he settled into the hollow by her side, the atmosphere grew quiet. The wind disappeared, the ocean's crash grew faint, and the sun was warm. Tom was beginning to sink into a peaceful drowsiness when Brigid spoke.

"Do you feel anything?"

He opened his eyes and snapped upright, as if he'd been caught dozing in school. He hadn't quite heard what she'd said. Reluctant to ask for the question again, he punted.

"Ehm, well. What do I ... "

"Feel." She continued facing forward, but smiled. "I was asking to know if you feel anything."

"Oh. I do. I do feel something." Tom braced his hands on his knees, frowning at the pile of rocks, knowing 'sleepy' was surely not the emotion she was after. "Calm. I feel quite calm, I suppose. Calm, and relaxed, and—" Giving up, he puffed a sigh. "I haven't a clue what I'm meant to be feeling at all. I'm sorry."

She rolled her eyes at him. "Be easy, Tom, for all love. I wasn't meaning to set a test for you. I was only curious. You're not obliged to feel things."

Relieved, Tom shifted closer and looped an arm around her waist. "What sort of people lived here?"

"Nobody seems to know. Too many centuries have come and gone." Brigid looked over at the sprawling ruin. Her voice became low and deliberate. "It was important to them to be facing the north. I don't know how I know that. Or how I know this little hollow was important as well."

He looked again at the pile of rubble in front of them, trying to turn it into something that made sense. "Is it a shrine do you think? Maybe they prayed here?"

She said nothing, and appeared distracted, her brow furrowed with private thoughts. Tom followed her gaze, fixed on the northern horizon, but whatever had captured her interest there was lost on him. His attention had wandered back to the choppy waves frothing at the rocks below them when he felt Brigid's shoulders tense and slip from beneath his arm.

"It wasn't for praying they came. The women came here

to talk. I know, because I can feel them here." Her dark eyes flared, challenging him. "It isn't the sort of thing you believe in, sure I can feel that as well, but it's something you ought to know about me, and now you do. I feel things. Sometimes I see things, too. Sometimes I look at people and see shapes and figures and shadows around them, and sometimes I see the shapes and figures where there are no people at all."

Her nervous, defiant expression was one Tom had already learned to recognize. She expected him to laugh at her. He could tell she was steeling herself, her face so stiffened against ridicule that he felt a deep personal grievance against anyone who'd taught her to expect it.

He wasn't prepared to say he could believe in what she described—spirits walking in the world amongst the living—but it didn't matter whether he believed it or not. It mattered that she did. Laughter was the furthest thing from Tom's mind. Taking her hand, he didn't even smile.

"Do you see them around me?"

"I do." Brigid pinned him with a stare, but the hardness faltered, then softened. "I do," she said again, gently. "But I haven't worked out what they mean. And sometimes instead of seeing things, there's a feeling—a sort of shiver in the air. It comes at me and works its way right in, until it's like a heartbeat inside of me, beating alongside my own."

"Does it not frighten you?" he asked.

"Never." Her reply was immediate, decisive. "I'm only frightened to death of losing it, if I leave here." One of her hands remained in his—warm and still—but with the other Brigid pulled at the grass between them, shredding and rolling the blades, staining her fingers with the scant juice they released.

"I don't know how I've come to be this way, but it seemed to start when I moved to the island." She spoke as though talking to herself. "I saw things here that other people didn't. It means having them think me a witch or insane or something worse, and so much of what I see has misfortune in it. If it's all from some power in this island only, shouldn't I be dancing for pure joy at a chance for leaving it? Why am I not wild to get away from the place? Is it not enough, even, to be in love—"

Brigid stopped, looking horrified. Her grass-stained fingers flew to her lips, but Tom's grip tightened on the hand still wrapped in his that was trying to pull away. He held his breath while they stared at each other, measuring the silence with the beat of his heart.

"I'm sorry," she whispered.

Tom ventured a small grin. "That you're in love? In the name of God, why? Unless you've someone else in mind I'm only delighted to hear it, and glad for the company. It's desperate, being in love all on your own."

Brigid smiled, but he could see the tears rising up in her eyes. "I'm not sorry to be in love, or for wanting to be with you. I'm sorry to be so afraid. I'll have to leave here some day, I know that; but I'm terrified over what I might lose. I can't imagine living without that part of myself. I can't imagine the loneliness of it."

Tom held her while she cried without a sound, trembling in his arms like some small, terrified creature, fragile and wild. The noiseless grief tore at him, but he couldn't help feeling grateful for a break in the conversation. He needed some time for his thoughts to catch up with his feelings.

She loved him. She wanted to be with him. Her exact words, and no mistake. For months, Tom had dreamt of hearing her say them, but could hardly believe it now that she had. In fairness, he'd envisioned hearing the words in response to his own. The fact that Brigid had beat him to it only heightened his astonished wonder.

His dreams took a new turn now as he thought about taking Brigid home with him, walking the fields with her, bringing her down to the village. He envisioned being together in the house, sitting snug by the fire, a tableau in which his parents were conveniently absent. Sure they'd fecked off to Galway, hadn't they? Or at least down the road. Their retirement plans suddenly seemed a less critical issue for him.

Brigid's lack of dowry concerned him even less. The challenge of presenting Seamus with a daughter-in-law whose treasure was the simple gift of her presence no longer seemed of any consequence.

Eager to put it all into motion, Tom wanted to propose on the spot, but he couldn't bask forever in a fantasy where all obstacles crumbled before him. As Brigid continued to sob, he understood nothing could be that easy. His delight became tempered by the knowledge of what he needed to do. It was the last thing he wanted, but he closed his eyes and did it anyway.

"It's okay," he murmured. "We'll carry on as we are, will we? But I promise you this—when you're ready to leave, I'll be waiting."

Tom could tell when Brigid registered what he was saying, and what it meant. At first she seemed to be crying even harder, but gradually the tears stopped. She lay limp in his arms.

"It isn't fair to you," she said.

"Ah, well. I'll manage. Only I'll need to sort out some way to visit more often."

"It isn't a bit fair."

"It's no bother." This was such a breathtaking lie that it seemed to stun both of them for a moment.

"I could live here alone, you know," she finally said.

Grateful she couldn't see him, he clenched his eyes tighter and forced a light reply. "You're killing me with this. I'll have you to know that, at least."

"I don't know if I'd want to, but I've thought about it."

She sat back to face him, and for a long moment seemed to be taking in more than what she saw in front of her. When her eyes again focused on his, Brigid looked surprised to see him still there, and then sheepish.

"I'm a madwoman. You don't say it, but you surely must be thinking it."

"Go on, now," Tom teased gently, leaning in closer. "Can you not tell what I'm thinking?" He brushed at the strands of hair that had fallen over her face. "What's it like, then, these feelings you have? Will you tell me?"

She regarded him thoughtfully, then reached for his hand. Guiding his fingers to her throat, she covered them with her own and hummed a long, low note. "The feeling of it is like that. Only there isn't any sound."

The vibration of her voice under his fingertips went through Tom like a sliver of lightning. Unable to resist its pull, he lifted her fingers away and pressed his lips to the same spot on her throat.

At first, Brigid's whole body tensed, but then she relaxed.

She pulled him closer, her fingers sliding around his neck and up through his hair. "You understand, but you're not able to believe in any of it, are you?"

Tom kissed her chin, and then each corner of her mouth. "I don't know whether I'm able, but I want to believe in it, for your sake if nothing else."

She took his face in her hands. "It's a good start. 'Oh Lord, I believe. Help my unbelief.' That's the book of Mark, so it is."

"Uh-huh. Good aul' Mark." Tom was anxious to move on to less weighty matters. "And what about yer man St. Augustine? 'Oh Lord, make me chaste. But not yet.'"

His mouth traveled beneath her jaw and along her neck. Then, he gently nudged aside her blouse, and felt her soft skin shiver under the heat of his breath.

15

While Tom's mouth was raising goosebumps every-where it touched, and his fingers reaching everywhere she'd allow them, Brigid made some surprising discoveries about herself. She wondered if she ought to be ashamed by how quickly her shyness had vanished, or by the instant under-standing of where she wanted his hands to be, and where he wanted hers. She'd assumed that when this moment came – if it came at all – she would find it a great, fumbling mystery. It was startling how familiar and instinctive it all seemed. She wondered if it was normal or only more evidence of her own oddness, and if Tom would know the difference. As soon as he offered her a chance to catch her breath, Brigid tried to see whether he did.

"I should be falling away with shock, I think."

"At me?" His eyes widened, surprised and worried. They hovered inches from hers – steady, a lovely shade of blue shot with silver.

"At myself, of course. It's not very modest behavior."

Tom laughed. "Says yer wan who swims naked in the sea."

Brigid felt the heat in her flushed face rise higher, and immediately his grin faded. "I'm sorry. If you're uncomfortable—"

"I'm not, though. Not at all. Sure isn't that the point?"

He looked confused. "Why?"

"Shouldn't I be? Uncomfortable?"

"But you're not?"

"No."

They looked at each other.

"Right so," Tom said. "We'll talk about it later, will we?"

"We needn't. No. And we're after talking enough right now, as well," Brigid said, and pulled him down to her.

It wasn't long before the layers of clothing between them became intolerable. Removing them without letting go of each other was an awkward struggle that had them both laughing, but as soon as they were pressed together, skin to skin, Tom's kisses became more urgent. Arms circled around him, Brigid felt the hardness of him and tightened her grip. Nervous. Excited. The pressure of her own breath rose. She heard it catch in hoarse gasps while her stomach shivered in an uncontrolled spasm. As her hips lifted to push at the weight against them Brigid felt a sharp pain that faded as a racing pulse filled her head, drowning out everything around her—even the roar of the ocean.

Much later, after the perspiration had cooled on their skin, they looked at each for a long, silent moment. Seeing Tom's smile—anxious, questioning—Brigid's heart swelled. He was afraid she might already be regretting what they'd done, but she could tell he was also just as worried that he'd disappointed her. She reassured him with a kiss that came close to igniting them all over again, but then pushed him gently back and settled into his arms.

She remained there, letting his fingers trace the groove of her spine, but after a few minutes shifted her head to look up at him. Mingled with his drowsy contentment, she could see a hint of the strain she'd noticed earlier.

Brigid ran a finger over his forehead. "You said you'd tell me about what's been happening at home, with your parents running away to Galway, and you left minding everything and killing yourself with work."

"Sure you make it sound fierce exciting. But it's not, really." His laugh ended on a sigh.

He hesitated, but once Tom began talking it spilled out of him, the story of his father, and of a relationship that had soured in recent years and seemed only to grow more contentious as time passed. Brigid could see how much it confused and saddened him, and that he'd pushed himself to the point of exhaustion, trying to prove his worth.

"He'll see how hard you've worked while he's been away," she said. "How well you've managed it."

Glumly, Tom shook his head. "I doubt whether it will make any difference."

He started to say something else, but then simply shrugged and remained silent, staring up at the sky. Below them, the rhythmic beating of the waves had grown fainter as the tide retreated, and a breeze carried up the briny smell of everything left behind in the shallows. After a few minutes, he ran his hand over her back. With his face still turned to the sky he smiled, his mood lifting.

"You're shivering. Shall I warm you up again?"

Brigid laughed and sat up. "I see how it is with you, Tom

McBride. A greedy charmer, so you are. The climb to An Cró Mór will warm us nicely, I think, and we need to hurry so as not to be late for the dinner Lis is cooking for you."

Tom groaned, stalled and thoroughly distracted her for several more minutes before accepting defeat. At her insistence, he removed himself while she dressed and tried to put her clothes back in order. When finished, Brigid found him wandering around the half-buried stones of the ancient fort.

"Have I managed it?" She spread her hands, indicating the state of her blouse.

"'A handsome woman is easily dressed.'" He chanted the proverb with a playful lilt, and at her dubious frown added, "Sure no one expects you'll be looking freshly ironed after a day's march to the end of this rock."

Tom grabbed the basket he'd left on the hillside, but after lifting it seemed to lose his balance. He caught at the wall and steadied himself while slowly adjusting the strap against his shoulder. It was no more than a few seconds and his face registered only mild surprise, but Brigid felt something – or more accurately, she could sense him feeling something.

"What is it, Tom?"

"Nothing really." He scanned the area around his feet. "Only it seemed like something was giving way for a second. Felt a bit peculiar. It's gone now, though." Tom looked up, grinning. "Do the spirits here like to give the ground a good shaking? They're having a laugh at me, maybe."

"I don't think so." The prickle of warning along Brigid's spine had not gone away. "Put down the basket, Tom."

"Why? Are you not ready to go?"

"It isn't that. It's … " She didn't know what it was. Something didn't look quite right and she felt afraid, but Tom appeared to be fine, and Brigid could tell he was mystified by her concern. She offered an excuse more benign than she was feeling. "I'm thinking we need to get a bacon sandwich and some lemonade inside you."

They spread the blanket in the hollow, and her vague anxiety began subsiding as Tom again demonstrated the volume of food he could put down. She had enough experience now to confirm he was turning every mouthful into muscle, but when he started on the third sandwich Brigid began to think she hadn't made enough. She nudged the scones forward, still watching him closely.

"You've had a hard time of it these past weeks, I think."

"Oh, not entirely," Tom said. He swallowed the last of the sandwich and after a satisfied sigh stretched out on the blanket, propped on his elbows.

"It wasn't so bad, until I lost the two farm lads we usually have around. One got appendicitis and then the other broke his arm—silly plonker. In fairness, I have to admit I enjoy running the place, making my own decisions." He scowled. "I can try something new without himself roaring away at me, saying I'm doing it wrong."

Brigid considered this last statement while sweeping the crumbs from the blanket. She moved to sit closer to him, tucking her feet beneath her.

"Maybe it's why he went away," she suggested. "To give you the run of it all. He could have been kinder about it, instead of goading and jeering at you, but it's not so unfair is it? Stepping away to see how you get on, working on your own?"

"Do you think so? I never looked at it that way." He quietly processed the idea, the scowl passing to a hopeful uncertainty. It loosened the tightness in his face, but left it shattered with weariness.

"Maybe you're right. I don't know what to expect when he gets back, though. It might be even harder."

"But you miss him."

"I do, really," Tom said, sounding sleepy, now. "I miss them both. Sure aren't they my family?"

He blinked, and his eyes were slow in opening. "Should we not be getting up that wee hill, now?"

"Not yet. We'll rest a bit." Brigid gently pushed him onto his back.

"Right. A few minutes, maybe." He closed his eyes and was asleep within seconds.

She lay on her side next to him, watching the rise and fall of his chest, reflecting on his earlier reassurance - that he wouldn't press her to leave, that he'd wait for her to tell him she was ready. The effect of his generosity was greater than he knew. In the act of offering that selfless gesture, Tom had been utterly revealed, and the rare phenomenon Brigid had last experienced in the presence of Dan O'Brien had happened again.

She'd seen his spirit, a narrow band of pulsing light out-lining every inch of him, and for all its brilliance, it was the strength, the shimmering power of it, that stunned her. Attracted her. It was a different sort of energy than she was used to, but as soon as she perceived it she began feeling its pull.

Careful not to disturb Tom, Brigid got up and began walk-ing. She felt restless, her heart drawn in two directions with no compass for understanding which was best for her. Moving away from the path, she descended the sloping southern cliffs to the opposite coast, ending up in another of her favorite spots – *Gleann na bPéist*, the Valley of the Worm. Sharks often swam in the waters there, and when they congregated, the undulating motion of their fins did resemble those of a great sea serpent.

There were none swimming there today. Brigid wandered through ferns, enjoying the whisper of their fronds against her skirt, and came to the large, flat rock that was popular with the islanders. Generations of them had carved their names into it. Some of the crudely formed letters were only a few years old; they were chiseled deep with sharp edges. Others were worn soft by decades of wind and rain, and still others had nearly faded entirely beneath stains of black and orange lichen.

So many years, she thought, running her fingers over the names. So many people. So many stories. Had any of them been like her, feeling the humming spirit of the earth beneath their feet, and in the air, rushing at them, moving through them? Had the island come alive for any of them as it did for her? If so, they'd had their entire lives to experience that strange pulse – absorbing it, learning from it – but she wouldn't. She would have to accept this. Someday.

"But not today," Brigid said. She gave the rock a final pat before straightening, and then started back towards the fort.

As she climbed the slope, Brigid heard a commotion in the sky. She looked up to see a flock of white sea swallows gathering overhead. Breaking into a smile, she quickened her pace up the hill.

16

It came to him in his sleep, and Tom connected it with fiddle music – four repeating notes at the highest register. He could picture the bowing technique required to play it, the rocking motion, the lift and drop of his wrist. The sound began at a distance but kept getting closer, building until it finally woke him, and he registered Brigid's absence before his eyes had even opened. She was probably near by, but at the moment anything beyond the reach of his arms seemed too far.

It had all happened so quickly. Almost too quickly, Tom thought. He'd been dreaming – well, in fairness, he done more than dream – about being with Brigid in this way for months. Alone in his room he had a better sense of how to manage it all, but when the actual moment was upon him, his brain had seemed to shut down fairly early. He'd allowed too much to slip past without giving it enough attention. Now, he couldn't wait to hold her again, swearing to linger over every moment and every square inch, and to remain alert to her smallest reaction.

Tom sat up and scrubbed at his face, wondering whether it was a standing stone or some fascinating rabbit hole Brigid had deserted him for. He could hardly blame her; anything had to be more interesting than watching him nod off like an old granny. He couldn't be sure how long he'd slept, but he was sitting in shade now, so it was probably at least an hour. An hour that could have been spent far more productively.

"You're an awful eejit, Tomás." The remark scraped in his throat. He reached for a bottle of lemonade while looking around for the scones and cakes, but although he couldn't remember eating a single one, there weren't any left. The tea towels she'd wrapped them in sat empty next to the basket with a few crumbs scattered around them. He grunted a laugh.

"She's after leaving me here to starve." He took a long pull from the bottle and finally registered the sound from his dreams. It had followed him out of sleep and now he recognized it as the cry of birds. Tom peered up at the flock in the sky. They were a blur of white against an azure background, flying low as they passed over him, heading south. He counted a dozen, but that number didn't account for the volume of the noise.

Another flock quickly followed, and then another, all of them appearing out of the north. He followed their flight path as they disappeared over the ridge and realized the sound was cumulative. A chorus had formed beyond the slope above him, growing with each new arrival. He craned his neck at the sound of the next flock approaching, and the bottle of lemonade slipped from his grasp. There had to be at least a hundred of them. When they passed less than twenty feet above his head in a riot of noise, no further clues were needed.

Jumping to his feet, he began scaling the steep hill. Wherever the birds were going, he imagined he would find Brigid there as well. When he reached the ridge, Tom scanned the horizon as he came up over the top of it and then froze, staring across a stretch of rolling terrain.

Hundreds of birds had gathered into a single, circling flock. He saw now they were sea swallows, flying at high speed, forming a wide funnel in the middle of the island—a living tornado. In a revolving pattern of pure white, with glimpses at black-capped heads and orange beaks, the birds raced around a single pivot point.

Brigid.

She was barely visible, sitting on the ground at the center of the swirling mass with her back to him, head tilted to the sky. Tom had never seen anything like it, nor had he ever heard anything like the cries of the birds as they wheeled in the sky above her head. Like their pattern of flight, they'd settled into the same song of high, chattering notes.

It was an astonishing sight, but it became even more wondrous when Brigid got to her feet. She stood motionless, and then spread her arms and began turning in slow counterpoint to the revolving swarm. The birds reacted immediately. A shiver ran through their formation. She raised her arms in salute as they started rising. Tom's breath caught in his throat as the hundreds of small forms spiraled into a blinding whirlwind, twisting and spreading as they shot higher, until they suddenly flew apart, scattering across the sky in fragmented shapes that turned south and disappeared over the ocean.

The quiet left behind was absolute. It smothered the wind and even the churn of the sea. The pervasive hush had something in it that was beyond Tom's power to describe.

When he had the use of his legs once more, he started towards Brigid, picking his way through a maze of heather, the tread of his boots squeezing water up through the boggy ground. He hadn't gone far when she turned, sensing his approach. It reminded Tom of the fright he'd given her on the White Strand more than three months ago. He wondered how he'd managed it, and if it was likely he'd ever surprise her again.

Brigid met him halfway. "Did you feel anything?" she asked, eyes shining. She was so beautiful, in ways he couldn't begin to count.

"I did, love." He folded her in his arms, his lips moving over her windswept hair. "In the name of God, I did feel something that time."

She rested her head against his shoulder and put her arms around his waist. "And to think it all started with a handful of scones and cakes."

They returned to the sheltered hollow for the picnic basket, and Tom made a final attempt to decipher the ancient stone formation he'd seen earlier. Brigid folded the blanket, watching him.

"It was a bread oven," she said, waving a hand at the small mound. "I'm certain of it."

"A bread oven?" Startled, Tom frowned at it and then began laughing. "Not a high cross or pagan goddess, but a bloody *bread* oven? Are you joking me?"

"And why would I lie about it? If I feel it's a bread oven, I'll not be telling you it's a high cross." She was laughing as well. "It doesn't matter, sure, because you don't believe in it anyway."

"I do, though." He rested a hand on the pile, his face pensive. "The funny thing is, I'm starting to believe in all of it."

～

When they arrived back at Lis and Sean's, they were both famished again after the long walk home. Eager to start the meal, Brigid helped transfer the food from the hearth. Lis had drawn heavily on their meagre savings to provide a fitting dinner for their guests - a goose stuffed with potato dressing and several side dishes. All of it was on the hearth, roasting in iron pots sprinkled with red-hot embers. When Brigid lifted the lid from one of them, the smell of onion and sage was glorious. She placed it on the table along with her own contribution—a pitcher of milk and another caraway seed cake.

"Lovely!" Tom murmured, eyeing the loaf as she placed it in front of him. "Will I get a taste this time, before the birds fly off with it?"

Her aunt had separated them, putting Tom on her left and Brigid at the end of the table next to Sean. She recognized it as a calculated placement, giving Lis the opportunity to bombard him with food and casual questions without hope of rescue. He weathered the onslaught bravely, but when the other guests piled on, Tom's replies became more guarded.

Annie and Jack Granville had once been Lis and Sean's neighbors, living in the cottage Brigid now occupied. They'd moved to Dingle several years earlier so their children could finish school. Annie looked as if the change agreed with her. She'd always been a pretty woman, and now she was a fashionable one as well, in a colorfully patterned dress and matching earrings. By contrast, her husband was a dour character, as colorless as she was bright, and in a flat cap and patched sweater, Jack looked as if he'd never left the Blasket. He'd been lucky enough to get a job at the Dingle creamery, and announced as the table was being cleared that he knew Seamus McBride.

Feeling sorry for Tom, and wondering how he'd handle the topic of his father, Brigid took a peek at his face. There was a hint of wariness in his smile. She continued gathering plates as they both waited to hear if the connection was a friendly one.

"From the creamery, is it?" Tom suggested. "He's there quite often."

Without answering the question, Jack lit his pipe, peering at Tom over the flare of the match. "He's done well for himself, your father. Manor house in Ventry, and all."

"Is it *those* McBrides, then?" Annie chimed in, eyes wide.

Tom laughed. "I wouldn't call it anything like a manor house."

"He did," Jack said.

"Ah. Right."

"How many cows have you, now?"

"We've thirty milkers."

Brigid couldn't help joining in the general gasp. Like everyone else, she'd had no idea of the scale of his farm. Tom's gaze swung to her and then away again. He looked embarrassed by their surprise.

Jack grunted and took another pull on his pipe. "Land?"

"About a hundred acres. Plus the peat bogs."

"You put some out to lease."

"We do, a good few fields."

"With turf rights?"

"Oh, leave him be, Jack." Lis thumped a teapot on the table. "Unless you're wanting to buy the place off him."

"I was only curious," Jack grumbled. "He's become a big man over there, Seamus McBride. A regular modern-day landlord. There are few enough in all of Ireland who've managed that. I was only wanting to know how he did."

Tom had been staring down at his hands. Brigid saw Jack's veiled mockery had perturbed him. At the caustic tone of this last observation he looked up, his mild expression still firmly in place.

"There's a fair bit of luck in it, sure, but I suppose it was mostly down to hard work." He met the man's eye with a steady gaze. "My father's worked hard all his life. He still works harder than any man I know."

"There now, Jack." Sean's low voice quivered. "Chew on that, why don't you?"

"Yerra, it's nothing to me at all." Jack chuckled as the remark tipped them all into outright laughter.

Each of the men had a stool or ladder back chair to carry when they departed for the céilí, and they met others doing the same as they climbed the path to the top of the village. They formed an odd parade, with Brigid and the other women following behind, carrying tarts and cups and plates for the tea that would be served near the end of the evening.

The venue chosen was Peig's old house. It was large enough to accommodate refreshments and a place for the women to talk in one room, and music and dancing in the other. When they arrived, Margaret's son, Liam, was racing around the yard in an overexcited lather. One of Mary's nephews was in hot pursuit and Tom was immediately pressed into service to surround and capture "the child", much to the boy's shrieking delight. Once inside, Tom was whisked into the center of the gathering to meet everyone else—particularly the musicians, who were eager to begin.

"I hear your lad from the town is a millionaire," Petey said, coming up behind Brigid as she was arranging the tarts.

She rolled her eyes. "Isn't it a fright to God that Annie Granville won't leave her husband at home when she's asked to a ceili. It's a lot of rubbish, Petey."

"Is that so? He's only a poor dirt farmer, tilling his little half-acre like the rest of us? No?" He laughed as she looked away, blushing. "You'll want to hold on to that one, girl. He'll have you in a house nicer than anything Dan O'Brien will be giving us. A manor house, mind you."

"I don't care a bit what sort of house he has."

Petey's voice grew gentle. "Of course not, lass. We can all see it's not the house you're thinking of." Seeing Tom approach, he winked at her and strolled back to the group of men he'd left gathered around the barrel of stout.

"Jayz," Tom groaned. "It's really not a manor house at all. Not by a long chalk. The father must be off his head telling anybody it is."

"Never mind." Brigid accepted the glass of cider he offered her. "I'm glad you stood up for him, though."

"So am I. And it's no word of a lie. There's none could say Seamus McBride is afraid of a day's work, and he won't ask a man to do anything he wouldn't do himself. Anyway," Tom indicated the musicians who were staring at them from the corner. "They're mad to get this thing going. Are you all right, here?"

"I am. Go on now, and show us what you can do with that fiddle of yours."

He glanced around the room and back at her, a threat of mischief in his eyes. Brigid knew he wouldn't embarrass her by trying to kiss her in front of all these people, but he was thinking about it, which under the circumstances was just as nice.

In their corner, the musicians made room and huddled around Tom, quizzing him on questions of style and the extent of his repertoire. He sat tall and straight in his chair with the fiddle balanced upright on his knee, and kept nodding agreeably. He appeared to enjoy this interrogation a good deal more than the earlier one. When the group was satisfied, chairs were adjusted, instruments poised, and at a nod from the séisun leader the first set began.

17

The faint reflection of the sun that had been hovering in the west, reluctant to give up the day, had finally winked out. The shadows had deepened to full darkness in the fields below Peig's house, and a damp, cutting wind – the knife point of autumn – had displaced any remaining hint of summer. It nipped at anyone who ventured outside the house, but couldn't be felt inside, where the overheated atmosphere approached a state of spontaneous combustion.

A turf fire had been lit earlier to combat the stale chill in the vacant house. As the drink went round and the *craic* escalated, the blaze was allowed to subside, but the embers still flared when gusts shot down the chimney, sending sporadic puffs of smoke into the room.

The musicians and dancers were still in great form, each inspiring the others to outdo themselves, and no one wanted to call time on the evening. One tune had just ended, but Fintan, the laconic, white-haired seisun leader from the upper village, announced a new one and they were away again. The musicians applied as much vigor as they had three hours earlier. They needed only a few measures of the tune to achieve a steady sound.

"Right, lads. Now we have it." He nodded at the young men waiting for his signal – Mary's nephews from Tralee.

The three brothers were used to dancing together and after counting off the beat they launched into a hornpipe. Moving in a triangular pattern, each of them took a turn showing off their footwork on the "flag of the fire." Their boots made the flat stone in front of the hearth echo with the crack of rhythmic steps.

From his place in the corner between a bodhran and a concertina, Tom was in good position to observe the dancers, but he was more interested in watching the men and women gathered around them. In the smoky glow of the oil lamps, their eyes were bright, their faces shining with perspiration. Spirited participants in their own right, they called out encouragements to the dancers and players, and the steady thump of their feet added a percussive accent to the music. Everyone was delighted with the evening, but in the faces of the islanders he saw a poignant intensity to their enjoyment, an eagerness to fix it in their memories. The Blasket had not seen such a gathering of young people in a long time, and possibly never would again.

Tom kept an eye out for glimpses of Brigid farther back in the room – sometimes recognizing her particular style of movement before he could clearly see her figure. Earlier in the evening, when someone had stepped forward to sing a lament of endless verses, they'd slipped into the darkness behind the house for a few minutes. He searched the crowd for her now, hoping for another such interlude.

"Go on, Tom. They're all yours, these boys from Tralee. Name it and make them hop for it."

With his mind occupied elsewhere, Tom almost missed the command from Fintan, but from the crowd's yips of anticipation, he knew what was expected. Having discovered Tom could play faster than anyone in the room, Fintan had been teasing the dancers, threatening to unleash his solo fiddle for a high-speed set dance, and now the time had come. Tom made a comical show of assessing Mary's nephews, and they smiled back, game for the challenge. In deference to the older man, and because Fintan was a wizard with a tin whistle, he swiveled back to the séisun leader.

"We'll make it 'The Noisy Curlew', but I'll need you to help me along."

They played at a ferocious rate, and a little past the halfway mark Tom added several unexpected ornamentations. The dancers registered surprise with small grins, but didn't miss a beat. When the tune ended there was glory for everyone as the spectators hooted and stamped their feet. Tom waded in amongst the throng to shake hands with Mary's nephews.

The tallest of them, a fair-haired man whose shirt was plastered to him, was panting and laughing. "That was grand, Tommy, but can you go the other direction, now? What about a slower one?"

Still looking for Brigid, Tom had other ideas, but the man's brothers joined the appeal for a slow air and the crowd took up the cause until he agreed to give them one. Back in his corner, he considered various options as he tuned the fiddle. Through a hole in the crowd, he finally caught sight of Brigid smiling at him from the back of the room. Gazing at her, he knew what he wanted to play, but wondered if he dared.

Port na Bpucai, "The Faeries' Lament" was the quintessential Blasket tune, and for all Tom knew the descendants of its author might be there in the room with him. The mythical stories surrounding its origin were varied. Some said the lonesome song had come from a mysterious, unseen woman on the island of Inishvickillane, others that it was the funeral dirge of a fairy host passing overhead. The least fanciful was that a Blasket fisherman had heard the sound of whales passing beneath the canvas of his boat, and had memorized their song. Tom found it the most plausible explanation for a tune that drew so much emotion from so little melody. It seemed an appropriate way to honor his hosts. Trusting them to accept it in the spirit offered, he decided to risk it.

The peculiar lament could be identified from its opening note, and when Tom closed his eyes and sent the long, mournful sound into the room, the crowd instantly fell silent. It unnerved him, but he'd committed himself, so he played on, calling the spirit of the sea into the lamplit cottage.

The tuneless character of the music gave it an uncanny quality. Feeling it tingle beneath his fingers and against his neck, Tom could imagine the spell a man might fall under, hearing this sound from some deep, hidden source trembling through his boat. He drew out the final passage so softly the whisper of horsehairs against the strings was as clear as the note they were playing. The deep hush continued until the tune faded out, and then a collective sigh passed through the crowd before they erupted in a roar.

The first thing Tom saw upon opening his eyes was Brigid, only a few feet from him, sitting on the floor at the front of the crowd. She wore a transfixed expression of wonder and respect.

"Thank you, Tom McBride. I'll say it again, so. You're after becoming a fine, heroic figure."

Somehow he was able to hear her quiet voice above the cheering. Moved by it, Tom bowed his head. It didn't matter whether anyone else understood the homage he'd intended to pay, as long as she did. It seemed her opinion was shared, though, because he was soon at the center of a group of islanders, being showered with appreciation. While the men were wringing his hand and the women clasping him in powerful hugs, Brigid spoke in his ear.

"I'll go and help with the tea now, and leave you to this pack of admirers." She took advantage of the confusion to give him a quick kiss on the cheek. He groaned, watching her disappear into the crowd, wondering when – for all love – would he get five minutes to spend alone with her again.

Deciding that no tune could adequately follow the *Port na Bpucai*, Fintan declared an end to the music, but the players found other ways to stay warm. After tucking his fiddle case behind a chair, Tom accepted a glass of whiskey someone pressed into his hand, but mistook it for cider. He took a large swallow and nearly gagged as the liquor burned down his throat. Spotting a pitcher of water on a table against the wall, he hurried over to it, and after draining every drop he fell into a chair, trying to recover.

A few minutes later, he was still trying. At first he blamed the whiskey, which he didn't drink often, and certainly not in great, glugging mouthfuls, but as he continued sitting with his back pressed against the chair, it became clear something else was wrong. For all his gasping he wasn't taking in much air. When he felt the tightness growing in his chest, Tom knew he was in trouble.

"Oh, God help me." A wave of fear cranked the vise inside him a few more turns as he recognized the unmistakable signs of an asthma attack. The first in over two years. Not without warning, he realized, remembering the dizziness he'd felt earlier near the ruins of the fort. Vertigo had always been a warning sign for him, but he'd been distracted enough to miss it this time. Even if he hadn't, what could he have done? What could he do, now?

Feeling lightheaded, Tom was afraid to move, but then noticed the pall hanging in the air from a combination of clay pipes and the smoldering hearth. Whatever air he was taking in was likely three parts smoke. As his groggy mind absorbed this he heard his name called in a sharp voice, and saw Brigid hurrying across the room to him.

"The smoke . . ." Tom began, but then stopped, afraid of wasting breath on explanations. She didn't seem to need them anyway.

"I know. Come away from it. Quickly." Her face was grim and he hesitated, seeing his own terror reflected there. Realizing she'd frightened him, she bent down and pressed her lips to his forehead. "It's all right, love. Come along with me, now. We'll just go into the fresh air."

Tom took the hand she offered and allowed her to lead him through the crowd. Once outside she guided him into a chair, but he couldn't stay in it. He felt better standing.

"This has happened to you before," Brigid said.

He nodded, hands braced on the back of the chair, using

all his energy to stay calm. "Asthma. I've had it my whole life."

"Have you medicine for it?"

Tom shrugged. He could recite several he'd taken over the years but none were worth mentioning, as they weren't available. There was no chemist here to supply them, no doctor or hospital he could ever reach in time. Panic only made things worse, but he felt it rising in spite of his efforts, because in the quiet darkness he could hear the straining wheeze of his breath, each sip and release becoming more rapid.

She was still talking to him, but Tom couldn't listen anymore. He lost track of where she was. Other people had joined them outside, but he didn't know who. He seemed to be losing track of himself as well. He thought he'd been pacing in front of the house, but then found himself braced against it, fingers digging into the whitewashed stone. He felt Brigid next to him, holding his face. Then he heard voices shouting. At him. Or someone else. He couldn't tell which.

⁓

Brigid had been fooled by the vision at first, thinking it the vestige of something already experienced, and it frightened her to think what might have happened if she hadn't recognized her mistake.

She'd been working in the kitchen with the other women, and was spooning out tea leaves when the spangling light in her eyes stopped her hand in mid-air over the mouth of the teapot. She saw Tom as he'd briefly appeared earlier near the fort—blurred and out of balance, facing her with an oddly blank expression. As she watched, the air in front of her grew murky, and behind it Tom's image began to ripple and recede. He looked submerged in water, sinking beneath its weight. She knew then that it couldn't be a memory or any vague premonition of the future; the urgency of her fear convinced her of that. It was here. It was now.

"Drowning. He's drowning."

"What's that, my dear?"

Mary looked up from the tart she was cutting, but Brigid was already moving. Spinning from the table she raced from the room, still clutching the spoon, dropping tea leaves like a trail of bread crumbs behind her. In the main room, she pushed her way through the crowd, searching, and saw Tom at the other end of it.

Of course he wasn't drowning. What had put such a mad idea into her head? He wasn't paddling about in the sea. He was right there, relaxing in a chair against the wall with a glass of whiskey at his elbow. Limp with relief, Brigid puffed an exasperated sigh.

"Mother of God. Why have I to be such a queer, fey creature?"

She was still scolding herself when she noticed what the raucous group around him hadn't. Tom wasn't relaxed. He was absolutely rigid in the chair, and his hand on the table had gone white from the force of his grip. He might as well have been buried under the waves because the air itself was smothering him.

Brigid hurried to him, and when she reached his side, her senses were alive to the shadows lurking in the atmosphere—pressing ever closer as the smoke clogged his throat. Her nerves screamed in awareness, but that was of no help to Tom. He was already stiff with fear, and she was making it worse. Brigid forced herself to speak gently as she led him to the door.

Outside, the tearing wind chased away any relief the fresh air might have provided. Tom could manage only a few laconic answers to her questions, none giving her any idea of how to help him. He couldn't keep himself at all in the ladder-back chair she brought from the cottage. He was up immediately, leaning over it, hands fastened to the finials on each side. Desperate, Brigid tried to see only his face and not the gathering darkness around him, but she could hardly bear watching Tom struggle. The cords in his neck strained with his effort to breathe, his face so white it seemed to be glowing.

Matters only got worse as the news spread that he'd been taken ill. The cottage began emptying. People filled the dooryard, concerned and curious, and all talking at once. Had a fever come over him? Was it a stomach ailment? Wasn't he choking on something and shouldn't someone in the name of God give him a thump on the back?

Tom retreated from them like a hunted animal. He wandered to the exterior wall of the cottage while Brigid kept the crowd at bay, but when she heard old Maras complaining that it was no wonder, that the quality of turf they were burning was no better than stumps of heather, it gave her an idea.

"Coltsfoot," Brigid said, testing the word, and then shouting it as she turned wildly, looking for Mary. Her house was closer than any other. "Coltsfoot! Mary! Where are you, for the love of God? Have you any coltsfoot in your house at all?"

"Oh, Brigid, I haven't." Mary appeared at her side, looking shocked and sorrowful. "You're right I think, it's the very thing the poor lad needs, and I haven't a speck of it, but maybe–?"

"Peig," Brigid finished her thought and began shoving away the crowd at the cottage door. "Of course. Didn't she always keep a great tin of it in the kitchen."

She did, and it was still there, sitting on a shelf above the kitchen hearth, filled to the brim.

The flower grew in patches all over the island. It was called "coltsfoot" for its large, verdant leaves, shaped like a horse's hoof. On the island, it was a common substitute for tobacco, which was often in scarce supply, but it was also used to ease chest ailments.

With help from Margaret and a few barked orders from Lis, the kitchen where they'd been preparing tea was cleared and Brigid steered Tom to a chair. It was difficult convincing him to go back inside. It was even harder persuading him to take the treatment, because the quickest means of getting relief from coltsfoot leaves was to burn them and breathe in the smoke. After piling the leaves into a tin cup and nestling it in a pan of glowing embers, she placed it on the floor.

"Trust me." Brigid caressed his face, oblivious to what any of those gathered around them might think.

The sight of the smoldering pan clearly appalled Tom, but he nodded and tried to smile. "Kill or cure," he gasped, and leaned forward over the rising curl of fragrant smoke.

Brigid noted that along with Margaret and Lis she'd automatically begun to recite a prayer, chanting an appeal to the Blessed Mother over and over. In the next room, the sound of cups clicking against saucers indicated tea had been served after all, but the conversation amongst islanders and guests was subdued.

The first sign that the blend of prayer and healing smoke was doing its job came when the bluish-gray cast in Tom's face faded and his natural color began returning. Before long, he was taking less desperate breaths. When it seemed the coltsfoot had done all it could and was only making him cough, Tom sat back in the chair, the very image of relief and exhaustion. Wiping at the sweat collected above his lip, he looked at the three of them.

"Sorry I worried you."

"Worried us!" Lis roared. "You've only had us eight parts demented with terror."

"I was nine parts gone myself." He grinned weakly at Brigid. "If not for you I'd be this minute in front of my maker, talking fast and making excuses."

Still too shaken for humor, Brigid crouched by his knees to look at him more closely. "Are you really all right, now?"

"Not quite," he admitted. "Comes on faster than it goes. Tea helps, if you can believe it, but it needs to be scalding and black as tar."

Margaret jumped to put the kettle on the fire while Lis went to get a teapot from the next room. Brigid stayed exactly where she was, watching him. Tom gazed back at her, his smile tired but reassuring. After a minute his eyes wandered to the table next to them.

"Is that an apple tart?"

∿

He was knackered. His throat felt raw and the muscles of his chest ached from the panicked effort to draw a breath;

but after a fortifying cut of apple tart, and several mugs of boiling tea so dark and bitter it puckered his tongue, Tom began feeling more like himself again. Seeing him restored also cheered the group sequestered in the next room, giving new life to the party. With the musicians tuning up again it looked as though the revelry might last until dawn, but Brigid was anxious to get him away from the place. As soon as Tom said he was fit for walking, she announced their departure. They were still at the kitchen table, sitting alone with Lis, with the connecting door closed tight against the danger of wafting smoke.

"You'll not need your thin scrap of bedroll, Tom," Lis said. "I won't have you lying on the damp ground inside my house. You'll take our bed, so."

"I certainly won't," Tom protested, mortified by the thought.

"Of course you will. We likely won't even be home until morning, so it's only standing empty."

"It's kind of you, Lis, but sure I'm not an invalid. I'll be grand with the bedroll."

She began a more forceful argument, but Brigid stood and tapped her fingers on the table.

"He won't need the bedroll, or your bed. He's coming home with me."

Still facing each other, Tom and Lis froze in synchronized shock. He wondered if his eyes might be popping even wider than hers.

"Lord have mercy, and give me strength." Lis hitched her head at the closed kitchen door and hissed at Brigid. "Be sensible, child. Do you realize how that lot would be talking by this time tomorrow?"

"They've always had a great deal to say about me."

"They'll have a great deal more to say now."

"What about it?"

Lis directed a sharp-eyed appeal at Tom – a wordless message so precise she might as well have shouted it at him. *Talk to her.*

Still floundering in astonishment, he shifted in his chair. Took a sip of tea. Scratched his nose and coughed. He darted a look at Brigid and found the view formidable. There were spots of high color in her cheeks, a slight flare in her nostrils, and a fierceness in her eyes that was … well … formidable.

Tom had none of her powers of foresight, but they were hardly needed. Propriety demanded that he reject her plan, mouthing platitudes about their reputation and suggesting she was being careless with it; and he knew if he did, it would humiliate her, and she would be lost to him. He sent her a small grin, hoping her uncanny mind would see all the love and admiration he intended with it, and without uttering a word, took another sip of tea.

They were alone on their walk down to the lower village and took the winding path slowly. Tom was still short of breath, but he'd recovered enough to comfort Brigid, who was berating herself as the sole source of all his troubles.

"You were already tired, I saw that as soon as you got here today, and didn't I, for a lark, only drag you up and over the mountains all afternoon."

"Ah, go on. Your little hill here hardly compares with climbing Mount Brandon, and I go pumping up and down hillsides all day at home."

"And you needed a rest from it, didn't you?" Brigid tossed

up her hands. "What am I like, at all? I can see everything else, but I can't see what's in front of my nose?"

Tom ducked his head away, hiding the smile he couldn't suppress. Privately, he thought fatigue had almost certainly played a role in triggering the attack. It made him less vigilant, and perhaps made him sensitive to levels of smoke he would usually tolerate, but there wasn't the slightest chance he'd admit as much to her.

"Stop, now. It's rubbish. Even if it wasn't, I'd spend a year in an iron lung before I'd trade those hours by the oul' bread oven."

"It *was* a lovely afternoon, wasn't it?"

He caught her arm and pulled her to him for a tender kiss. "I'll remember it for the rest of my life."

As they passed Lis and Sean's, Tom facetiously offered to nip in and collect his bedroll, and got a clip on the shoulder in response. It was cold inside her cottage. Brigid spent a fretful twenty minutes building the fire, apparently trying to balance the need for warmth against a sudden, pathological fear of smoke. Sitting on the edge of her bed, Tom watched impatiently.

"One of us will go mad, you know."

"It's nearly there. I want you to be warm."

"There's more than one way to get warm."

"There is. Get yourself into that bed, now."

With a sigh, Tom did as he was told. Once under the covers he lay on his side, feeling sleep stealing up on him. Eyes drooping, he watched her, worried that she'd tricked him and was planning to sleep right there on the floor, but then she gave a nod of satisfaction, stood up, and began to undress.

It was a methodical process—the apron, the blouse, the long dark skirt, all carefully removed and folded—until she stood naked before the orange-red glow of the hearth. Without any self-conscious cowering or false modesty, she hummed as she held out a cotton shift, warming it on all sides.

Watching the firelight illuminate her, Tom wondered if he was already asleep, and dreaming. He lay motionless, afraid the sight would dissolve if he moved or looked away. The spell was only partly broken when she pulled the shift over her head and climbed in next to him.

"Now. Good as a hot-water bottle, so I am." She drew his arms around her, giving the back of one hand a quick kiss. "We'll have no shenanigans, please, as you've only just got your breath back."

Tom gathered her in closer. "I may have just lost it again."

He nuzzled against her neck, capturing its softness, the salty flavor of her skin. Testing himself, he inhaled, and took in the fragrance of warm cotton in one deep, satisfying breath.

18

She'd never slept with the heat of another body warming the bed, but Brigid quickly noticed its absence upon waking the next morning. Dozing in chilly solitude, she finally opened her eyes and turned her head to look around the room. She saw a fire dancing in the hearth. Surely it couldn't have lasted through the night. Tom must have stirred it to life, but there was no sign of him now.

Swinging from the bed, she shivered when her bare feet touched the ground. The damp had already absorbed the sand she'd scattered the previous day to dry the cottage floor. On tiptoe, Brigid scampered to the flagstones in front of the fire. She stood warming herself and smoothing the tangles from her hair, wondering where Tom had gone, and then heard the faint sound of his voice coming from the byre. He seemed to be carrying on a conversation with someone.

Tom's soft banter stopped and his face lit up when he saw her standing in the doorway. "Thanks be to God. Sleeping Beauty is on her feet again."

He was sitting on a low stool, the sleeves of his sweater

rolled to the elbows, milking her cow. Giving the animal's flank a gentle thump, he grinned. "Farmer's holiday. Only one cow to milk. The two of us are having a chat about you. Starlight was anxious, as you're not usually such a layabout, and I was explaining you'd had a busy night, stopping some tedious fool from suffocating, so she'd have to make do with me."

Starlight swiveled her head. Her eyes, with their fringe of luxurious lashes, conveyed a magisterial tolerance for the break in routine.

"I'm sure she could have waited." Brigid reproached her with a frown, which the cow dismissed with a snuffle. "As you are the one who nearly suffocated, you're meant to be resting as well, not working."

"Resting? Sure haven't I been asleep half the time I've been here?" Tom put the stool against the wall and moved the pail of milk away from Starlight's shifting feet. Then, with murmured encouragements, he gave the cow a slow rub-down, hands running over her spine, gently pushing at hips and ribs. Brigid was intrigued by this patient performance.

"What are you doing?"

"I like to check while I've got them standing still. See if anything isn't the way it should be." After examining Starlight's eyes and coaxing her mouth open for a peek inside, he gave her flank a few gentle pats, which sent her ambling from the byre with a rolling, stately gait. "She's fine, and lucky to be so well looked after."

"And you? Are you feeling better?"

"Oh, I'm back in form, all right. I swear it's the truth," he added, palms raised. "I feel fine. You'd know if I was lying anyway, I suppose?"

"I would. Of course," Brigid said, although that was a fib in itself. She couldn't depend on seeing things whenever she wanted to—it didn't work that way—but she wasn't going to tell Tom he might have the power to deceive her.

"Careful," he said as she came closer. "I'm a bit soggy. It's been bucketing rain since sunrise."

"I can see that." Brigid ran a hand through his hair, noting how much darker it became when wet. She caught the smell of damp wool and shaving soap as she lifted her face to him. "You needn't have gone out in it. You could have stayed with me."

Tom conceded the point, humming as he kissed her. "If you'd been awake, I would have done, but you ought to be grateful I was up so early. I needed a wash-up and a shave, so I crept over to Lis and Sean's to collect my kit, and every step taken with the fear for the stink they'd be giving out. I was wondering if I'd be allowed inside the door, but in the end there was nobody there at all—at five in the morning, even! I had time to toss the bedroll around the floor and drink a cup of tea before anyone got home. They arrived just as I was getting on with the shave, looking like I'd never been anywhere else."

"What did Lis say?"

"Sure what could she, with the husband right there, and Granvilles filling up the place, only raking in the eggs and rashers?" Tom looked delighted with himself. "I got a queer look from her, but she could hardly ask where I'd spent the night. So, I've saved your honor, and stopped the gossip in its tracks. All because you island people are mad for the all-night ceili."

"And where do they think you are now?" Brigid raised an eyebrow.

Tom nipped at her ear. "They don't give a toss where I am. They're after collapsing into their beds. Won't be stirring for hours, I'd say."

"Good. Come in and get yourself dry." She pulled him to the door.

Eventually, they decided it wise to make an appearance at Lis and Sean's. The rain was still coming down as they prepared to leave her cottage, and before stepping under the cover of the coat Tom held up for her, Brigid stood in the doorway, looking out at the white-capped waves.

"I'm thinking the naomhógs might not be able to leave at all, today."

She felt a thrill at the prospect of having him stay longer—maybe for several days if the weather remained unsettled—but the delicious feeling evaporated when she looked up and saw Tom's face as he twisted to stare at the ocean.

"Jaysus. I could be stuck here for days."

As soon as the remark left his lips he seemed to understand how it sounded, and quickly swiveled back to her, embarrassed.

"You're anxious to be away, I think," Brigid kept her voice light, hiding her disappointment.

"No, of course not. That's not—I'm sorry." Tom's apology sputtered into silence, but then he tried again. "It's only that I told Jamesie he needn't go 'round to the farm for the afternoon milking. Like an eejit, I never thought I'd be stopped from getting back to do it myself. That doesn't mean I'm anxious to leave, though. If I had any choice, you couldn't get me off this island until I could take you with me."

"I was only teasing, Tom." She stepped from the doorway into the shelter of his coat, preparing to hurry with him through the rain.

"You believe me, don't you?" he asked.

"Well, of course. Why wouldn't I? Will we run for it now, before we're wet through to the bone?" She forced out a reassuring laugh, but knew neither of them had been entirely truthful this time.

She knew Tom viewed the Blasket as a rival for her affections, but he'd seen the evidence of its beauty and Brigid thought he'd begun to understand why it attracted her, but now she realized his attitude had changed again, and it was no wonder. The characteristics she loved most about the island—its wildness and lofty isolation—were the very things that had nearly killed him last night. If they hadn't found the coltsfoot? Or if it hadn't worked?

Before he'd mastered the reaction, she'd seen Tom's fear at the idea of being trapped there. She could sense his growing aversion to the island, even if he wasn't entirely aware of it.

He couldn't wait to get away, and she couldn't bear to leave, and that paradox forced Brigid to recognize something she'd allowed herself to ignore. The two of them were nothing alike, and never would be. No matter where she went, she would always be a queer, unearthly character, with ideas so different from his own. Wouldn't that, in the end, make her a misery to him?

What now, then?

She didn't know how to answer the question, but a dark premonition of sorrow settled in her mind as they splashed across Lis and Sean's muddy dooryard.

Upon arriving, they found a few other neighbors had come to visit the Granvilles. Everyone sat around the hearth while the rain popped against the thick felt roof of the cottage. As mid-day approached, Annie Granville was persuaded to sing, with Tom's fiddle to help her along. Brigid followed Lis to the kitchen to help prepare another meal for everyone.

"It's good we have the fiddle, anyway," Lis murmured. "Poor Annie can't hold a tune to save her life."

Brigid nodded. "She makes up for it with volume, God love her. This is a gorgeous piece of ham, Lis. Where have you been keeping it?"

Her aunt gave her a sidelong glance. "I haven't been keeping it. It was on the table this morning when we got home. I can only guess your lad pulled it from the bottom of his rucksack. The one standing over there next to his bedroll," she added, with a hint of sarcasm.

"Oh." Brigid kept her eyes on the ham. "That was very generous of Tom."

"Hmm." Lis sank her small hatchet into a turnip and banged it on the table. "And how generous have you been with him, I wonder?"

"Lis!" Brigid tried stoking her indignation into a rage, but without warning found herself in tears instead. "Go on, then. You can think I've become a woman without morals if you like, but I love the man, Lis, and he nearly died in front of my eyes. He'll go away soon enough, but last night I wanted him with me. I couldn't stand having him anywhere I couldn't hear him breathing."

Her aunt quickly wiped her hands on her apron. "Oh, my treasure. I'm sorry. Hush, now." She picked up a tea towel and gently wiped the tears from Brigid's face. They both glanced over at the hearth, but all attention was still on Annie, doing her full-throated best with verse four of *The Pretty Milkmaid.*

"I'm sorry," Lis said again. "I know you love him, and sure even dogs in the street would see he's paralyzed with adoration. Of course he'll go away today, but isn't it agreed, then, between the two of you? I'd have such a weight off my mind if you were settled."

"It isn't agreed, but he gave me an understanding."

"An understanding that's not an agreement? I've no idea in the world what that means."

Brigid felt her cheeks growing warm. "He made a promise to wait for me."

"Oh, Brigid." Lis braced her hands against the table, her shoulders slumped.

"I'm still too afraid of leaving here, Lis, and of who I'll be once I do. I'm afraid I won't know myself anymore."

"And how long is this poor lad meant to be waiting for you to get up the nerve to find out?"

Giving no answer, Brigid picked up the knife and continued slicing. At her aunt's sigh of hopeless resignation, she gripped the handle tightly, struggling for composure.

"You can't hold him to that sort of promise, lass. You can't stand here and tell me you love the man and then do that to him."

"I know I can't," Brigid whispered. "And I won't."

The naomhógs had been expected to leave for Dunquin by noon, but nature had disrupted that plan. The rain was still coming down after they'd finished dinner, and although he was trying to hide it, Brigid knew Tom was nervous. She could read it in the tautness of his muscles while she cleared the table around him.

"Maybe Jamesie will check in, anyway," she said. "He must know the naomhógs can't travel with the wind like this?"

"He might. If the wind is blowing in Ventry as well. You seem to have a different class of weather over here. I must have heard a dozen stories about it last night." Recognizing the note of sarcasm in his tone, Tom looked up at her with a quick grin. "Anyway, I'm not opposed to spending another night here with you."

Brigid managed to return his smile, but her spirits continued sinking. Whether today or tomorrow, each passing hour brought her closer to a moment she didn't want to face.

In the early afternoon the weather broke, and when Petey came by to say the boats would be able to leave after all, Tom puffed a sigh of undisguised relief. With little time left, Brigid couldn't be bothered with artifice in getting him alone again.

"Come with me, now," she said. Without a glance at anyone else in the room, she walked out the door with Tom close behind.

His arms were around her as soon as they were inside her own cottage, but he quickly sensed something was wrong.

"What is it?" Tom pulled back to look at her.

Drawing on every ounce of strength she had, Brigid kept her voice steady. "It won't do, Tom. This arrangement. It's generous of you, but it isn't any use."

"*Whisht.*" He ran a thumb over her lips. "It's a different sort of courtship, I'll grant you that, but we've managed fairly well so far. I'll do better with the letter-writing, I promise, and somehow I'll find a way to visit more often."

"You'll visit a place you don't like coming to, and go away again without getting what you came for, and I'll have to see the disappointment in your face. How long can that go on before we hate the sight of each other for the unhappiness it brings?"

Sighing, Tom cradled her against his chest, kissing the top of her head. "There isn't a thing in the world that could make me hate the sight of you. Can you not understand that? I'm prepared to live with disappointment for a while. I've promised to wait, haven't I?"

There was so much comfort in his voice, so much strength in the arms circled around her. Pressing her cheek against the scratchy wool of his sweater until she felt his heart beating beneath it, Brigid wanted to surrender to it, but Lis had reminded her of what she'd already known. It was cruelly unfair, forcing him to return again and again, waiting for her signal. As much as she wanted him to wait, Brigid couldn't hold him to an open-ended promise. With her head still against his chest, she squeezed her eyes shut.

"That's just it, Tom, don't you see? You've made your promise, but I've given none in return."

Immediately, Brigid felt the contraction, a shiver of tension rippling through him, and heard the change in his voice.

"You said you loved me."

"And I do, but I said something else as well—that I can't bear leaving here."

"Of course, and I'll not ask you to when you're not ready, but when the time comes, and everyone else is leaving—"

"I could live here alone," Brigid said quietly. "I've said that already as well, and what does it matter, really? I've been thinking about it all day, Tom. I wish I could be different, but whether it's here or somewhere else, I can't help wondering if I'd do better to keep to myself."

"Wait a minute, now." He held her by the shoulders, searching her face. "What are you saying to me? That you want to live alone? That you'd prefer it?"

She dropped her gaze, unable to look at him any longer. The confused anger in his eyes frightened her. As Brigid began to wonder what in the name of God she was doing, she became dimly aware of some sort of commotion outside, raised voices calling out and others responding.

"I don't know what I'm saying," she said. "Only that the two of us are nothing alike, and I think you shouldn't hold yourself to such a promise when it might—"

"When it might come to nothing." Tom dropped his hands and stepped back. He took a stuttering breath. "So, you'll make no promises. That's what you're telling me, is it? Here, there or anywhere, you still won't choose me. You'll hide away in this godforsaken place, or maybe look for a fairy circle somewhere and wander around it, talking to birds and dolphins and watching for ghosts. You'd rather grow old and demented, alone, because you think it's a better way to pass a lifetime than spending it with me?"

The biting mockery stung deeply. Brigid felt the blood draining from her face, realizing she'd made a terrible mistake. She'd only succeeded in hurting him, and he'd paid her back with interest.

"You don't understand," she whispered.

"No," Tom agreed, his voice cracking. He looked away from her. "It's fairly clear I don't, isn't it?"

Neither of them spoke as he paced back and forth, his face unreadable. At last, putting his back to the rough mortared wall next to the hearth he sank to his haunches and stared at the floor. Brigid groped for a chair, shaken by how thoroughly her intuitive powers had deserted her.

After a long moment, Tom lifted his head, but before he could speak her cottage door trembled with the force of a pounding fist. It flew open, crashing against the opposite wall. Petey and Mícheál stood on the threshold. As they slowly walked in Petey removed his cap—a simple gesture, but so out of character that Brigid's heart froze.

"Tom. Your uncle Patsy has just arrived into the harbor with his trawler. It's your father, lad. He's had a heart attack."

19

*T*he events of the next eight hours fell from his memory as soon as they happened, along with every word Tom spoke or heard spoken to him. Some of the details returned later, hazy but discernible – the sight of his uncle's grim face as Petey's naomhóg approached the trawler; the mad confusion at Dingle pier, with friends gathered and eager to help, nearly begging to be given a job to do; the family members in front of Regan's, sorting out which cars were going to Galway and who would be riding in them.

Oddly enough, he remembered a particular moment during the drive, bumping along the road somewhere between Limerick and Ennis. He sat slumped in the back of a Ford Prefect he didn't recognize. He supposed it was a loan from one of Patsy's friends. His uncle was driving it, and his aunt Beryl was in front next to him. When Tom turned his face from the window, after looking at nothing he could recall, she was twisting around to look at him. She'd already done it countless times in the past three hours, her eyes holding the same expression of pity each time, and all Tom could think was that her lipstick was the brightest shade of red he'd ever seen. It was pointless, the snapshot of a moment of no importance, and yet it narrowly missed being his most vivid recollection of that entire day.

The clearest one was equally strange—a vision of the wooden floor in the waiting room of the Central Hospital in Galway. It had a design in it, blocks of rectangles hitched in a V-shaped pattern that reminded Tom of waves. He remembered how the floor seemed to be moving as he held his mother in his arms, collapsed and sobbing against his shoulder while she repeated over and over that he was "gone, already gone. Your father is gone."

Gone.

He recalled the dizziness of it, and of tightening his arms around his mother as much to stop himself from falling down as to give her comfort.

Listening to it described to him, Tom decided that his father had likely drawn his last breath while they were foostering around the unfamiliar streets, trying to find the hospital. It was shattering, of course, arriving too late for any last words, or a final goodbye. He knew it because everyone kept telling him so, but Tom was too numb to feel shattered. He only felt strangely awkward. Here they were, an entire caravan of McBrides, on the scene and ready for the vigil, and nothing to do but turn and go home again.

They'd descended on the hospital like an invading army, sixteen of them, counting all the cousins, and still they hadn't all arrived yet—his brothers were still on the boat from Liverpool. Adding in his mother's Galway relatives they formed a disorganized crowd looking for a purpose. The hospital staff eventually took the matter in hand, coaxing them onto benches lining the walls and bringing in extra chairs. Then, they served tea and biscuits.

Tom sat on one of the benches with his elbows on his knees. A lemon odor of wax rose from the line of cresting waves in the floor. He focused on the flowered china teacup, holding it in his calloused hands like a chalice, until his mother squeezed his arm.

"We'll go see him now, will we?" Her lips trembled with the effort to smile at him.

"We will, Ma. Sure." Tom hadn't understood that was an option. He wondered if people thought it queer he hadn't asked, and whether there were other things he didn't know about that he ought to be doing. He turned a questioning look at Patsy, sitting next to him, but his uncle only gave him a gentle clap on the shoulder.

They rose together, and were immediately joined by his uncle Lorcan, the eldest of Seamus and Patsy's brothers. He was a grizzled old farmer with a habit for coming out with uncomfortable truths and doing precisely what you wished he wouldn't. Tom generally found him entertaining, but his mother couldn't abide the man. He put an arm around Eileen and they left the waiting room, the arthritic Lorcan loping after them with his typical, bow-legged swagger.

"Alice," he called out to his daughter, when they met her in the hall. "We're just off to see the body, now."

Eileen flinched at the blunt announcement, and Tom tightened his grip on her. Less than an hour ago, Seamus had been a husband and father, but now had become simply a "body." His father was dead. His head had cleared enough to form the words, but the idea seemed preposterous, its meaning too big to absorb.

They were directed down a long corridor to a cool, cement block of a room. Both its walls and ceiling were painted a serene blue, as if to evoke something of the celestial. A full-color statue of the Blessed Mother, its plaster lined with cracks, sat on a pillar in one corner. Otherwise, there wasn't a stick of furniture to be seen until two nurses wheeled the bed into the room.

They drew the sheet in a graceful, coordinated movement, and although Tom had tried to be prepared, he was startled. His mother wept softly, her body heavy against him. The silence continued, and his tension rose. Just as he was picturing himself snapping like a rope with too much weight on it, Lorcan honked loudly into a handkerchief.

"Sure it doesn't look like him at all."

"Lorcan," Patsy rumbled in warning.

"I'm only saying—"

"I know, but that's enough, now."

Privately, Tom agreed with Lorcan. He'd never seen Seamus asleep, and had never realized how much of what he recognized in his father was down to his ever-changing expressions—his mouth twisting in laughter, eyes fired with anger, eyebrows raised to project a lordly self-satisfaction.

The lifeless figure he was looking at conveyed none of that. It might have been the face of a stranger.

Overcome with emotion, his elderly uncle couldn't help himself. "Jaysus, he'd gone quite bald, hadn't he?"

"Lorcan," Patsy snapped, his voice cracking as he draped an arm around his brother's shoulder. He met Tom's eyes, both of them struggling with an unhinged laughter. Then, the last of the fog he'd been trapped in for hours cleared, and Tom felt the tears on his face.

⁓

"Crikey, the place is solid black in there." Tie askew, and with an air of triumph, Dillon McBride came through the door onto the back patio. He was carrying a tray with four brimming pints in one hand, and a half-bottle of Powers in the other. "They'll be on each other's shoulders in another minute. Feck it, Tom, will you ever take the tray and not just your own pint, before my arm breaks in half?"

"Yeah, yeah. Sorry, Dil. Here, take yours." Tom handed his brother a Guinness, gave another to Jamesie, and the last to his brother Garrett.

It hadn't taken long for his brothers to enforce their customary rules of engagement. One was that the youngest should do whatever the others tell him, if he knows what's good for him. Tom didn't really mind it. He was just happy to have them there. For most of the previous day, he'd been surrounded by crowds and was often their focal point, but he'd only stopped feeling lonely early that morning, when Dil, Garrett and Hugh had walked in the door. The four of them had never been demonstrative with each other, but there was affection in the handshakes they exchanged – gripped a bit tighter, held a little longer. It brought Tom more comfort than any of the tearful embraces he'd endured until then.

After the initial confusion at the Central Hospital, one of his mother's sisters had organized the coffin and a hearse to bring Seamus home again. A long line of family cars followed it from Galway down to Ventry, creeping through a hammering rain and stiff winds, turning heads in every town along the way. It was an impressive procession that his father would have thoroughly enjoyed. When they reached home, a battalion of neighborhood women had already turned it into a wake house. They'd simply taken the place over, and Tom couldn't even fall into bed until one of them had finished snapping clean sheets onto it.

The onslaught had been constant ever since, and he'd long ago lost track of events. Jamesie had offered to do the farm chores alone, but Tom refused to let him, desperate to do something that felt normal. The two of them had just finished cleaning the barn and had retreated to the back patio with Dillon and Garrett. After continuing throughout the day the rain had finally stopped and the patio – built into the hillside with a mortared wall around it – provided shelter from the gusts of wind blowing over the pasture.

Dillon took a seat next to Tom on the flagstone steps. "Do you realize about eight out of ten of that shower of eejits in there are relatives?" He gave Tom a friendly elbow in the shoulder. "Did you know that?"

"I did, of course." Tom smiled, swatting his arm away. "Sure I see them more often than you. Did they not recognize you, then, Dil? I suppose you do sound more like a Brit than an Irishman these days."

"Why are there so many of them, I wonder?" Garrett was sprawled in a chair, his long legs stretched and crossed at the ankles. "How is it more haven't emigrated by now?"

"It seems the McBrides haven't the taste for it. Most of

them anyway," Tom added.

"Rubbish. They haven't the imagination for it. Present company excluded, of course." His brother raised his glass to Tom and Jamesie.

"I've imagined it, all right," Jamesie said, nibbling at a torn fingernail.

"Have you?" Tom was surprised and more than a little skeptical. His friend blushed.

"Well. I turned it over in my mind, like."

"You may get your chance, Jamesie." Dillon said. "Hugh has set his mind on clapping Tom into a trunk and bringing him back to Liverpool. Maybe he'll take you along as well. McBride's Builders is always hiring, these days."

Jamesie looked stricken. "Liverpool, Tom?"

"Don't listen to him." Tom felt a protective fondness for his credulous friend. "Where is Hugh, anyway?"

"Locked away in Dad's office," Garrett said. "He couldn't wait to run his eyes over the accounts."

Trying to hide his irritation, Tom took a long pull from his glass, but fooled nobody. From his pocket, Dillon brought out one of the clay pipes that were being handed around by the dozen, and put it to his lips.

"Lord have mercy." He struck a match and raised an eyebrow at his older brother. Garrett winked in return.

"You look as though you swallowed a pip, Tom. What's the matter?"

"Nothing. I'm only thinking he might have said something to me, first. I look after the farm accounts. I'm after doing it near two months now with no bother."

"Is that so? All of two months is it?"

"Two months is what I said, isn't it?" His brothers looked startled by the retort, and Tom hung his head. "Sorry."

"Take it easy, Tomaisín," Ruffling his hair, Dillon offered the pipe, and then remembering, snatched it away. "Ah, jayz, what am I like. Is it playing you up still, the asthma?"

"Not often, but . . . yeah, once in a while." He huffed a mirthless laugh and looked out over the back pasture. The grass, still wet, sparkled in the twilight. The blades projected the vivid green of summer, but the damp air smelled of autumn – withering oak leaves and windfall apples. He wondered what the weather was doing in the Blaskets.

Near the end of the long drive back from Galway, he'd made one attempt to remember what had happened during his last few minutes on the island. He tried to recall what he and Brigid had said to each other in parting before he raced down to the boat slip, and was almost certain they hadn't said anything at all. She'd rejected his promise, or at least had refused to give one of her own, which amounted to the same thing.

He could have tried some gentle persuasion, but the last words Tom remembered from their exchange were his own, scathing and cruel. She'd shared the most essential aspects of her life with him, trusting him to understand or at least respect them. In return, he'd done what others had often done before – mocked her and the things she treasured – and then he'd left without a word of apology. In a single outburst he'd revealed how little he comprehended her, and how small he was compared to everything she valued.

The enormity of what this meant added a slug of pain to the load of grief and guilt he was shouldering, and it was so intense Tom had to back away from it. He hadn't allowed himself to think of Brigid again until now, but as soon as her face appeared in his mind, despair overwhelmed him. He grabbed the bottle of whiskey and got quickly to his feet.

"Back in a bit. I need a walk."

Taking the flagstone steps two at a time, he climbed up into the pasture and strode away from the house. He stood facing the ocean, sipping the whiskey, trying to keep his mind empty while the wind beat against him. After a while, Jamesie appeared at his side.

"They've gone awful dry down there on the patio." He gestured at the bottle of Powers. Tom nodded and handed it over, but Jamesie made no move to leave. He uncorked the bottle and took a swallow. They stood without speaking for several minutes, passing the whiskey back and forth, until Jamesie at last broke the silence.

"Jaysus, that's an awful looking sky. Diabolical, really. We're in for a spell of it, I'd say."

Following his friend's gaze, Tom raised his eyes skyward and had to agree. The dark, dense cloud cover felt oppressive. He shrugged, indifferent, and Jamesie regarded him sadly.

"Are you all right, Tommy?"

"To be honest, I'm not sure."

"I was thinking, if you'd like to send a note off to Brigid—"

"Thanks, but there's no need. I'm fairly certain she'd rather not hear from me."

"Ah, jayz. Right." Jamesie heaved a long sigh. "Can I help at all?"

Tom gave him an incredulous, sidelong glance.

"I didn't mean—not with her...mother of God," Jamesie

sputtered. "With anything else, like."

Tom felt the stiffness in his face give way to a faint grin. "You've helped already, Jamesie. Will you stay on for a while yet?"

"I will. Sure isn't my entire family inside your house? I've no reason to be going home."

"Good. Go on now, and take the lads their whiskey. Give me half an hour to see what Hugh is getting up to and then we'll have some music."

Alone again, Tom stood for another few minutes in the pasture. Turning in a circle, he looked in every direction, from the top of the hill down to the rocky cliffs of the shoreline, feeling the last of his boyhood draining away. It belonged to him, now. Every animal and hill of potatoes, every rock and field, every speck of earth beneath it all.

The legacy of Seamus McBride had become his own.

20

As he came through the front door, a low, droning wail greeted Tom, freezing him in place. Even knowing what it was, the sound was enough to rattle his nerves. The tradition of *caoineadh* - keening over the dead - had largely died out, but his cousin Eithne had asked to revive the custom for her uncle. Predictably, the same conclave of women who'd guided every other event so far had latched onto the idea.

"Are you sure you want this, Ma?" Tom had asked Eileen that morning. Exhausted by grief, she'd waved a hand in vague acceptance.

"What harm? Eithne loves a bit of drama, but she means well."

He'd understood his cousin to be the solely appointed *bean chaointe*, but if volume was any measure there was more than one "keening woman" in the house. Heading in the direction of the parlor, Tom slipped through the crowds, wanting to be sure one of the moaning voices was not his mother's.

The parlor, where his father had been laid out, was unlike any other room in the house. Its walls were painted a luxurious, royal red, and the Victorian-style couch and surrounding chairs were upholstered in green velvet. Instead of the usual rough-cut hearth, there was a ceramic stove beneath a decorative mantlepiece, and above it, a massive 19th-century oil painting depicting the Madonna and child. It was the one room in the house that had come fully furnished when Seamus bought it, and it was the main reason people thought the McBrides wealthier than they actually were.

People had been visiting the room in small, quiet groups throughout the day, but it was jammed now. The assembled crowd seemed spellbound by Eithne. She'd been joined by two other young women and they were carrying on a guttural chant beside his father's coffin, while his mother sat nearby.

Except for an hour when Hugh had persuaded her to lie down, Eileen had remained in a chair next to the coffin all day. Expecting an inevitable collapse, the brothers had taken it in turns to keep an eye on her, but Eileen's stamina had outlasted theirs. It was close to eight o'clock but she was still sitting there, her expression calmly tolerant.

Tom found Patsy slouched against the wall next to the doorway and his uncle raised his glass in a discreet salute.

"I don't know how she's standing it. Jaysus, I'm near to climbing the walls meself."

Tom gave the keeners a wincing glance. They looked theatrically disheveled – deranged, even. Eithne's sparrow-like figure was enveloped in a tattered black shawl, and her hair had been teased into a wild rat's nest of flaming red.

"Should I tell them to pack it in, do you suppose?"

"If you're brave enough. I'd be afraid of my life to even try."

Tom edged his way around the room to his mother, who

took his hand and peered up at him with her habitually worried frown. "You look so pale, Tom. Are you feeling all right?"

"I'm fine, Ma." He crouched down, leaning closer to her ear. "Is this not driving you mad, though? Will I have them stop?"

"Don't bother; I've this minute told them to finish all this business before Father Mahoney gets here. I hope we've some of that cherry brandy he likes? Maybe I should check."

"I wouldn't worry. We've more liquor inside this house than a distillery. I've no doubt he'll find a drink he can choke down. Are you okay for everything here? I'm going to talk with Hugh for a bit."

"I'm grand, love." She gave his arm a firm pat. "Get them all back here for the rosary, though, Tom."

"I will. Promise."

Tom wound his way back through the shifting mass of mourners, who became steadily louder the farther they got from the parlor. He arrived at the door to his father's office and paused, wondering if he should knock, but then gave an impatient sniff.

"Divil a bit. I've more right to be in there than he does."

He compromised, giving the door a few taps while opening it. As usual, a stir of chilly air and the smell of damp plaster assaulted him as he walked in the room. The soot-clouded lamp was turned to its brightest setting, throwing more shadow than light across the nearly empty room.

Hugh stood with his hands braced on the desk, squinting down at an open ledger covering the top of it. He looked up at the sound of the knock, and seeing Tom, his pinched scowl turned to a smile. He angled his head in the direction of the continuing wail.

"Are you joking me? A *bean chaointe*, even?"

Tom grinned back. "No joke. 'Tis in the manual."

"Tell me we're not paying ready money for that racket."

Tom closed the door before answering. "I don't think so. Unless Eithne needs bus fare to get to her audition at the Abbey Theatre."

Hugh laughed. "I'm glad you're here. I was about to go looking for you. Fancy a pint? Have that if you like. I told Dil I didn't want it, but he brought it anyway." He waved at the glass of stout sitting on a table near the door.

"No, I'm all right." Tom came to stand on the other side of the desk, the annoyance he'd felt already evaporating. He could never stay angry at Hugh.

Of all of them, his eldest brother bore the strongest physical resemblance to their father, and he had an even sharper mind for business, but his temperament was more like their mother's. Hugh was a mild-mannered worrier. He suffered from ulcers, his russet-brown hair was already thinning, and his face had a jowly puffiness that spoke of too much time spent indoors, and too little sleep. He was only thirty but seemed older, and since Tom was the youngest by eight years, he'd always regarded him as an adult.

"Have a seat." Hugh pulled a heavy chair around to the front of the desk. Tom dragged another one forward from the wall and they sat facing each other.

"Hard to believe he's gone, isn't it?" his brother said gently.

"It is."

Tom looked away, and then down at his hands. This was another topic he wasn't allowing himself to think about very deeply. He'd thrown it into a corner of his mind, piling thoughts of inconsequential rubbish around it to keep everything out of sight. Hugh rested an arm along the length of the desk, fingers tapping idly against the wood.

"You've come across the will by now, I suppose."

Feeling close to dangerous territory, Tom nodded. He'd discovered the will a few days after his parents had left for Galway, in the top drawer of the desk. It seemed placed there intentionally, to ensure he would find it. Despite the years of fractious discussions about it, he hadn't really expected the document to hold many surprises, but was still relieved not to find any when he read it. Each of his brothers had been left an equal, lump sum of money. The house and land had been left to Tom alone, with the stipulation that his mother would have an annuity, and would have the option to live in the house for the rest of her life.

"I've seen it, yeah. Is it bothering you?" He eyed Hugh warily, but his brother's expression was reassuring.

"Not in the way you think. Dad settled something on the three of us a long time ago, when we each emigrated. We always knew he'd leave the farm to you. I'm only hoping to persuade you not to hang on to it."

Tom gaped at him. "What are you saying? That you want me to sell it?"

"It's worth considering. Sure it's an awful lot of work, just to have something to eat at the end of the day. Can you not see how hard it would be to manage this place on your own?"

Bemused, Tom recognized that at one time he would have been offended by the comment, regarding it as a statement of his own inadequacy, but he had little left to prove to himself where the farm was concerned. He felt no anger towards

Hugh; the remark only reminded him how long his brothers had been gone, and how little they understood what he'd been doing for the past several years. His smile was wistful, patient.

"I've a notion how to go about it, Hugh."

His brother chuckled. "Ah, right enough. I imagine you do, at that. Listen to me, though." He leaned forward, his large brown eyes serious. "Come to Liverpool. Think about it, at least. The construction boom is roaring away since the war; we can't put the houses up fast enough and I'm short on foremen. If I'm being honest, you'd be worth more to me than the other two put together. Dil only wants to arse about and go for pints with the men, and Garrett has too much of the oul' fella in him. He's a bollocks and his men can't stand him. You're a born leader, Tom, and you know it. It may have driven Seamus crazy, but it's the very thing I need."

Tom didn't know any such thing. He lifted his head and stared at Hugh. "What are you talking about? What drove him crazy?"

"That you got results without being the hard-driving manager he wanted you to be. From the time you were thirteen years of age, every farm lad working here—fellas twice your age, or more—would do anything for you. Seamus had to yell, but you only had to ask, and never twice. Yer man Jamesie? Thick as two planks but sure he'd sooner die than disappoint you. That's a rare thing, Tom, to be the sort of man people want to follow, not because they're told to, but because it makes them feel good. Dad didn't understand that. He couldn't see how you did it or why it worked, and he wouldn't trust it. He was afraid you were too soft, not serious enough. Thought he needed to make a man of you." Hugh gave him a sympathetic smile. "That's not news to you, though."

"The last part? No. It isn't news. But the rest of it?" Tom took a deep breath. "Why are you telling me this now? It would have helped to hear it sooner, Hugh. I might have –"

His voice faltered, thinking about his quarrel with Seamus six weeks earlier in the calving shed, neither of them realizing their words would be the last of any importance they would say to each other. He stood up, feeling shaky.

"I will have that pint, after all."

After getting the glass from the table, he took a long swallow and walked around the room with it. He could no longer hear Eithne and her friends, thanks be to God, but there was still a buzz of conversation in the house, punctuated by rumblings of laughter. If Father Mahoney had arrived the rosary would start any minute, but Tom couldn't leave the room yet. He was busy re-interpreting his entire relationship with his father based on the information just received.

"I'm sorry," Hugh said, watching him pace from one corner to the next. "I should have said something earlier, I suppose. I didn't think it would matter that much. The funny thing is, Tom, you're actually tougher than the lot of us. It may sound mad, but I think it was the asthma that did that for you."

Tom pivoted to face his brother, his scowl incredulous. "It does sound mad. It's nearly killed me more than once."

"I remember, believe me. I can still picture that night in the middle of winter. Da wrapped you up and flew away with you on the back of a horse to St. Elizabeth's. I think you weren't even five years of age, yet. You both came back the next morning, knackered. He fell into a chair with you in his arms and just broke down crying, he was that relieved.

Scared us nearly to death. Do you remember it?"

"I do," Tom said softly. It wasn't the panicked race to the hospital or the arrival home he recalled, but the ride back. Seamus had given him an enormous currant bun covered in white icing. He remembered eating it while his father held him snugly against his chest, and sang every verse of *Róisín Dubh*. Tom smiled at the memory, feeling his throat tighten. He would have been happy to ride the horse all the way to Dublin that day.

"Here's the thing, though," Hugh continued. "Those attacks were terrifying—for all of us, but mostly for you, of course—but after you'd been through a few bad ones, there wasn't much else that could really frighten you, or break you. We all admired that about you. Seamus included." he added.

Tom came back to his chair and sat down. "I'm not sure I know what you're getting at with all this."

Hugh shrugged, as if the answer were obvious. "That you were a great lad, and you've become a fine man, and I need fine men working with me. You'd do well over there, Tom. Don't answer now. Just think about it, and think about where you'll be in another fifteen years if you stay here—a bachelor farmer living in this great big house with your elderly Ma. Because you haven't got a girl, I'm guessing?"

At Tom's stuttering, red-faced confusion, his brother sat up straighter, eyes wide. "Oh, hang on a minute. You do have a girl?"

"I don't think ... I'm fairly certain she's not ... never mind. Doesn't matter."

"Well who is she? Tell me that much, anyway."

Mercifully, before he was forced to make an answer, the

office door banged open and Garrett's figure stood silhouetted on the threshold.

"*Oremus.*" He intoned the Latin in a singsong chant. "Now
Father Mahoney has had his fill of brandy, he wants to be
getting on with the program. So, 'let us pray,' lads. Find your
beads and proceed to the parlor in a good, orderly fashion."

21

Peering into the bucket at her feet, Brigid saw there was little more than a pint of milk collected there. She gave each of the teats one last pull, but it was clear Starlight had given all she could—at least for the morning, and perhaps for the day.

"It's all right, love," she said, seeing something in the cow's large brown eyes that looked like apology. "You've done your best. I can't ask more than that."

Brigid ran her hands over the animal, giving each flank a slow, exploratory massage. She did it every morning now, imitating the motions she'd watched Tom use. Starlight enjoyed the attention, and the ritual—with its daily resurrection of a happy memory—gave Brigid some comfort as well. This morning, the probing of ribs and hip bones told her nothing she didn't already know. Starlight had lost weight; but sure hadn't they all?

The beginning of September had looked so promising—sunny days, mild breezes and a welcome extension of summer temperatures—but the weather that blew in on the day after the céilí had swept all that away. The lobster season abruptly ended and the mackerel fishing – the season the islanders loved best – never started. Before the month was out the community had also lost a fair share of the potato crop.

It had happened two weeks earlier, after a series of relentless storms had subsided into an impenetrable fog. Brigid had welcomed it at first. After so many nights of shrieking wind the silence came as a relief; but it's persistence, and the muffled, cotton wool quality of it, soon began to feel ominous. The second morning after its arrival, what little peace it offered was shattered, when she was shocked awake in the half-light of dawn by her uncle. Sean's fists pounded wildly on the door while he roared at her.

"Get up and out to the fields, girl. There's blight coming on the crop. It's taken the Daly plots already, and Keane's as well. We'll lose them all if we aren't quick about it."

The mere mention of a blight was enough to send a shudder through Brigid. It was a fearsome, fast-moving enemy and had led to the starvation of an entire generation a hundred years earlier. She'd never known it to strike the Blaskets, but the current conditions were ideal for an infestation – unseasonably warm and windless, and a fog so wet it soaked through to the skin.

She'd spent sixteen hours in the fields that day, along with every other able-bodied man and woman, working in grim silence. While the fog persisted she was sometimes unable to see anyone around her, but Brigid could hear the grunts and harsh breaths as her neighbors dug into the earth, urgently forking up potatoes and carrying them away before disease could settle on them. It was stunning how quickly it had spread, and heartbreaking to watch the wooden expressions of the islanders as they ripped the spoiled plants from the ground – black and rotting – and carried them away to be destroyed.

They saved a good deal of the crop before the wind began raging again, but much was lost, putting even more strain on a food supply that was already running low. The constant gales had kept the naomhógs on land for weeks. No crew could take a boat across to Dunquin and hope to survive the journey.

So the islanders waited, keeping careful inventory of their dwindling pantries. With the radio telephone knocked senseless since the night of the céilí, they were completely isolated from the mainland, and from each other as well. Each family hunkered in their own house, and Brigid imagined the tableau in every one of them was the same. They gathered around the hearth, and prayed for a break in the siege.

For a few minutes that morning, a wan glimmer of sun had led her to hope their petition had been heard, but opening the door of the byre Brigid saw the clouds had already smothered it. A misting rain was falling again, but the wind wasn't quite as fierce, so she stepped outside, hoping her cow would follow. Having spent much of the past several weeks inside, living on handfuls of oats and the apples Brigid fed her, she was in need of grazing.

"Come here to me now, my treasure," she called softly. "Look at all this lovely green grass, only waiting for you to make a meal of it."

Starlight stood in the doorway, unconvinced, but once coaxed from the byre she quickened her pace along the path, heading for the pasture at the southern end of the island.

Ignoring the rain Brigid followed, grateful for the chance of a walk without fear of being tossed like a feather on an angry current of air. She hurried to keep up with Starlight, and after rounding the corner of an empty house at the edge of the village, she nearly collided with Margaret coming the other way.

"Oh, Margaret, I'm sorry! It's a wonder Starlight didn't knock you right onto the ground, she's that anxious to get a mouthful of grass inside her. I'm delighted to see you, so. How have you been keeping? You're all well, I hope? You and Padraig and the child?"

For Brigid, this was nothing short of babbling, but she was desperate for a little human contact and conversation, no matter how idle. Huddled inside for five days straight with only the cow for company was too much, even for her quiet temperament. It was hard on her spirits, as well. They were heavy enough with the weight of all her sorrow and regret, but the forced seclusion had taught her something that pressed them lower still. She was no longer in love with solitude, not this type, anyway—the kind that stretched out into the future without ever feeling the touch of a hand on hers, or a whisper of warm breath against her neck. It was a painful lesson, and one she'd learned too late.

The last time the men had rowed out to Dunquin, nearly a month ago, she hadn't allowed herself to hope for anything, but when the mail bag had been emptied, and Lis morosely confirmed it contained no letter from Tom, Brigid knew she'd been fooling herself. Her grief was physical, a stabbing pain that reached everywhere, and she couldn't hide it from her aunt, no matter how hard she tried.

"His head is all over the place, taken up with the care of his father. I'm sure of it," Lis said, not sounding sure at all. "Will you not choke down your pride and write to him instead?"

"It's nothing to do with pride," Brigid said, her head aching from the effort of holding in her tears. "Only I think it's best to just leave it. We've hurt each other enough, I'd say."

The weather had ended any further trips to Dunquin, as well as any more arguments from her aunt, but even if there was a boat that could carry a letter to him, what could she say to Tom, now, after she'd pushed him away?

Forcing the question from her mind, Brigid took a breath, preparing to burble another stream of hectic nonsense at Margaret, but then stopped, seeing the look of haggard fear in the woman's face.

"Tell me. What is it? What's happened, Margaret?"

"Liam. My own little one." Margaret spoke softly, the words nearly carried away in the wind. "A few days ago, he slipped in the dooryard and caught an awful gash on his arm. I think it's infected, Brigid. There's redness spreading all around it, and now a fever has just come on this morning."

"Oh, Margaret."

Brigid knew what they each were thinking. The parallel was too painfully obvious, the comparison inevitable, but it was Margaret that finally said it, her voice rising in anguish.

"What are we to do, at all? Isn't it just the same as Seanin Kearney. Has my boy to face that as well, now? Sickening and fading away with none to help? And why him, for all love? Sure aren't there rakes of old men up the road, waiting to be called. God only wants to take the youngest away from us."

"No more of that, now." Shaken by the words, and the

power they might have to summon the thing they named, Brigid put her arms around Margaret, holding her in a tight embrace. "We won't think of it. We won't speak of it. Go back to him, now. Put Liam into bed and let him lie quiet. I'll get Lis and we'll be over to you in a few minutes."

They arrived at the Daly's house on the heels of a fresh shower of rain, and she and Lis spent the day there, mostly soothing Margaret, as there was little to do other than keep Liam quiet and watch the hot red streaks spread slowly up his arm. By evening he was listless, the fever still climbing, and they convinced Margaret and Padraig to move the little boy to Brigid's house. Their reasoning was unspoken, but clear to everyone. She lived closest to the path leading down to the boat slip.

As the night wore on, everyone in Brigid's house – and a good few were gathered – fixed half their attention on the drama inside and the other half on the weather. There was nothing to be done in the darkness, but in the morning, they would look for the first sign of a pause, any hint of a calm in the atmosphere. At a moment's notice, the women were ready to swaddle Liam into a bundle fit for travel, and the men at the kitchen table, clustered around Padraig, had the naomhóg ready and waiting.

"We need only an hour. No more than that, to get across." Sean's gruff voice was low and reassuring.

Padraig nodded, eyes fixed on the table and his folded hands on top of it. Brigid brought over a pot of tea. Setting it down, she gently persuaded him to unclench his scarred, calloused fingers and wrap them around a mug instead.

A scant sixty minutes. It was so little to ask, she thought, not for the water to lie smooth as glass, but only to become less murderous. Brigid thought perhaps her prayer for a calmer sea might be more quickly answered if offered while looking at it. She wrapped herself in a shawl and told Lis she was going outside. Incredulous, her aunt started to protest, but then shook her head and sighed.

"Be careful, at least, and for the love of God, stay on the path."

She did stay on the path at first, but the night wasn't as black as she'd expected. There was no moon, and certainly no starlight to be seen through the blanketing clouds, but still a faint, violet glow made her surroundings visible. Brigid couldn't tell what was making it, unless it was the turbulent surf itself, creating its own light as the waves slammed into the cliffs, exploding on impact into white froth and mist.

She said her prayers while walking, and then wandered out onto a grassy area sitting high above the Blasket's small harbor. It was an unconsecrated graveyard. This was where the islanders had once buried infants – those who had not lived long enough for baptism, because there were so many things in the world that could stop a tiny heartbeat, and the priests were all so far away.

Brigid stopped at one of the sunken grave markers, trying not to think of little Liam. If it came to the worst, he would not lie here. His own baptism had been a joyful event for the village, as had his first tooth, his first steps. He stood in for all the children that had once run through the village and scrambled over the hills. Every milestone in his young life had been marked and celebrated as a blessing. By all of them. Would he be taken from them as well? Were they meant to lose everything?

Her own sense of loss was magnified by a growing fear that she was falling out of step with the island. Lately, its power seemed to be shrinking away from her. She felt as if she'd been pushed to the wrong side of a threshold, and for the first time an idea crept into her mind that would have been unthinkable, even a week ago. Maybe the island didn't want them here any longer. Maybe its spirits had a craving for solitude that had finally grown stronger than their fear of loneliness. If so, it was a clash of desires she understood, a decision she could respect. Brigid wished she could have been braver when presented with a similar choice.

Tilting her head, she looked up at the low, violet-hued clouds overhead. Attempting to see the night sky behind them was like trying to glimpse her own future. As often as she'd prayed for it in the last several weeks, no vision would reveal itself, so Brigid could only look at the past, regretting everything she'd said to Tom in the last minutes they'd spent together. She longed to have them back again, to replace every word spoken in fear with one of affirmation. Of acceptance.

She had no expectation of any such grace. After clinging to solitude all her life it seemed she would be left with loneliness, not because it was the path she'd chosen, but because when the chance for a different one was offered, she'd refused to make any choice at all.

22

*I*n the weeks following his father's death, Tom came to understand grief as a confusing and unpredictable state of mind. For a while, its impact felt more like a glancing blow, because a rotating cast of mourners had assumed much of the burden for him.

First, there had been the weeping disbelief of his relatives, and when that lot had dispersed they were seamlessly replaced by a parade of visiting neighbors. It was the usual assortment of busybodies, fastening onto drama as burdock attaches to a passing sweater. To go with their long faces, they arrived at the door offering everything from canned preserves to pig's trotters as their entrance ticket. Some were people Tom barely recognized. His mother appreciated the distraction, but he found their condolences – breathed while clutching his wrist in a talon-like grip – oppressive. He fled to the rain-soaked fields as soon as courtesy allowed, and returned only when he could see them starting down the hill again, their clucking sighs amplified in the heavy air.

"Ah, the poor pet. She hasn't an eye in her head for crying."

"Desperate. Is she thinner, did you think?"

"I don't know at all, but sure she'd no trouble with those biscuits of yours."

Ironically, it was just as the entertainment value of their private tragedy waned that Tom discovered he was out of step with everyone else. The extended family members from four counties were back in their homes getting on with their lives; his brothers had returned to Liverpool, and the village population—having done their duty and satisfied their curiosity—were turning their attention to some fresh spectacle. It seemed the world's grief for Seamus McBride had played itself out, but for Tom it was only beginning. The force of his father's personality had been an all-encompassing fact of life, and though small in stature, the man had filled every room he ever entered. Coping with his absence was like trying to fill a hole that grew bigger each day.

His mother understood, of course. The two of them, at least, were on the same wavelength—the last attendants at the vigil, watching the candles burn down. The commonplace rituals were hardest for them to face, and the kitchen table was a spot they'd particularly avoided. They took their meals on trays, sitting by the fire, but after a few weeks Eileen took a step forward. That evening, she laid the tea on the scarred wooden table, and stopped Tom from taking his usual place in the middle.

"You don't belong there anymore," she said, keeping a tight grip on the chair as he reached for it. "Take his seat."

Unable to answer, he shook his head and focused on the fragrant steam rising from the stewpot. He glanced at his mother's hand when it covered his.

"Will you have me sit facing an empty chair, love? You're the man of the house, now. Take the seat he meant you to have. He knew you were ready. Didn't he tell me so himself, the very day we left on the train."

Tom knew she meant well, but the words rang hollow. It seemed Seamus had been comfortable sharing them with everyone else—his brother, his uncle, his mother—but not with his youngest son, who'd been waiting years to hear them.

Although it only sharpened the edge of his grief, Tom couldn't help wondering if his father's retirement would have softened him. Hugh's recollection of that snowy horseback ride to the hospital years ago had been painful, because it brought to mind a man he'd nearly forgotten. The one who'd consoled him with iced buns and old songs, who'd whittled toy soldiers for him, and who'd taught him ... well ... everything.

The two of them had been pals once, right up until the day his brothers left home, and transferred all the weight of their father's expectations onto Tom's young shoulders. Seamus had driven him hard after that, and their relationship suffered the consequences of his impatience and biting skepticism. Maybe eventually they would have settled back into the friendship of his boyhood. He couldn't decide if the idea was comforting or distressing, but it didn't matter. He would never know.

However difficult the apprenticeship, Tom couldn't deny the effect it achieved. Seamus had prepared him well. He had no fears about the responsibility facing him, but now, on the brink of assuming the role he'd been groomed for, he was no longer sure he wanted it, and that did frighten him.

After he and his mother finished eating, they took up their usual places on either side of the hearth. Since the funeral,

Eileen had refused to go to bed before midnight, when she could be sure exhaustion would carry her quickly into sleep. Tom had been keeping her company while she reminisced and told old stories. Many he'd heard before, but some were new—like her memories of growing up in Galway City.

She'd be returning there, soon. True to his word, a few days before the heart attack his father had placed a deposit on a small bungalow in the Salthill neighborhood. Something needed to be done about it one way or the other. The owner would likely return the money, considering the circumstances, but as often as his mother repeated an expectation of that outcome, she sounded less certain each time. Tom also found it suspicious that she didn't want him traveling to Galway with her.

"There's no need, really," she kept assuring him. "You've so much to do here. Your uncle John will meet the train. He'll help me with whatever needs doing, and I'll be home again in no time at all."

Tom remained doubtful. The bungalow was only a few streets away from two of her sisters and their families. He thought there was a fair chance she'd decide to keep the place. Like so many other things, he didn't know how he felt about that. He stood behind a chair next to the fire, fingers drumming against the back of it, and looked down at Eileen.

"Will you be all right, Ma, if I go out for awhile?"

Eileen's brow puckered. "Oh, Tom. Where do you want to be going at this time of night?"

"I don't know, really. Somewhere."

With uncertainties piling up around him, he felt he'd go mad if he couldn't get out of the house for a few hours.

Before guilt could overwhelm his determination, he bent to give her a quick kiss and hurried from the room.

"I'll go for a pint at the Swallowtail, maybe. Just the one. I won't be late."

Although the Swallowtail was less than a mile away, Tom grabbed the keys to the truck on his way out the door. The rain had finally stopped, but the wind was stirring ripples over sheets of water in the pasture. The ground was too saturated to absorb another drop. When the battered Ford sputtered awake on the third attempt, he sent it coasting down the narrow dirt path, bouncing as it shuddered in and out of the puddled potholes.

At the intersection with the main road he stopped, undecided. He let the idling engine grumble while he thought. After a minute, Tom pulled the wheel to the right, away from the Swallowtail, and drove towards Dunquin.

⁓

A few miles before the village, Tom pulled off the road into a parking area tucked beneath Dunmore Head. It was the most westerly point on the Irish mainland – a bluff jutting from the end of the peninsula like the cocked thumb of a hitchhiker, headed for America. The tires crunched over the graveled surface as he moved farther off the road, and after swinging the truck to face the edge of a steep drop-off, Tom switched off the engine. He stared out and down at Coumeenoole Beach, flat and wide as it spread up the coastline.

The beach bore a slight resemblance to the Blasket's White Strand. Its red-cliffed shoreline had a similar shape, but the likeness ended there. He doubted its ragged coves could be sheltering a marvel like the one he'd discovered on a sunny day in June.

Strengthened by fierce gusts, the tide had reached right up to the base of the cliffs, but now it was retreating, and in the darkness the slick, wet sand looked like polished stone. Without taking his eyes from the scene, Tom fingered the two pieces of mail in the pocket of his jacket. They'd been crammed there for two weeks, and he still didn't know what to do with them.

He drew them out of his pocket and shuffled them in his hands, one over the other, and then looked down at what had landed on top.

It was the Liverpool postcard. His brothers loved bragging about their adopted hometown, and the card presented a collage of photographs highlighting its superlative feats of engineering. There was the Royal Liver Building, which Hugh had boasted was the first to be built with reinforced concrete. Next to that was a picture of the city's immense cathedral, and in the center, pride of place went to a depiction of the Queensway beneath the River Mersey—"longest underwater tunnel in the world", he could hear Dil exclaiming.

The card had an inscription on the back: *Post this when you're on you're way, and we'll meet you at the dock!* Each of his brothers had signed it. It was stamped and addressed to Hugh McBride, Chapel Road, Liverpool. A month ago he would have laughed and tossed the card into a drawer, or even the trash, but when he'd found it on his dresser after they'd left for the train station, he hadn't done either. Instead, he'd propped it with the written side facing out on the table next to his bed.

Every morning his brothers' names were the first thing he saw when he opened his eyes—an invitation renewed daily, chipping away at his resistance.

Beneath the postcard lay the second item—an envelope, containing something that could hardly be called a letter. Slipping the page out he rubbed the paper between two fingers, not looking at it. It was too dark to read, but he remembered what was written there.

Dear Brigid,
I wanted to write, only to say how much I wish

Since writing those lines, he'd made no further progress, unable to complete even that single, half-expressed thought. What was he wishing, after all? That she could be different than she was? Or that he could?

He put the page back into the envelope and threw it onto the seat next to him, along with the postcard. To clear the fog of his breath from the windshield he cracked a window open, and then sat listening to the wind whistling through it while he watched the ocean's rolling retreat. After a few minutes Tom gave the handle of the door a savage pull, shoved himself out of the truck, and began walking up the steep, grassy slope to the top of Dunmore Head.

The rounded hilltop contained two monuments in stone. The first was ancient, a 5th-century pillar inscribed with letters from a primitive Irish alphabet. The second was more recent—a shelter constructed as a watch post during the war. Tom walked past both and continued to the end of the bluff, where it descended again, and narrowed into the shape of a ship's prow aimed straight at a conical shape just off shore. It was the last, vestigial piece of the mainland, a grass-covered rock called The Lure, and far beyond it lay the shadowed outline of the Great Blasket.

He picked his way around slivered rocks that looked like the teeth of a giant, protruding from the ground in a crooked line. Tom chose one that was reasonably flat and sat down. Hunched forward, elbows on his knees, he looked out at the island. He could just make out the larger houses at the top of the village. They looked like splashes of white paint on a black background. The cottages on the hillside below them couldn't be seen at all.

It wasn't the first trip he'd made up Dunmore Head, nor the first time he'd gazed across this turbulent channel of the North Atlantic. He'd come several times during the summer, following the same path, sitting on the same rock, but like the clear, sunny days he'd chosen for those visits, his thoughts had been brighter then, and filled with hope.

He remembered again the last words he'd spoken to Brigid. Even then, in the midst of his angry confusion, he'd seen how they'd hurt her. Tom wished he could take them back, but even if he could, it wouldn't change the truth she'd hinted at. In the end, she would choose to remain alone, not only because he'd shown himself as incapable of understanding her as everyone else, but also because his love wasn't enough. Brigid was tapping into something he couldn't compete with. He couldn't begin to comprehend it, but thought maybe the heat and light it delivered was something that ordinary, human love could never equal.

If that were true, there was little point of prolonging the

pain with letters. The future he'd envisioned a little over a month ago was made of things he'd already lost. The one in its place was beginning to look like a dull, lonely road, and Tom knew he needed to find a new one. He thought maybe it should start with the Liverpool postcard, but his heart refused to accept the idea. It was still fastened on the island he couldn't stop staring at, three miles out in the sea.

It was only a looming shape now, black against a slightly lighter sky; even the houses he'd seen earlier were invisible. It was late and his mother would be getting anxious. Tom straightened and braced his hands against the rock, but as he stood up, a flicker caught at the corner of his eye. He scanned the horizon, and a moment later saw it again. A wink of light at the southern end of the island. It went out, but then reappeared, and after flashing intermittently it steadied. He didn't think it could be an oil lamp. The distance was too great to see a flame that small.

Tom frowned, squinting at it while the whisper of an idea floated into his head. An instant later, there wasn't a shred of doubt as the wind caught at the small light. It blossomed into a towering fire, a red conflagration that illuminated the tip of the island.

"Holy mother of God."

He leapt to his feet and began to run, dodging around rocks as he sprinted across the bluff and down to the truck. After getting it started he yanked at the wheel, tires spinning on gravel as the truck shot out onto the road and raced towards Dunquin.

At this hour of the night, with the post office closed, Tom could think of only one place where he might find a working telephone. Following the coastal road, he shifted gears and floored the accelerator, ignoring the truck's whining protest as it rocketed out of each winding curve. The route turned inland as he neared the town – a scattered settlement of houses set back from the road with acres of rolling landscape between them. Tom sped past the homes, all of them shuttered and dark, with curls of chimney smoke hinting at the lives sheltered inside.

After a final, careening left turn he landed on a long strip of dirt next to a two-story building of mottled concrete. A sign painted on the eastern gable identified it as Kruger's Guest House. There was a low, bunker-like addition attached to the end of it, and although it had no sign Tom knew it was the town of Dunquin's general store, and its only pub.

He came to a skidding stop in front of the door and tumbled out of the truck. His boots sent up a splash as they landed in a shallow lake of water standing in the yard. Tom quickly searched the horizon. The island was visible from where he stood, but a rise in the landscape ahead obscured its southern end.

He ran to the pub's entrance, a vision of the fire still vivid in his mind if not his line of sight. Inside, he found a sparse crowd gathered in a dim smoky lounge, but the bar itself was like a beacon in the fog. The mirrored wall behind it was lined with shelves holding glasses and bottles of every shape and size, all twinkling in the reflected light from the lamps on the counter. Next to one of the lamps stood a man with the physique of a boxer, pouring out a glass of whiskey.

The half-dozen men lining the bar looked up in surprise as Tom burst through the door. Ignoring all of them, he went straight to the bar and the broad-shouldered barman behind it.

"In the name of God, ring for the lifeboat. The Blasket has the signal fire lighting. It's after going up like a bloody gasworks explosion."

23

The debate about lighting the signal fire had started while Brigid was out walking. She arrived back at her cottage to find everyone but Margaret gathered around the table. Their solemn conversation stopped abruptly when she opened the door. For a few seconds they stared at her in silence, but then Sean's creased face relaxed.

"It's Brigid."

"Of course it is, and who else?" Lis sounded relieved as she waved a hand at her. "Brigid close that door before the air gets in to shiver the child. What have you been at, for all this time? Wandering around in the dark. You nearly looked like a stranger just now. Come here and sit with us."

Without waiting for her reply, they shifted to make room for her and turned back to their discussion. Brigid felt a surge of love for their familiar faces, and their tolerant acceptance of her.

"It's shifted now," Sean was saying as she joined them. "The rain has stopped and the wind will likely settle enough for us to go in a few hours."

"And what if it doesn't settle enough?" Brigid asked quietly. Her uncle began to reply, but then rubbed a hand against his stubbled jaw and sighed.

"We're losing time as it is." Padraig's voice was low and filled with anguish. "Why not light the fire for someone to see, while there's still hours of darkness left? It's now or never, I'd say. It'll do no harm, and in the name of God it will do us no good tomorrow night."

No one contradicted Padraig, but Brigid knew they were all aware of the risks involved for a signal fire in these conditions.

From her place at Liam's bedside, Margaret pressed a hand to her mouth, and her half-stifled crying sent a spasm through Padraig's slumped shoulders. That settled the matter. Sean looked at Petey and Mícheál. Both men nodded and got to their feet, but when Padraig started to rise, Mícheál gently pressed him down into his chair.

"We'll see to it. Stay with your family."

Without another word, the men buttoned their heavy jackets and started out for the storehouses. With no trees to provide a supply of timber, the islanders continuously gathered up every stick of driftwood they could find, dragging it up from the beach, plucking it from the sea into their boats. A portion of everything found was placed in communal storage for emergencies such as this.

Brigid had offered to collect lamp oil from the houses in the village while the men were gathering the wood. She wrapped herself again in the damp shawl she'd hung to dry just moments before and took the iron pot from its place by the hearth. Before leaving, she sat for a moment with Margaret and Liam. The salve they had applied to his arm filled the cottage with an odor of camphor, but it seemed to be doing nothing to reverse the spreading infection. The boy's swollen arm was bright red from wrist to elbow, and the skin around the wound had an unnatural sheen.

Putting a hand on his forehead, Brigid closed her eyes and sat motionless, waiting, but her palm remained cool against his skin. There was no tingle of heat, no flash of insight. She didn't know whether to be grateful or distressed that the child's fate remained hidden to her. Feeling as helpless and uncertain as everyone else, she murmured a quick prayer, and after kissing Margaret's bowed head she slipped out of the cottage.

~

To communicate with anyone they couldn't immediately reach, the people of the Blaskets had used signal fires for generations beyond counting. Whether targeted at another island or the mainland, they served as calls of distress and sometimes of warning, and sometimes they carried more precise news. Lis still talked about the night many years earlier when relatives of the O'Cearna family sent a signal from Dunmore Head on the mainland. She remembered the anguish of watching it with Neilí Uí Cheárna's children. The fire bore the news of her death at the hospital in Dingle. On a happier note, her aunt also talked about the dramatic events that led to a signal fire announcing Brigid's arrival in the world.

Her mother's labor had been difficult. When it continued at length without progress, the women became frightened, and Sean had organized a crew to go for the doctor. Under a threat of rain, the men rowed out on a choppy sea, keeping an eye on the island as they pulled at the oars. Halfway across Blasket Sound they saw what they'd been hoping for—a blaze rising up from the White Strand, broadcasting a safe delivery. The crew immediately turned for home, arriving just ahead of a wind-driven storm that would have surely capsized the boat. Sean had once joked that her mother had nearly been the death of him, but Brigid had saved his life.

She watched her uncle now, moving gingerly as he and the other men added bricks of peat to a structure that was beginning to look like a church steeple.

"Mind yourself," he barked at Mícheál, who'd stumbled over a half-buried rock.

"How am I meant to be minding anything," Mícheál grumbled, "With the night black as pitch and the wind only cutting the chest straight out of me. And how is it none but Brigid had the sense to carry a lamp?"

He stopped, ostensibly to remove his cap and give his forehead a scratch. Brigid thought it was just an excuse to give his racing heart a chance to recover. A fall could have easily led to a tumble down the steep hillside and over the cliff.

None of them had needed to be told where to go. It was important for the fire to be seen, of course, but after catching the attention of someone on the mainland, it was equally important that it be understood. This was why they were all creeping about on the rounded knob of *An Gob*, the headland at the southern tip of the island.

It was a treacherous place to be on such a night. The wind alone was terrifying, with haphazard gusts testing their strength and balance. The acute angle of the slope added another element of risk. The grass was slick, and the wet ground was spongy in many places, rock hard in others. The men worked with exaggerated patience, each step planted with force before allowing their foot to accept the weight of it.

Their nerves had become strained. It was madness for them to be there at all but they had no choice, because it was the one spot on the island where a correct interpretation would be guaranteed. Everyone knew that a fire from *An Gob* meant dire emergency. It was a blunt, unequivocal cry for help.

Petey took Mícheál by the arm, guiding his brother back to the job at hand. "You'll have plenty of light soon enough, please God," he said.

They worked without further conversation, needing only gestures and a few curt nods to communicate. At each stage of the construction they waved for Brigid to bring the oil, which she sprinkled like holy water on the growing pile of fuel. She'd called at every house in the village to collect enough paraffin, but even with a pot full of it she feared they wouldn't get the fire lit. Everything was wet; even the air felt thick with moisture.

Along with the oil, their hope lay in the dryness of the fuel and the art of its arrangement, a patchwork of driftwood and peat enclosing a central core of sticks and dried heather. When it was built to their satisfaction, the men began a mild argument about starting the fire.

"Light the middle first, I'd say."

"We'll have it knocked over. There's no gap wide enough to get an arm through without bringing it down."

"But sure wasn't that the point of the heather, and all? The driest bits at the center."

"The heather should have gone 'round the outside."

"Well, it's in the middle now, isn't it?"

"What does it matter, when the whole lot is after soaking in paraffin?"

"It was the middle taking most of the paraffin."

"Oh, will you ever stop, the three of you," Brigid snapped. The men turned and peered through the darkness at her. She raised the flame on her lamp. "I've a small enough arm; and as I'm the only one with the means for lighting it, just you hand over that torch and maybe we'll have a fire before the sun comes up."

The men exchanged a sheepish glance, and Sean reluctantly gave her the long thin branch he'd propped against a rock. After setting her lamp on the ground, Brigid lowered the branch through the glass chimney's narrow opening. The oil-soaked rag tied to the end of it ignited immediately, sending up a sharp odor that tickled her nose and bathed them all in a flickering orange glow.

Taking a tighter grip on the slender, flaming branch, she looked out across Blasket Sound. She knew Dunmore Head was somewhere in the distance. At this spot on the headland they stood exactly opposite its massive, sheer-sided bluff. Its form was invisible, though, as was the rest of Ireland. She lifted the branch higher, expanding the perimeter of her shadowy circle of light, but only by a bit. Everything beyond it remained a blank realm of darkness. Hoping she could stir up something bright enough to pierce it, she walked to the steepled pile and threaded an arm through the widest gap she could find.

It caught slowly at first, the heather crackling as it smoldered and smoked, but the interior glow grew steadily stronger. The men looked on nervously while she searched for more gaps. She circled the structure, jabbing the makeshift torch into the kindling piled at its core. Just when it seemed she'd done all she could, Brigid felt the wind stir around her feet, and then heard an odd noise, like a long, toneless groan. It was the air, rushing between the cracks, being drawn in to the hot center of the fire. An instant later the draft was pulled skyward, and a towering explosion of flames leapt straight up through the pointed tip of the structure.

The transformation stunned Brigid into paralysis. She stood rooted in place as the billowing fire reached for her, and came to her senses only after feeling a strong arm tighten around her waist. Diving at her, Sean jerked her away from the flames, but the force of it knocked Brigid off balance. She landed against his chest and they fell together, hitting the ground hard. Breathless and disoriented, Brigid tried to get her bearings, but it was already too late. She clutched at the ground, feeling the slippery, wet grass slide between her fingers as she plunged down the hillside.

24
෨

Giving no reply, nor any sign that he'd even heard Tom, the barman placed a glass of whiskey on the counter. In reaching for it, a ragged old farmer stirred up a strong odor of himself – liniment, sheep dung, and unwashed drawers. He maneuvered the glass to his lips with both hands and gave a sidelong glance at Tom, who tried again with the barman – louder this time.

"Do you not hear what I'm telling you? There's a signal fire on –"

"Sure I'm not deaf, lad. I've heard it twice, now."

The codger found this remark hilarious. Laughter and phlegm rattled his throat in equal parts while the barman replaced the cork in the whiskey bottle and offered a tolerant smile. Tom recognized it as a special one reserved for drunks and eejits. He'd used it himself on a few occasions at the Swallowtail. At the same time, he also recognized he was talking to the *fear an tí*, the "man of the house" – Muiris Kavanaugh, himself.

Known far and wide by the nickname gracing the side

of his guest house, Kruger Kavanaugh was the Dingle Peninsula's homegrown celebrity. He'd been born in Dunquin, emigrated to America, and had returned years later wreathed in stories of adventure. He'd been a publicity man on Broadway, a bodyguard to Eamon De Valera, and there were hints of a connection with the late-but-still-notorious Al Capone. Tom decided a shift to a more deferential tone might be in his best interest.

"Mr. Kavanaugh, I wouldn't come here telling lies to you. You can't see it from here, but if you'd only walk up the road a bit–"

"I can see the whole island from the field out the back."

With effort, Tom kept a tenuous grip on his self-restraint. He began urging a quick trip to the field to verify his story, but then a man his own age–fat, ruddy-cheeked and clearly a regular–stumbled in through the back door, still struggling to button his fly.

"Jaysus, lads! There's fire on the Blasket! Bloody inferno, so it is."

"Is that right, Andy? Well, I suppose we'll go have a look, then, will we?" Kruger shrugged at Tom, eyes twinkling. "Fair play, lad, and what's your name, now?"

"Tom McBride."

"From Ventry? Son of Seamus?"

"I am…was," Tom stuttered, his agitation briefly interrupted. The routine was still too new, too much for him to know how to handle.

"Grand fellow altogether. I'm sorry for your trouble, and I meant no offense." Kruger extended a large, muscular hand. "Only I never trust the first thing a man tells me if I've never laid eyes on him before."

Tom smiled, accepting the handshake. "I can't argue against that."

Kruger glanced around the room, which Andy's announcement had emptied in less than thirty seconds. "Blighters. You can be sure half will run off without settling. Right so." He tossed his towel on the bar. "Let's go see this big fire, anyway."

They walked out the back door, and discovered the news had spread quickly. There were far more people gathered in Kruger's field than had been in Kruger's pub. Arms swinging, the burly man stumped through the wet grass and Tom followed, barely remaining upright on the lumpy terrain while his head swiveled towards the island. When it came into view, the fire still looked immense, even at this distance. The wind out of the north played with the flames, allowing them to sink and bulge before again yanking them skyward into high, twisting tendrils.

They reached the middle of the field and stared along with the others gathered there, until a man at Tom's elbow broke the spell of silence.

"Seems unnatural," he said, raising his voice to be heard above the wind. "Like that holy burning bush out of the bible."

Tom turned to see it was the fellow who'd laughed at him earlier and sourly thought he looked old enough to have shared a drink with Moses. Calculating how much time had already passed, he scowled at the man's nervous amazement.

"It's a signal fire, and I'm after saying it for the third time, now." The howling gale offered a good excuse for shouting. "They meant for us to see it and send help. What more do you need? Can we not, for the love of God, ring for the lifeboat? There's at least an hour gone, now. "

"The size of it, though." Another raised voice, behind him this time. "Could it be a plane crash, even?"

Tom wanted to take them all by the throat and shake sense into them, but Kruger put a hand on his shoulder—a friendly, iron-hard grip.

"A Messerschmitt is it? Some German doesn't know they lost the war, maybe?" He grunted a laugh, and began steering Tom back across the field. "Well, just you keep an eye on it, Johnno, but I'd say yer man from Ventry got it right the first time. I've not seen it for many a year, but when the islanders set a fire at *An Gob* it means they need help, and they need it fast."

Upon re-entry, the empty pub seemed to give off an even stronger scent of stale beer and tobacco, but Tom was grateful to be back inside. After the buffeting roar of weather against his ears, the quiet interior felt like a monastery. Kruger slipped behind the bar and then out of sight as he began shifting things around beneath it. Tossing his jacket onto the bar, Tom swore under his breath.

"Have you a telephone here in the lounge?" he called out, pacing restlessly. "We're wasting time."

"You have all the exchanges off by heart, do you?" The innkeeper reappeared, holding up a telephone directory.

"Oh. I don't, no. Sorry."

"For a man who only happened to notice a fire during his evening drive, you seem fairly keen about all this, Tom." Kruger looked as if his own remark reminded him of something. He frowned, concentrating, then a glint of understanding surfaced and he appeared to be suppressing a smile. "It's a common name—'Tom.' We've more about the place than I can count, but I'll wager you're the one who fell in love with Brigid O'Sullivan."

Startled, Tom stared at him. "How—" He swallowed the question, smiling faintly as the answer became obvious. "The post office. Eva."

Kruger nodded. "Mad for the chat, she is, but I had it off the islanders as well. They turn up here whenever they're in Dunquin, to pick up supplies and get the gossip. They don't often have much of their own to share, so that was a juicy bit of news. Gobsmacked about it, so they were. They say she's an odd little thing, a bit mad, maybe."

"She's not mad," Tom snapped. "She only sees things most people can't—now please, will you ever get the Coast Guard on the line."

"Right, I'm going immediately." Kruger thumped a bottle of Powers on the counter, inviting him to take a small glass—emphasizing the "small"—and then went through the connecting door to the main house.

Tom leaned against the bar but ignored the whiskey, pre-occupied with his thoughts. The islanders intended the fire to be a distress call, that was clear enough, but beyond that, what did it mean? With one foot flexing against the bar rail, his knee bounced spastically as he considered the possibilities.

Someone was dangerously ill—Brigid? Someone had been seriously injured—was it her? The odds were greater that it was one of the more elderly islanders, and he felt only a passing flutter of shame for hoping this was the case. Still, her name re-surfaced in every scenario he thought of, along with the memory of her voice, her laugh, the way her skin felt beneath his fingertips.

The pub's customers trickled back from the field, along with a good few who hadn't been there earlier. They congregated at the end of the bar to share theories and stories, and he ignored them as well. By the time Kruger returned, another hour had passed and Tom's elbows were planted on the bar, fists pressed against his head. Lifting it to meet the innkeeper's eyes, he went rigid.

"Are they coming?" he asked, needlessly. From Kruger's solemn face he knew they weren't.

"Took forever to get through, only to find out the lifeboat got called out two hours ago. A distress call came from somewhere south of Dursey Island. Fellow at the station said they likely couldn't make a start this way until tomorrow afternoon."

"Tomorrow afternoon is too late! We bloody well need to be doing something now!"

The outburst had the same effect as a gunshot. All conversation stopped, and in the pause that followed Tom felt the attention of every man in the room turning to him. A furtive glance at the mirrored wall behind the bar confirmed their heightened interest.

One of the men cleared his throat. "Have you relations on the Blasket, then?"

Deflated, Tom hung his head. "Not relations, but … friends. I've been to visit a few times. I brought Mr. Dan O'Brien from the Land Commission over to meet with the islanders. He needed a boat to take him from Dingle and I … "

He trailed off, remembering the sunlit brilliance of that day. As the trawler closed the distance he'd watched the island grow bigger, entirely innocent of what it would soon mean to him, and of everything that would follow when summer ended.

Outside, the rain suddenly began again. The noise of it hitting the puddles covering the yard made it sound as if a brook was running through it. He felt a hot pressure growing behind his eyes, and kept them fixed on the aged wood of the bar. It was dark—the color of Guinness itself—and coated with the sticky membrane of countless spills and splashes. He picked at a splintered crack for distraction, but it wasn't any use. Without a sound, and for the first time since the day his father died, Tom found himself weeping.

"All right, lads. Have the whiskey and take a table." Kruger pushed the bottle down to the men who'd grown quiet at the end of the bar. "Give us a bit of space."

They obediently trooped off to a table in the corner of the lounge. As they settled in and shared out the bottle, their subdued mood shifted back to bantering conversation.

Arms spread, Kruger braced himself against the bar and waited. Tom scrubbed at his face and took a deep breath, and then exhaled it with a startled puff as his gaze fell on Kruger's hands. Most of the ring finger was missing from one of them. Guessing his thoughts, the innkeeper raised his hand and wiggled the stump in a good-humored salute.

"Lost it during the war." Kruger grinned. "Mind you, I didn't say 'in' the war. I was in Holland at the time. Long story." He lowered his hand, and when he spoke again his gruff voice was gentle. "It won't be her, Tom. There's more than a few on that island well and truly ready to meet their maker. Mark me if He isn't calling one of them home, tonight."

"Would they think that an emergency, though? Would they call for help on a night like this, for an old man sleeping away his last hours on earth?"

Kruger had no answer for this, and Tom had no time left to wait for one. He pulled his jacket from the bar. "Right. I'm going myself."

The innkeeper's gasp ended as a snort. "You're a selkie, then? You'll get into your seal skin and swim to the Blasket?"

"I'll get into a trawler and drive to it. My uncle has a boat in Dingle harbor and I know how to manage it. There's a GP there I know how to manage as well, because he was nearly my personal physician. I was in his office at least once a week growing up and he made a fortune off me, so I'd say he owes me a favor."

"Personal physician." Kruger gazed at the connecting door to the main house. "Hang on. Give me a minute."

"I don't have one to give," Tom said, but he did hang on, thinking if a man like Kruger Kavanaugh had an idea it was worth waiting to hear. It didn't take long before the man gave a curt, decisive nod.

"Ever hear of Ethel Merman?"

Tom shrugged, exasperated. "An actress, isn't she? Musicals?"

"That's her. Hell of a woman. Great fun, and," Kruger showed a palm, forestalling Tom's irritation. "Her personal physician is this minute fast asleep in a room right next to my own. From New York. Came for the fishing but he's been sat in this bar most of the week, drinking martinis and watching it rain. Hardly set foot on the boat he's got waiting for him, anchored right off the pier here in Dunquin."

Tom's eyes narrowed skeptically. "What kind of boat is it?"

"A trawler, if you can believe it, rented from Pat Doyle over in Ballyferriter, who was supposed to be dragging him around in it." Kruger laughed. "Pat's been here every day as well to commiserate and match him drink for drink. Says it's the first time he's ever been paid for a piss-up."

They looked at each other, and the idea unfurled like a scroll between the two of them.

"Will he do it, do you think?" Tom asked.

"He won't want to, but I'll talk him 'round."

"Right. Give it a lash, and I'll wait here." Tom's attention wandered to the clock behind the bar. "Oh jayz, is that the time? I need the telephone myself. My mother will be up the wall by now."

25

The crank-operated telephone was on a wall in the entrance hall of the guest house. Before climbing the stairs to rouse the doctor, Kruger gave vague instructions for its operation, then took the lamp and disappeared, leaving Tom in the dark to fumble with the contraption. He got it to work eventually, got a call through to the Swallowtail, and when Jarlath Fenton bellowed a greeting in his ear, it seemed like a small miracle.

He needed a slightly bigger one when the receiver was passed to Jamesie, who was dumbfounded at hearing Tom's voice on the line. While that amazement lasted it was impossible to tell him anything, but once he began paying attention Jamesie rolled through a number of reactions in quick succession. First, he laughed, thinking it was a joke, then he became anxious for Tom's sanity after realizing it wasn't, and at last his mood shifted to horrified resistance once he understood what Tom wanted. It was the first time his friend had ever balked at anything he'd asked him to do, but Tom had to admit it was an outrageous request, one he shouldn't be making at all.

"What am I meant to be telling her?" Jamesie demanded, sounding aggrieved and panicked.

"The truth," Tom said.

"The truth!"

Tom clamped the receiver against his ear. It was hard to believe the noise wasn't carrying to every corner of the guest house.

"Including what, if you don't mind? What does she even know about Brigid?"

Tom held his breath for a beat or two, and then released it. "Nothing. I've never said anything."

Jamesie's voice rose an octave. "Have you gone mad entirely, Tommy? You're asking me to tell a woman who just lost a husband that she'll likely lose a son as well, because the eejit's after sailing into a storm, only to see if the girl he's in love with – a girl she knows *sod-all* about – needs his help."

"I know you shouldn't be the one telling her, but I haven't any choice. It's better to be honest the first time than to be changing the story later."

"I'll get no chance for another story. Your ma will gut me like a fish, or else she'll fall over dead the minute the words are out of me mouth."

"Eileen is made of fairly strong stuff. She won't collapse," Tom said, but offered no comment about how his mother might treat the messenger of such news.

Hearing voices upstairs, he knew there wasn't much time left. As he began pleading his case with greater intensity, the despair Tom had been struggling for weeks to resist surfaced like something explosive, unstoppable. His own personal signal fire.

"Listen to me, Jamesie. I'll not deny I'm out of my mind, but in fairness I've been losing it for a long while now. I haven't a clue at all what to do with myself. I could stay, I could emigrate. I could build houses in a city or milk cows the rest of my life. I could go this way or that but it doesn't make a blind bit of difference what I do, because it's an empty life I'll keep plodding through until it's finally done. The only thing that makes it worth thinking about is her. Knowing she's there, that she exists, even if she's not with me. It might be the only comfort I'll ever get, and I've had a good two hours now to wonder if something's happened to her. I won't sit here wondering any longer."

Impatiently, Tom jammed the heel of his hand against one eye, determined not to give way to emotion twice in one evening. At the other end of the line he heard the usual pub noises—raised voices, coughs, a concertina playing. It provided some reassurance the line was still engaged until Jamesie spoke again, gently this time.

"I'll walk up to the house, so. I'll stay with your ma, will I? And see to the cows, until you're back safe. I'll have no choice, anyway. You'll arrive and find me turning on a spit over the fire."

Tom gave a shaky laugh. "Thanks, Jamesie. It's an awful thing to ask, and I'm sorry. I'm sorry for doing this to Ma, as well. It isn't fair to her; she should have heard it from me. I suppose she'll think I'm a coward."

"Rubbish. That's the last thing anybody thinks about you, Tommy. Take it handy out there, and please God we'll see you soon. "

The bell on the phone box emitted a soft jingle as the line disengaged and Tom clapped a hand over it. He stood motionless, collecting himself, until his restlessness forced him to start moving again. He considered returning to the pub for the glass of whiskey offered earlier, then rejected the idea, having no appetite for the conversation that would come with it. He stalled, but then began to feel uncomfortable walking up and down the dark hallway of someone else's home. All he needed was for Kruger's wife to appear in hair rollers and get the fright of her life. He'd just decided to go outside and pace in the rain when a door opened somewhere above him and then softly closed, followed by quiet footsteps.

Kruger descended, the lamp held out in front of him, illuminating the stairs along with his large, square frame. Reaching the ground floor he put a finger to his lips and motioned Tom ahead of him, giving him no opportunity for a proper look at the man following behind.

A half-hour had passed and the pub was deserted and dark. The last man out had doused the lamps, leaving a pungent, oily odor hanging in the air. A pile of coins had been left on the bar beside the empty bottle of Powers. Kruger huffed a surprised satisfaction. He set down the lamp he'd been carrying, and at the same time the man behind him stepped into view, like a shadow peeling away from its host.

He was quite a bit younger than Tom had expected – a slender man, probably ten years older than him and a half-foot shorter. He had thick, dark hair that looked glossy in the lamplight, and his face had an olive-toned smoothness. He didn't look at all like a man who'd just been shaken from a sound sleep. His eyes were alert, full of sharp, slightly nervous curiosity. Kruger nodded at them each in turn.

"Dr. Isaac Frum, physician on the Upper West Side,

Manhattan. Mr. Thomas McBride, farmer on the upper southern coast, Ventry.

"Mr. McBride." Dr. Frum shifted the bag he was carrying and shook hands with him. "I thought you'd be older."

"Ah. Right." Tom shrugged, declining to mention he'd been thinking the same thing.

"Kruger says you know your way around a boat," the doctor continued. He spoke quickly, with a dry wit and nasal accent that reminded Tom of American comedians he'd heard on the radio. "He also says weather be damned, and that I shouldn't be worried in the least. I hope that's true, because I can't swim."

Tom grinned. "Then I suppose we'd best stay in the trawler."

∿

During the drive to Dunquin pier, they shifted from Irish to English to accommodate Dr. Frum, but Tom spoke very little, and said nothing to the doctor at all. He felt a bit guilty for obscuring the danger involved in their mad adventure, but it didn't stop him from conspiring with Kruger to keep the man from thinking too much about it. Tom played his part by keeping his mouth shut, Kruger by running his from the minute they left the house. He rabbited on nineteen to the dozen about mutual acquaintances in New York and where to get the best *knish*, which – only from the context of the conversation – Tom understood to be something to eat.

The chatter went on as they continued on foot, down a steep, concrete ramp that descended in a switchback pattern along the side of the cliff. Its final turn bisected the wide pier, creating a protective, circling arm around an area where several naomhógs were stored.

Tom helped Kruger carry one of the boats to the opposite side of the pier and lower it into the water. Even in the sheltered cove the waves were lively, slapping at the boat's light, canvas frame, trying to yank it away from the landing, but Tom held it steady while Kruger offered the doctor a helping hand. At this point, the scales finally fell from the eyes of Isaac Frum. As he looked at the naomhóg, alarmed outrage replaced his mood of cooperative tolerance.

"No, no, absolutely not. This was not the deal. I'm a city boy from the Bronx, but I can damn well tell a trawler from a rowboat."

"Not at all, Isaac. This is only a … taxi-service, like." Kruger jabbed a thumb over his shoulder. "The trawler is there, a few hundred yards away."

Still suspicious, Dr. Frum walked to the end of the landing to see for himself. While he stood peering through the darkness, Kruger dropped the charade of hearty confidence, his own alarm obvious in the question he spat from the side of his mouth.

"Bloody hell, Tom. Are you sure about this?"

"I am." Tom's reply was immediate, but his level of anxiety was by no means low. With the boat bouncing under them like a Connemara pony, he realized the ocean was wilder than he'd expected. It didn't matter. With or without Isaac Frum, he was taking the naomhóg to the trawler, and that trawler was going in to the Blasket.

Dr. Frum returned, medical bag held stiffly at his side, and Kruger smoothly took up his role again. "You saw it, then?

Great huge thing. Come along, now. It'll be fine. Yer man here knows what he's doing. He's a first-rate captain."

Tom could see the man wasn't fooled by any of the soft talk, and was giving no indication that he intended to get in the boat. Ignoring Kruger's outstretched hand, the doctor turned his intelligent, piercing gaze on "the captain."

"How do you know this can't wait until morning?"

"I don't," Tom said, "but sure isn't that the point? If we don't know what the trouble is, isn't it safer to figure it can't wait?"

"Safe for who? We're the ones risking our lives here. Based on pure speculation."

"Fair point," Tom conceded. While appreciative of the effort, he couldn't bring himself to mimic Kruger's bland reassurances, and berated himself for listening to him in the first place.

He would have done better to head for Dingle. His own doctor would have been easier to convince, would have understood it all sooner than this. He shouldn't have expected a rich American doctor who caters to the stars of Broadway to understand the particular desperation of a poor, forgotten population. It was too late to correct the mistake, now. Growing resigned to the idea of doing his best alone, Tom continued to hold the man's gaze.

"Have you learned any Irish on your holiday, Dr. Frum?" he asked. "*Bóthrín na Marbh*. It means 'road of the dead.' That's what the islanders call the path leading down to their wee, half-built boat slip. They carry the coffin through the village, and down that road, then everyone left on the Blasket stands there on the shore, watching while a crew rows it across the

Sound. They come to this pier, and carry the coffin up to the cemetery on the hill. I'll not try to convince you this trip isn't dangerous, but I will ask you to imagine standing here in a few days' time with your rod and reel, waiting for the islanders to clear a coffin off the landing, so Pat Doyle can row you out to get on with your fishing."

Having nothing further to say, Tom looked away, turning his face to the Blasket, reflecting on all he'd learned about the place in the last six months. For the first time, he truly understood what it meant to her. What it meant to all of them.

The fire at *An Gob* was beginning to lose some of its height and strength, reminding him again of how much time had passed. He coughed to shift the tension clenched in his throat, and then grabbed at the concrete edge of the pier, catching his balance as Dr. Frum stepped into the boat and sat down without a word.

26

It seemed like she'd been falling for hours. Her body felt impossibly light, as if touching nothing at all, and Brigid had no way of distinguishing the ground from the sky. It was all one, a darkness containing nothing she could recognize as she fell. Panic swept over her, but then retreated, replaced by a calm acceptance, an odd, resigned peace – then, she slammed against the boulder.

If she'd been sliding head-first it would have killed her just as quickly as a fall from the cliff, but from the impact Brigid realized she'd been tumbling sideways. She hit the rock as if turning to embrace it – her left shoulder connecting first, followed by a hip, and then a thigh as she rolled forward and over it. It didn't stop her, but it slowed her momentum enough for Sean to catch up to her.

With no thought for his own life he'd been half-running, half-sliding down the hill himself, and as Brigid landed on the other side of the boulder he threw himself on top of her. For a few more seconds they continued falling, arms and legs entangled, until Sean finally managed to sink his hobnailed boots into the ground and bring them to a stop.

They lay side by side, and after a few sobbing gasps of air Sean rolled up to a sitting position and anxiously hovered over her.

"Are you hurt, Brigid?"

In a state of dazed shock, she sat up and shivered at the sight in front of them. They'd landed less than twenty yards from the edge of the cliff.

"I don't think so. What about you?" she asked, and was relieved to hear her uncle's rumbling chuckle.

"Fairly pulverized, but no bones broken."

Petey and Mícheál had started down the hill at a more cautious pace. Sean gave them a wave of reassurance, calling for them to stay where they were, and then collapsed onto his back to stare at the sky. They remained silent for several minutes, listening to the roar of the fire above them. Sean swiveled his head to look at her.

"I'm too old for this nonsense, child."

Brigid nodded, understanding that he wasn't only referring to their hillside gymnastics.

"It's odd, I suppose," he continued. "A man my age, wanting to leave home. It gives me the fear, right enough. I've not known any other life, and there's no coming back, once it's been let go." He sat up again, and even in the darkness she could see his pale eyes glistening. "I know you're disappointed with us, Brigid, but it's been a hard life as well, and getting harder still. Until the end of my days I'll be missing this island, but I'm hoping you can understand. I'm hoping you'll forgive us."

"Sean." Brigid laid a hand on his shoulder. "You've not

disappointed me, and there's nothing you've ever done in your life that needs forgiving; I know it for a fact, and I know you're right. I've been stubborn and foolish, and living inside my own head for too long. It's time I learned to live in the world. I mean to try my best. If Dan O'Brien finds no cottage small enough for me, I hope you and Lis might tuck me into a little corner of yours?"

Sean smiled, his face brightening. "We'd be only delighted to have you, love."

Taking his extended hand Brigid stiffly rose from the ground, and felt her body already beginning to ache as they ascended the hill. When they rejoined Petey and Mícheál, each of them indicated their relief with faint smiles, but no one spoke a word about what had happened. In a community where a similar catastrophe could happen to anyone, the narrowly avoided death was a subject no one cared to discuss. Brigid was grateful for the unspoken rule of etiquette. Silence suited her just now. She wanted to sink down next to the fire, hoping its purifying heat might restore her, and she wanted to be alone with her thoughts.

"Go on to your beds now," she said, forcing some energy into her voice. "I'll stay minding the fire for a while."

Concerned for her, the men put up some resistance, but she could see they were exhausted – from their physical efforts and also from the emotions of the evening. At last, they allowed her to shoo them away. They followed the worn path up the slope where it connected with another leading back to the village. Brigid watched them go, and when their figures blended into the shadows she settled on the ground and stared at the fire.

Her entire body was throbbing now, but she felt grateful for the bruises. Every muscle and bone had played a role in her salvation, but Brigid also couldn't stop thinking about what she'd felt in the seconds just before hitting the rock—a sense of release, of peaceful acceptance. What did it mean? Was it simply self-protection, her mind shutting down, becoming numb to its own terror? It couldn't mean she'd wanted to die. Surely not. Could it?

Once it had surfaced, Brigid found the question itself frightening. The idea that she might have welcomed death in that small slice of time—however brief—appalled her. It also made her feel fragile, threatened, even—as if she'd uncovered the symptoms of a disease that could make an end of her.

Shivering, she moved to sit against a boulder that was closer to the fire. The sight of it, burning high and strong, cheered her a bit. They'd done a fine job with it. Anyone on the mainland within a mile of the coast couldn't fail to see and recognize the flames. Someone would ring the Coast Guard at Valentia to send the lifeboat. Brigid wouldn't give up hope, for Liam or herself. She simply refused to. She burrowed into her shawl, and after pulling her skirt over her knees and wrapping her arms around them, she rested her back against the rock and fell asleep.

When she woke, her thick shawl was soaking wet from a soft, misting rain that had begun while she slept, and the quality of the darkness had changed, which suggested the night was more than half-spent. The state of the fire also confirmed these observations. The flames were low, and she wondered if there'd been time for anyone to see the signal before the rain extinguished its strength. With the long iron

Sean left behind, Brigid rolled and pushed the unburnt wood to the center, then picked up her lamp and started for home.

She took a path back to the village that ran closer to the shoreline. At the intersection with a smaller trail that led up to her cottage she paused and then walked past it, drawn by a whisper of intuition back to the place she'd started from hours earlier. She stood on the section of cliff above the harbor, trying to guess what had pulled her there. Maybe it was to close the circle she'd opened. The night had been a mixture of sorrow, confusion and fear, and had left her drained of something vital. Maybe a return to the spot where it began could make her spirit whole again.

She waited, but again felt nothing. There was no tingling prescience, or rush of energy. No completion. With a fresh sense of loss, she turned back to the path but then froze, and felt a shiver traveling down her spine. Shrouded in mist, no more than fifteen feet away, a figure stood near the edge of the cliff. It was a man, tall and slender, and from the rain jacket and trousers he wore – stylish, a bit like the clothes she'd seen in the Sears catalogue – Brigid knew he wasn't from the island.

He was facing the sea with his back to her, and either he hadn't noticed her or was pretending not to. Gradually, her startled fear dissolved as she studied him. Had the lifeboat arrived while she'd been sleeping? For just an instant, Brigid thought he looked like Tom, but then saw this man wasn't anything like him. He was more muscular, a bit taller, and his hair was nearly as dark as her own. Still, there was something about the way he stood – straight but relaxed, easy with himself – that made her think of Tom.

While she was still watching him, the man turned away

from the cliff. He began slowly walking towards her, still not looking at her but clearly searching for something. After a few more steps, he stopped, and when his gaze swept over her with no change in expression, she hitched in a long, shaking breath and held it.

He wasn't looking at her because he couldn't see her.

There was little more than the length of her arm separating them now, but he was turned a little away from her. Standing motionless, with his head angled to one side, he appeared to be waiting—patiently, thoughtfully. When he swiveled slowly to face her, Brigid suddenly understood what she was seeing. Her body began to tremble, and then she heard herself quietly crying. It was so far beyond anything she would have thought possible that she wondered if it could be true. She desperately wanted it to be, and felt she would never know for sure if he didn't see her. She needed to be seen, needed him to find her.

And then all at once, he did.

It was only the space of a few heartbeats, but his dark, pensive eyes—a mirror image of her own—locked on Brigid, and she saw them widen in awestruck wonder. He looked at her, saw her, and knew her.

The outline of his figure was already fading into a spray of ocean mist rising over the cliff, but there was no mistaking his tender smile—it was so much like his father's. In the final seconds, after Brigid could no longer see him, she heard his voice—a low, melodious whisper in her ear.

"You told me that you knew me before I was born. I always wondered what that meant."

Falling to her knees, Brigid rocked forward, head bowed. She wasn't sure how long she remained there, with the vision cradled in her heart like the gift it was, but at last she rose from the ground, transformed.

Still shaking in every limb, she sensed something else was about to happen. It wasn't him again – she somehow knew that experience would never be repeated – but turning to face the sea Brigid saw what had tugged at her awareness. A small, irregular flash of light, barely visible in the pre-dawn darkness, but drawing closer.

A boat.

27
∽

*L*ighter, younger and more agile, Dr. Frum was much easier to get into a trawler than Dan O'Brien. Tom installed him in the wheelhouse while he scrambled around in the rain. He was frantic to get underway, but forced himself to slow down when the bucking vessel nearly pitched him overboard for the second time. This was not his uncle Patsy's trawler, and to go haring about without making sure he understood the difference could turn a dangerous trip into a suicidal one.

Beyond that, Pat Doyle was a slob—too many mangled fishing nets, too much cocked up rigging, too many loose parts rattling around the deck that could fly through the wheelhouse windows and decapitate them. The one useful item he discovered amongst the rubbish was a pressure lamp. It was the floodlight variety, a type used to light temporary airfields during the war, and it had a full supply of paraffin in its fuel tank.

He and Dr. Frum worked on it together, and when they finally got the thing to flame into life it nearly blinded them both. Tom locked down the glass-fronted lid, and with a length of rope secured the lamp to the main mast, where it sent out an impressive light. He next worked at getting the engine started. All of it took longer than he wanted, but at least the rain had stopped by the time the trawler was ready for departure.

Tom wished he could say as much for the wind. He lowered his head into a blast of it as he weighed anchor, and then made his way aft to the naomhóg, still riding alongside, pitching up and down like a rollercoaster. He untied the hitch line from the rail and tossed it down, giving a wave. Kruger caught the rope and lowered the oars, calling up for him to go, but Tom refused to move. He imagined the evening was only a small blip on the spiking timeline of Kruger Kavanaugh's adventurous life but he still waited until the innkeeper was safely back at the pier before stepping into the wheelhouse and throttling forward.

As they moved into the deeper water of the Sound he estimated the wave surge to be five feet at minimum. That was higher than anything he'd ever experienced, but Tom assumed the same strategies he and Patsy had used for smaller squalls would serve for a larger one. The difference was a matter of degree – or so he hoped.

Knowing he lacked his uncle's many years of experience, Tom navigated with fixed concentration and a sense of humility. He settled for slower progress, tacking into the wind as if the trawler had sails aloft, doing his best to keep the prow at a forty-five degree angle to the waves, and throttling down to a crawl whenever it surged over a cresting swell.

It made for a zig-zagging route and a bumpy ride. Tom had the ship's wheel to cling to, but although he called a warning ahead of each lurch, Dr. Frum came off the bench he was seated on more than once. Fortunately, there wasn't much space for him to tumble around and hurt himself. Unfortunately, the third time he flew off the bench he ended up crashing into Tom, who had to fight to stay upright as the doctor dropped to the deck.

"Jesus and Mary. Between us and all harm." He reached down with one hand, fumbling to help the man up while keeping his eyes glued straight ahead. "Are you all right there, Dr. Frum?"

Muttering obscenities, the doctor climbed to his feet and wedged himself back into the corner. "Still in one piece – so far, anyway."

Tom felt a growing admiration for the man. Whatever fear he might be experiencing, the doctor was doing a good job of hiding it behind a facade of dry humor.

"Thank you for doing this," Tom said quietly. "I'm sorry for not saying it earlier."

"How could I refuse? You made a compelling case, Mr. McBride."

"I'd prefer it if you call me Tom, if that's all right. Whenever you say 'Mr. McBride' I nearly look around for my father."

"Sure, but consider yourself lucky. My father was a doctor, too; we shared a practice. He got to be Dr. Frum, and I had to be "Young Dr. Frum." He died a few years ago, but the older patients still call me that. Makes me feel like a twelve-year-old."

Tom took his eyes from the ocean long enough to glance at him. "You have other patients? Does Ethel Merman not keep you busy?"

Dr. Frum sniffed and flapped a hand as though swatting

a fly. "Ethel Merman keeps everyone busy, but I did not take up medicine to stare down the throats of Broadway singers. I see her and a few other hypochondriacs once a month in the Manhattan office. I get paid a ridiculous sum of money, and then I go back to the Bronx and see patients with actual problems."

Tom nodded. "Fair enough."

"What about you? You're a sailor who farms, a farmer who sails?"

"Both, I suppose, or neither. I'm not really sure, anymore."

Frowning, Tom pulled his attention back to the task at hand. Some of the darkness had begun leaking out of the night sky. Ahead of them, the outline of the Blasket had grown sharper, even as the signal fire continued sinking into embers, but wherever the waves were not stirring it into whitecaps the water was black as ink, and deceptively fluid. He knew there were hard, immoveable objects lurking ahead, and the searchlight he'd tied to the mast wasn't doing enough to distinguish them.

"I'll tell you this, anyway," he said. "You're about to become a doctor who sails. I'm going to need you to take the helm before long."

Dr. Frum stared at him. "I'm taking the helm. And you're going where? Over the side?"

"The lamp needs more fuel pumped, it's gone too dim."

"I see. I see." The doctor nodded, his face expressionless. "You're quite a joker, Tom. A real Henny Youngman. Know who he is?"

"I do, yeah, but I'm not trying to be funny."

"You're hilarious without trying. How about I go pump

up the lamp?" Dr. Frum moved forward on the bench and Tom caught him before he could topple onto the deck again.

"I think it would be safer for me to go."

"You realize I'm Jewish, right? Know how many Jews belong to the New York Yacht Club? Exactly zero. I don't even know how to fish. Kruger insisted I'd love it, but I was never so glad to see it rain in my life. I was happy paying Pat Doyle's bar tab, hoping I'd get through the week without ever putting a foot on this damned boat. We are not a water-loving people, Tom. God had to part the Red Sea before we'd go near it."

Tom smiled. "You're quite a comedian yourself."

"Sure, sure. Laugh it up. You don't know the mistake you're making. The last decent sailor we had was Noah."

"You'll be in good company, then." Tom beckoned with a jerk of his head. "Come here now, Dr. Frum, 'til I tell you how to steer this thing."

"*Oy.*" Arms spread wide for balance, he stepped gingerly over to the wheel. "Isaac. Just call me Isaac. The longer I'm on this boat, the less I feel like a doctor."

～

"That's nothing like the Valentia lifeboat, I'll tell you that for a fact."

"Nothing like. Far too small. A trawler, maybe."

"I've never before seen a trawler with a spotlight on."

"Some different class of boat altogether, maybe."

"Sure it could be. Who can tell, at such a distance?"

"I'll wager it's a trawler."

Brigid gritted her teeth, willing herself not to roar for them to shut their foolish mouths. In her excitement, she'd hurried back to her cottage with the news of the approaching boat, and word had traveled from house to house until everyone in the village was awake and gathered on the bluff above the harbor, all of them spouting nonsense.

The light shining from the main mast of the vessel—whatever type it was—was driving most of the debate. While a lifeboat would certainly have one, it was true that a spotlight on a trawler was unusual. As a further oddity, it seemed in danger of falling from the mast. While the boat labored over the waves the lantern swung from right to left in crazy, haphazard arcs.

Brigid found she couldn't take her eyes off the darting shaft of light. Its effect on her was powerful, as though a knob was rotating inside her, drawing her muscles to the tightness of a bow string. When the boat veered and sailed due south for several hundred yards, the light disappeared entirely until the course had been corrected. By the time it shone out again, Brigid's hands ached from being so fiercely clenched.

"It's not attached to the mast. I think someone is holding it." As soon as the words left her mouth, she saw the dark outline of a figure braced against the mast behind the lamp, and the reason for the spotlight's uneven motion became obvious. "He's using the light to give directions. It must be someone who knows the harbor. He understood it would be dangerous. With the sea this wild, it would be hard to tell whether he's looking at a rock or—"

She stopped, her breath catching before she repeated the words to herself. "Whether he's looking at a rock or something else."

An intuition shifted to an idea, and the idea unfolded as truth.

"It's Tom."

Lis looked at her as if she'd lost her mind, but then her face softened. "I don't think it can be, love. Tom lives in Ventry, remember. He wouldn't have seen the fire from there. How could he know?"

"It's him," Brigid said. "I know it is." She grabbed her own lamp from the ground and ran.

The descent to the harbor was like moving through a tunnel. The upended naomhógs, arranged in a line along each side of the lane made the journey down through the rocky gap darker and more narrow. Temporarily sheltered from the wind, she could hear the rainwater running off, dripping in a stream through the tufted grass clinging to the side of the cliff. Brigid could no more slow her steps than she could make the earth stop turning, but the path felt slick as ice beneath her shoes. After a few near tumbles, she kicked them off entirely and hurried on, trusting the grip of her bare toes to keep her upright.

Sean and Petey were already at the landing slip, preparing to launch a naomhóg to meet the boat and carry its passengers to shore. Hearing their conversation as she got closer, Brigid understood they'd decided it was definitely a trawler, and from its hair-raising progress towards the harbor they were wondering what manner of sailor was steering it, and also who would be rescuing whom. Brigid gave them a fright as she came bursting out of the darkness behind them.

"It's Tom."

They spun to stare at her, and in their faces she read the

same concern Lis had shown—as if they expected her to break into a gibbering fit. She didn't care.

"Will you ever stop gawping at me," Brigid exclaimed. "Look out of your two eyes at that trawler. Can you not see the man standing there, plain as day?"

They all looked together. The smallest hours of the night had passed, and although the scene out on the ocean was still colorless, the trawler was sharply outlined in the hint of pre-dawn light. As it drew closer, the figure standing on its rolling deck became more visible.

Sean's eyes widened. "That's Tom McBride right enough. How is it he's not been thrown overboard, standing out at the mast like that?"

"He's fastened to it." Petey said. "I can see the rope tied around. In the name of God, he's as mad as you Brigid. Where did he come from, I wonder?"

"What's it matter?" Brigid said. "Will you not put that naomhóg into the water now, and ... "

She trailed off as the shifting lantern swept up from the sea and stopped when it found her, fixing her for several seconds inside a pale, blue-white gleam. She stood facing Tom, feeling the light as a tangible presence, like the brush of his lips against her hair. Brigid lifted a hand—in greeting, in welcome—her palm cupping the air as though already feeling the warmth of his face.

28

Tom had pumped every remaining ounce of paraffin into the pressure lamp. He could only pray the fuel—and his luck—would last until they reached the spot he was aiming for, a few hundred feet off shore.

Unlike earlier trips, there was no dinghy bouncing along behind the trawler. That logistical detail had not occurred to him until they were well underway. Presumably, someone on the island would be awake and be on the lookout for a response to the distress signal. He was sure a trawler staggering left and right like a cockeyed inebriate was not at all what they expected.

To be fair, aside from a botched tacking maneuver that sent them hurtling south for several tense minutes, the dim view Isaac took of his own seafaring skills had been overstated. He was a timid helmsman, but given the conditions that was better than overconfidence. For a man without experience and shouldering a reasonable fear for his life, the doctor had performed better than Tom had any right to expect. As long as the directions were simple and the gestures exaggerated, Isaac was able to keep the trawler on a more or less steady course.

Another minute would get them to the mooring spot, which Tom thought was about as long as he could continue holding the lamp, lit or not. He'd spent no more than twenty minutes on the deck but it felt like hours. His fingers were numb from the sea spray that continuously soaked him to the bone, and the rope he'd circled around his waist to hold him to the mast had nearly cut him in two a few times.

Emerging from a curtain of fog, the trawler lurched a few feet closer to the Blasket and Tom finally got a clear view of the boat slip. The full light of dawn wouldn't come for another hour, but enough of it had bled into the sky to make the figures standing on shore visible. They stood next to a naomhóg that was placed near the end of the ramp, upright and ready for launch.

"Thanks be to God," Tom whispered. He lowered the lamp and felt the tension he'd been carrying for the past hour begin to loosen.

They'd made it. For the first time, he allowed himself to acknowledge they easily might not have. The strength of his relief, and sheepish guilt—for endangering his own life along with that of a man he'd only just met—left every stretched nerve quivering. It also cleared his head, making room for a different kind of anxiety.

The fire at *An Gob* had served its purpose but was merely a crude signal, the announcement of a story yet to be told. With the island looming before him, Tom realized how much he feared the tale waiting for him—but hadn't hearing it been the purpose behind the entire reckless enterprise? He could hardly avoid it now.

Raising the lamp again, he tried to hold it steady. The light was no longer blinding; it had just enough strength left to reach the shore. Tom couldn't identify the men, but when the beam jumped away from them and swept up the ramp, it illuminated a figure he would have known from a hundred miles away.

Caught in the dim glow, Brigid looked like a being made of air and light—skin the color of moonlight, hair flying dark and wild around her cheeks. Facing him, she stood motionless, but then raised a hand and stretched it, as if threading the trembling light through her fingers.

The sight of her knocked Tom witless. The rope around his waist kept him from falling when his knees buckled, but the lamp fell out of his hands, and the sound of shattering glass brought him to his senses. He had just enough time to send Isaac a signal to reverse engines before the flame sputtered out. Pulling at the knots to free himself so he could drop anchor, Tom pressed his spine against the mast and closed his eyes, trying to pin down the feeling that washed through him. Relief, of course, but not only that. Was it joy? Gratitude? He decided it was a combination of the three and maybe more besides, and the name for all of them together was "salvation."

Once the trawler was firmly anchored, Tom waved to the men on shore. They slid the naomhóg into the water and climbed aboard, then locked down the oars and started rowing. The waves weren't the alarming, spiking height they'd been earlier, but the small boat still almost disappeared each time it crested a rounded swell and rode into its trough. Tom watched their slow progress and could barely contain his impatience. Resisting the urge to bark at them to *put your bloody backs into it*, he grabbed one of the safety lines and groped his way back to the wheelhouse. Once inside, his ears rang in the sudden silence, their workings battered by the relentless noise of weather. He found Isaac still at the wheel—white-faced—reeling in a state somewhere between terror and triumph.

"You'll never make me believe this was the first time you've done this," Tom said. "You were brilliant. And I'm grateful. Truly."

Drenched, and with every move releasing a fresh cascade of water, he held out a hand. After a slight hesitation, Isaac managed to peel one of his own away from the wheel to shake it.

"I'll never believe I let you talk me into it. I'm still not sure how you did." The ghost of a smile tugged at Isaac's lips before settling into a frown. "You're hypothermic."

"I'm what, now?"

"Hypothermic. You're glassy-eyed and your teeth are chattering like castanets."

"Castanets?"

Isaac sighed at his confusion. "You're losing body heat. Take off the jacket. And the shirt, and the ... what the hell are those, long johns? Take those off too."

Privately, Tom felt sure he was shivering from something other than cold. He also couldn't see how taking his clothes off would make him any warmer, but Isaac had become a physician now. His wise-cracking anxiety had evaporated, and the clipped instructions he delivered carried an authority it seemed best not to refuse. As a compromise, Tom stripped to his waist. Using the remnants of a shredded jib sail, the doctor worked briskly, rubbing him down as though he were a steaming plow horse that had been worked too hard. It did the job. Tom's fair skin reddened under the assault but his teeth stopped their incessant rattle.

"Feel better?" Isaac gave him a clinical stare.

"I do," he admitted. "Thanks."

Seeing Tom reach for the soggy clothes he'd dropped next to his feet, the doctor gave them a kick into a corner.

"Again with the jokes. Here, put this on. At least it's dry." He handed Tom his overcoat and buttoned up his own sweater—a loose and well-worn shaker knit cardigan—waving away Tom's protest. "This thing is warmer than any coat I ever owned. My father's lucky sweater. The Dodgers never lost when he wore it."

"But—" Tom swallowed the rest of his objection, hearing a voice hooting from the trawler's port side. He shrugged himself into the coat—it was a few sizes too small—and hurried out of the wheelhouse. Isaac grabbed his medical bag and followed. Reaching the side and peering down over it, Tom saw Sean and Petey struggling to hold the naomhóg steady as it bounced against the trawler.

"That's really Tom McBride, is it?!" Sean looked as if he still doubted it, even though their faces were less than ten feet apart. "You're not telling me that fire was lighting up the sky all the way to Ventry!"

Tom raised his voice to be heard above the wind. "I've no idea, Sean, as I wasn't in Ventry when I saw it."

Isaac was at his side now, having awkwardly pitched himself from the wheelhouse. He fixed a white-knuckled grip on the backstay as though he intended to snap the line in half while Tom called down introductions. "Sean, Petey, this is Dr. Isaac Frum. He's over from America."

"From America!" Petey roared in disbelief.

"He's been on holiday, staying at . . . .mother of God," Tom broke off helplessly. "I'll give you the story later, will I?"

"Later sounds good," Isaac muttered. "Later sounds spectacular."

Tom put a steadying hand on his shoulder before continuing. "What sort of trouble are you in over here?"

He still feared the response to this question. Since he'd seen Brigid standing on the shore, the unbearable dread gnawing at him had retreated, but every other name on the island was known to him as well; he could summon the faces of all their owners. He'd been sifting through each one, wondering which had been struck by misfortune. The answer from Sean, delivered in a broken voice, shocked him to the core.

"Liam," Tom said, repeating a name he hadn't even considered while the weight of it fell on him like a stone. "The child. Their only child."

"Who's only child?" Isaac asked.

"Everyone's," he said softly.

The lively little seven-year-old was Margaret and Padraig's son, but he was also the pulse of every heart on the Blasket. He was their little man, and they loved him fiercely. The night of the ceili, he'd watched Liam make his way around the main room of Peig's house, and had seen the eyes of weathered Blasket fishermen grow tender as they took turns pulling him onto their laps. The thought that this source of joy might be taken from people who had so little to draw on was appalling, but Tom didn't have long to think about it. Sean's description of Liam's condition had transformed Isaac. Bristling with a sudden, fearless energy he was pulling at Tom's elbow, hissing terse commands in his ear.

"We have to hurry. If the infection spreads through his bloodstream I can't do a damned thing. I have not shlepped myself across the sea in a typhoon to be useless, so let's get in the boat, for God's sake."

By now, Tom was accustomed to following the man's orders. He swung himself over the side without another word, hung there until his boots felt firm on the small, rocking vessel, and then carefully lowered himself into the naomhóg.

"Wait," he called out, seeing Isaac beginning to throw one leg over the rail. "Let me have your bag first, and then I'll help you down."

Steadying his balance, he reached up for the medical bag and handed it to Petey, but when Tom turned back to the trawler Isaac was already on the way. Trying to imitate Tom's movements he backed himself down, feet scrambling for purchase, but at the critical moment an errant wave bucked the naomhóg against the larger vessel. Isaac crashed onto the slender latticework of the hull, which sent up a shuddering crack at the impact of his feet, and then he began falling backwards.

With a panicked cry Tom made a desperate, off-balance grab for him but missed, feeling only the brush of his fingers against the thick sweater as the momentum carried him forward. There was time enough to share one startled glance before they both toppled into the space between the two boats and sank beneath an angry, frothing sea.

⁓

Horrified by the sight of history repeating itself, Brigid drove the heel of her hand against her mouth. If the scream rising through her throat were allowed to escape, she thought it might never stop.

She'd watched, just as she had on that first day they'd met, as Tom stood silhouetted against the murky, pre-dawn horizon, holding himself steady in the rocking boat. Once again she saw him reach a helping hand to a man who was a stranger to her, and once again that man had lurched into the boat, arms thrashing, and set it off balance.

The first time the tableau had played out as farce. Brigid had smiled at the sight of Tom and Dan O'Brien, sprawled on the deck of the trawler in the fading sunlight, collapsed in laughter.

There was nothing funny about what she was watching now. Just as on that bright day in June, Tom grabbed for the rail of the trawler, but this time he missed it entirely. Brigid watched in disbelief as he and the stranger fell together and dropped out of sight.

Sean and Petey scrambled to catch them, and then scanned the water where they'd fallen in, but after a minute they sat back, and appeared to be frozen in shock. Facing each other at either end of the naomhóg, they were rigid as a pair of standing stones, but an instant later Brigid heard Sean's rumbling baritone mingled with Petey's high-pitched tenor. They started yelling—both at once, both incoherently—as they twisted themselves in every direction, searching.

"Can you see them at all? Are they under the boat?"

He wasn't speaking to her, but the screeching pitch of Petey's voice cut through the wind and carried over the water to Brigid. She'd already run down the concrete ramp and now stood at the very bottom of it with the sea water surging around her ankles. It would be reckless as well as useless to go farther, but the only thing preventing her from plunging into the ocean was the knowledge that once she was in it she would no longer be able to see it. She needed to stay where she was, to keep sweeping her eyes over the water, to keep looking for them.

She'd been alone since Sean and Petey had rowed out to the trawler, but didn't remain so for long. Within minutes there was barely room to stand on the boat slip as half the village appeared, descending the steep path in small groups until a dozen or more were gathered in a solid mass. Hearing a raised voice shouting orders, Brigid glanced back and saw the crowd parting to allow the passage of two more naomhógs, each carried by a two-man crew. With their glistening hulls turned to the sky they looked like long, dark beetles creeping down the path.

Everyone stood in near silence as the naomhógs were turned upright and eased into the water, and then rowed out of the small harbor. Sean and Petey had moved away from the trawler now. Brigid watched the three boats spread out in a line to cover more territory, and sensed the subdued atmosphere around her.

It was unusual for a gathering to be so quiet. Usually, there was no shortage of chatter and debate, of suggestions and arguments for one course of action over another, but there was none of that, now. The hushed voices served as an expressive symbol, confirming what they all knew. Every island man who was able for it was on the water now, aiding the search. There was nothing more to be done.

29

The first clear thought Tom had as the waves covered him was counterintuitive – in fact, it was more instinct than thought. He had to get away from the boats, or more precisely, from the space between them. Every second spent bobbing around in the narrow channel increased the odds of being trapped below the surface, or of having his head cracked open like a walnut before he could be pulled to safety.

The same was true for Isaac, but Tom couldn't warn him of their danger because the boiling chaos of foam and water made any communication impossible. He couldn't see the doctor but could feel his arms and legs moving in frantic slow motion, bumping against him. With no other options available, he caught the doctor's wrist in a tight grip and pulled him forward, hoping his head was above water. With his other hand he began clawing his way along the length of the naomhóg.

He intended to work his way around to its opposite side, but as soon as they reached the boat's prow and began making the turn, a strong current grabbed them. For several minutes they bounced helplessly over the whitecaps and Tom quickly lost all sense of direction. He tried to get his bearings, but reflexively closed his eyes as a breaking wave slapped against his face. The sour-salt taste of the sea filled his mouth. He felt Isaac's wrist slide from his grip, tried grabbing it back again, and came up with nothing.

Moving within reach of the boat's solid presence, Tom had remained calm, but feeling his grasping fingers close on empty water in every direction badly frightened him. Thrashing in a circle, he looked for Isaac, the naomhóg, the trawler, but the movement only brought on a new crisis. He couldn't move his arms. He was still wearing the too-tight raincoat Isaac had insisted he put on, and now it had become wrapped around him like a straitjacket. Kicking his legs, Tom fought to free himself, trying to keep his head above the surface, until at last another instinct told him to stop struggling. He took a deep gulp of air, and allowed himself to sink.

Once underwater, Tom felt calm again. The ocean wasn't completely silent—it had its own uniform sound, a steady note thrumming in his ears—but the roaring wind and crashing of waves against rock no longer tormented him. Now that he was motionless the folds of the raincoat loosened again. He slipped it off easily but continued to float beneath the surface, feeling oddly peaceful. Was this what it was like when you gave up on your life? Is this how it felt to drown?

The thought itself seemed to spark something in him. Images began cascading through Tom's head like a stuttering newsreel. He saw the fields around his house. A fall of waving, black hair across a cream-white cheek. A sky full of sea swallows. A sea-green cockleshell in the palm of his hand.

And music. Fiddles, bodhrans, concertinas. Music everywhere, and the images of rough hands turning nimble as they worked the instruments.

He broke the surface with the sight of all of it still before him, returning to a realm of noise and confusion. It was disorienting. Tom could see nothing at first, but gradually his eyes focused. He saw the Blasket's White Strand far ahead, and a fair distance to the left of him, he could see the trawler, along with three naomhógs spread out in a line next to it. Somehow, the swirling current had carried him north.

Treading water he turned in a slow circle. The sky was growing lighter every minute, making it easier to see the emptiness around him. Tom tried to keep his mind blank as he searched, tried to force down his growing sense of horror and its accompanying weight of guilt and recrimination. He revolved again and again, but finally had to acknowledge he was alone. He twisted, intending to hail the boats. After riding over one mountainous swell he settled into its trough and waited for the next to lift him, but then straight ahead he saw the figure of Isaac Frum tumbling towards him on the crest of a following wave.

His arms were still flailing. Tom was nearly overcome with relief at this evidence of life. The wave came on so fast he nearly missed his chance, but managed to snag the collar of Issac's cardigan as he flew by. In spite of the sudden weight that pulled at his shoulder, threatening to pop the joint from its socket, he held on, gasping.

"Lucky sweater. In the name of God, be lucky now."

The loops of wool thinned and stretched and dug into his fingers, but they held. With his momentum reversed, Isaac turned and automatically grabbed hold of him, desperate for the safety of something solid.

"Stop," Tom shouted, drawing back before the doctor pushed him underwater. "You'll have the pair of us drowned."

"I can't swim," Isaac shouted back.

"I know that, but you can float, can't you? You'd be dead by now if you couldn't. Listen, I understand it's not easy, but you need to relax. I can't help if you're trying to climb on top of me."

"Relax!" The doctor was close to hysteria but with a supreme effort he stopped lunging at Tom. "What are you going to do?"

It was an excellent question. Tom looked to his left again. The boats were even farther away now, and shouting seemed like a waste of energy.

"Teach you to swim," he said.

∼

The wind-driven current had carried them over to *An Trá Bhán*. Brigid would never know what made her turn her gaze north to the expanse of ocean in front of the broad white beach, but when she did, the figures in the water immediately caught her eye. They looked tiny and doll-like, but they were unmistakably human. She didn't take the time to point, or cry out, or tell anyone what she'd seen. Brigid simply turned and ran, ignoring the startled cries of those she shouldered aside on her way up the path.

Lis and Mary followed her, moving more slowly. They didn't know what it was all about but had long ago decided that—peculiar as she was—Brigid was nearly always worth paying attention to at moments like this.

She raced along the path to the White Strand, her feet hitting the sand as the first coral hues of dawn appeared, lighting the peaks of Mt. Brandon on the mainland. She ran to the hard-packed shoreline, and then up the beach to the end closest to the village, and continued straight into the ocean. She could see Tom clearly, now. He was bare-chested, but the man with him was fully clothed. They were within fifty yards of the shore, but too exhausted to see how close they were. Tom was struggling to keep his companion afloat, but they were foundering, sinking into the surf like a ship taking on water.

"Tom!" Brigid's skirts billowed around her. She was up to her hips, fighting to stay upright as the waves tried to knock her down. "Tom, look at me! You're nearly there."

He hadn't heard her, but was still moving forward, tugging the other man along as if trying to swim while hauling a sack of potatoes. He was almost on top of Brigid before he saw her, and when he did it looked as though he might have escaped drowning only to be struck dead with amazement.

"You've reached the shallows, Tom," she shouted to him. "Put your feet on the ground, now."

Her words registered slowly. Tom stared at her for several seconds before he seemed to understand. He managed to stand, but the inert form next to him made no such effort. He pulled the man up and staggered a few feet before a wave knocked them both down.

Brigid surged forward, reaching them at last. She put an arm under the stranger's and together she and Tom dragged him to shore. They stretched him out on the sand where he lay flat on his back, motionless, eyes closed. Tom collapsed next to him, his forehead resting on one arm.

His chest was heaving for breath and Brigid became even more frightened. She knelt and gently rubbed his back. "Are you all right, Tom? Are you not able to breathe? Is it an asthma attack?"

Tom's response was muffled against his arm, but then he rolled onto his back, looking faintly alarmed. "Jaysus, it never even crossed my mind. A good thing. If I'd thought about having one, I surely would have done. What about Isaac, though. Is he breathing?"

"Isaac?" Brigid turned for a closer study of the man she'd forgotten about as soon as she'd dropped him. He was short and slender, with a smooth complexion and dark hair. She couldn't begin to imagine who he was, and wasn't sure if he was breathing or not. Tom rolled up onto his knees next to her and hovered over him, his expression anguished.

"Oh please, dear God, he isn't gone? He can't be dead, and me the cause of it?"

The man's eyes remained closed, but his lips twitched into a small smile. "He ought to be, but he isn't. And for what are you feeling guilty? I'm the one who knocked us out of the boat." The smile disappeared as he opened his eyes and frowned at Tom. "You have asthma?"

Tom choked on a convulsive gasp. It sounded too relieved to be a sob, too painful to be laughter.

"I do, but not at the moment."

"Where the hell is my bag?" The stranger suddenly sat up, fully alert, and turned a sharp-eyed glance on Brigid. "Have you seen it?"

He was speaking in English, at a rapid pace and with an accent she'd never heard before. Flustered, Brigid looked at the sand around them.

"A bag?"

"It's safe in the boat," Tom reassured him. "See, they're bringing it in, now."

Looking in the direction he'd pointed, Brigid saw Sean and Petey were pulling hard at the oars and had almost reached the boat slip. Tom extended a hand to help pull the stranger to his feet, and then finally introduced him.

"Brigid, this is Dr. Isaac Frum. We saw the signal fire from Dunquin, but the lifeboat at Valencia had been called away. Isaac is staying at Kruger's and he agreed to come with me."

She accepted the handshake the man offered and found the grip of his thin hand stronger than she'd expected. "Thanks be to God. We're grateful to you, Dr. Frum. We've a little boy here who's desperately ill. We've tried everything and none of it has done him a bit of good." Unaccustomed to speaking English, Brigid formed the words as carefully as she could, but then couldn't go on with it. Overwhelmed with exhaustion and emotion, she lapsed into a stream of Irish, turning to Tom as the tears rolled down her face.

"It seems months since we could put a boat on the water. There's been no fishing at all. The storms have never stopped, and when Liam fell into a fever we nearly lost hope altogether. Now I can hardly believe what I'm seeing. I can hardly believe you're here, Tom, and I—"

The rest was muffled against his chest as Tom's arms went around her, pulling her into a tight embrace. "It's all right, we're here, now. I'm here." He drew back, and she could see the tears in his own eyes as he cupped her face in his hands.

"Don't send me away again," he whispered. "You have my heart shaken to bits. You don't have to marry me. You can go anywhere you like or nowhere at all, but please don't send me away, Brigid. I can't bear it."

"Never. I never will." She stroked his face, pushing the wet hair from his forehead. "I let you slip from my hands entirely, Tom McBride, but I won't ever let it happen again."

30

*H*e felt half-frozen by the time they arrived, but there was no shortage of warmth showered on Tom and Isaac when they reached the village. Brigid's struggle to help them through the waves and onto the beach had been visible from the boat slip, and by the time the three of them reached her cottage, the naomhógs had already landed and everyone was assembled in her dooryard.

Lis ushered them inside and started scrubbing them with tea towels while others rounded up blankets and stirred the turf fire into a blaze. During all this activity a steady stream of visitors cycled through the small room, bringing refreshments and advice, eager to participate in the continuing drama.

In a quieter corner, Tom stood behind Brigid with an arm circled around her waist, unwilling–unable–to let go of her. They shared a cup of hot sugary tea with a slug of whiskey stirred into it, and watched anxiously, along with everyone else, while Isaac examined his patient.

After exchanging his water-logged lucky sweater for one of Sean's dry ones, the doctor had shown no interest in hot drinks, and no patience for anything anyone wanted to do for him. All he wanted was his medical bag, which he'd snatched from Petey's hands before hurrying over to Liam. They watched him frown in concentration, his slender hands moving with quick self-assurance while he peppered Margaret with questions. When he was finished, he crouched down to face her directly. After speaking with her for another minute, Margaret nodded, crying softly. Isaac gently touched her arm and straightened. He summoned Tom and Brigid with a jerk of his head.

"Get all these people out of here. I need boiling water and clean cloth." He gave the two of them an appraising look. "I have to open his arm and drain it. It's going to be messy. I need one of you to sit with his parents, and I need the other one to help me. I don't care which, just make up your minds and be quick about it."

Tom reasoned that an old friend would provide more comfort than a new one. After a few frantic minutes, the cottage was emptied of all non-essential islanders and Brigid sat by the hearth with Margaret and Padraig while he stood at Isaac's side. The kitchen table had been moved to the bedside. It held a few pots of hot water, strips of cloth and various items from the medical bag that he couldn't identify.

"Are you a surgeon?" he asked.

"Of course not." Isaac glared at him. "Are you a nurse? More importantly, can you handle the sight of blood? If you faint, you're no good to me."

Tom smiled. "I won't faint. I'm a farmer. I've been covered in blood up to my shoulders more than a few times."

Having offered this bluff reassurance Tom felt a greater

obligation to remain steady, but it was indeed a messy business. In a procedure that ended not a moment too soon, he passed the clean items from the table to Isaac and accepted them back soiled, as the doctor drained, cleaned and sutured the infected area. When he'd dumped the last strip of cloth into the pot of bloodied water, Tom's stomach was churning.

Weakened by fever and soothed by a local anesthetic, Liam remained unresponsive during the ordeal, but after Isaac had injected the first dose, the miracle of penicillin began doing its work. The boy's temperature gradually returned to normal. A few hours later, he opened his eyes and smiled at his mother, and then he and his physician shared identical expressions of alarm. Margaret had thrown herself into Isaac's arms, sobbing out her gratitude.

∼

Mary arrived not long after Liam had been bundled up and carried home in his father's arms. Brigid was sitting at the table with Tom and Isaac, all of them arranged in varying positions of exhaustion. She was wearily thinking about the hospitality owed to strangers and travelers, especially to one who had just saved the life of the island's only child. The least she could do was give the man a hot meal. Resolved to her duty, Brigid braced her hands on the table, and saw Mary standing in the doorway.

"*Muise,*" Mary said. "Ah, the poor lambs. You look perished, the three of you, but it's the doctor I've come to collect. Will you come down to the King's House now, Doctor, and take your ease? There's everything you could want ready and waiting for you. You'll have a hot bath and we'll get a morsel of something into you, and maybe a nice cup of tea as well, and then you can have a good long rest."

Isaac appeared utterly charmed by Mary. She'd delivered the earnest invitation to him directly with a wide smile and a trilling, musical inflection, but since every word was in Irish he had no idea what she was saying. He appealed to Brigid with a confused bleary-eyed smile.

"Mary is inviting you to stay at the King's House," she explained, in English. "She's fond of hosting visitors who come in to the island."

Privately, Brigid wondered if Mary had more than one motive in mind in whisking Isaac away. There was a particularly bright twinkle in her eye this morning.

"The King's House?" Isaac's dark eyebrows shot up. "Is there a king in it?"

"Well, there isn't. Not anymore. There's only Mary, the princess. She's the daughter of the last king of the Blasket."

"The princess. Sure. Where the hell are we, anyway? I feel like I'm in a fairy tale." Isaac smiled at the petite, white-haired woman who was still beaming at him. "It would be an honor, Princess Mary. As long as you don't mind entertaining a socialist."

Mary gave a satisfied nod and turned, waving for him to follow. "Ha! Here, now!" She sang out in English. "Come to bed."

When Isaac was gone and the two of them had stopped laughing, Brigid realized she and Tom were finally alone. At last. His eyes met hers. From their shining contentment, she assumed he was having the same thought. He reached across the table to take her hand and then frowned, rubbing it gently.

"Your hand is freezing with cold, love. Are you all right?"

"I am. It will warm up soon, I'm thinking."

Tom drew her forward to sit on his lap He cradled her hands, kissing them, and then grinned. "Do you know, I've only just learned the quickest way to get warm is to take all your clothes off."

"Is that so, now?" Brigid rested her forehead against his, smiling.

"It is. Would you believe it?" His mouth moved along her face, hovering close enough for her to feel his hot breath on her skin.

"Well then, stop dawdling, Tom McBride. Take them off, so. Come to bed."

Her own bed was not an option as it still bore the evidence of Isaac's grim surgical procedure, so instead they covered the flagstone with a pile of blankets. Kneeling in front of the hearth, they took their time, undressing each other slowly and stopping to caress the places revealed as each layer was removed. By now, Brigid had entirely forgotten about her tumble down the hillside of *An Gob*, but once Tom had uncovered the resulting bruises he eased her gently onto her back and planted a soft, cautious kiss on every one of them. When finished, he returned to her face and gazed down at her.

"I loved you the very minute I ever laid eyes on you," he said, his voice husky.

Brigid laughed, even as a tear spilled from each eye and slid down to tickle her ears. "It took me a bit longer."

"Did it? How long?"

"Oh, maybe half an hour."

"*Och.* Heart of stone."

His mouth covered hers, urgently now, and Brigid shivered as his fingers traveled down her stomach and slipped between her legs. It was different this time, she realized. Before, they had been preoccupied with the newness of it all and with their own reactions. It had been as though they were making their way along an unfamiliar path, eager for the discoveries it promised but careful of their footing with every step.

This time, they focused on discovering each other, and as the journey continued Brigid spared no thought for the ground beneath her.

She had faith it would hold them.

31

No matter how many blankets were piled over it, the large flagstone was not nearly as comfortable when they woke up on it four hours later. Tom had a few ideas for working the soreness out of their backs that Brigid agreed were remarkably effective.

Once they were limber again, it seemed a shame to bolt up too quickly when they were so warm and comfortable.

With her head on his chest, Tom lay with his eyes half-closed, facing the window, sifting strands of Brigid's dark hair through his fingers and noticing the endless slap of the wind against the roof of the cottage had stopped at last. A minute later he opened his eyes wider.

"Mother of God. Can that be the sun?"

Brigid lifted her head to look. A small square of light was creeping across the beaten earth of the cottage floor, and they stared at it as though watching the approach of the Holy Ghost.

"It is," she said, and settled against him again with a contented sigh.

It was Starlight's insistent groans that eventually got them out of their makeshift bed. In all the excitement, no one had thought to milk her that morning and she was fed up with waiting. While Brigid heated some water for washing and started the porridge, Tom went out to the restless cow and greeting her fondly.

"Hello, old girl. Do you remember me, at all? We had a lovely chat together a few months ago."

They had another one now, after he'd settled onto the stool and pulled the bucket forward. His own cows were used to this, by now. Tom found it useful–relaxing, even–to think out loud in the quiet morning atmosphere of his barn, while the stream of milk rang against the metal bucket in a steady, rhythmic tempo. He thought it might be the clos-est he would ever come to what Brigid experienced when she was communing with all the wild power of the natural world– except that she usually did it silently, whereas Tom was talking all the time.

"What do you think about a trip across the water, Starlight?" He grunted a laugh. "Not much, I'll wager. Sure that will be a lark, getting you into a boat and along the road to Ventry. We'd best leave it until summer I'd say."

The shooting stream of milk stopped abruptly as Tom paused, brought up short by this thought. There were so many details he hadn't even begun to consider yet, and how to move a cow across Blasket Sound was least among them. He was getting ahead of himself.

The cow shifted impatiently and he looked up at her, absently patting her side in apology.

"Jayz, what am I thinking at all? I haven't actually asked

her to marry me yet. I'll need to do something about that, I suppose, won't I?"

Tom thought he had plenty of time to talk through how he might approach that critical bit of business, but Starlight was finished sooner than he expected. He was surprised to see how little milk she'd let down. After setting the bucket aside he began his customary inspection of the animal, this time with greater attention.

The evidence of malnourishment was obvious, which made him realize it was just as obvious in Brigid herself. He'd noticed she'd lost weight, but the reason hadn't taken hold in his mind, until now.

Tom felt a hot flush of shame at the thought of the hardship she'd endured over the past two months – that all of them had – while he and everyone else remained oblivious to it. There was no shortage of hardship on the mainland, to be sure. A good share of Ireland's population lived in grinding poverty; but he doubted there was any spot in the country where an entire village was at this moment starving.

He carried the bucket inside, where Brigid was lifting the bubbling pot of porridge from the fire. Watching her, Tom forgave himself a bit for his lack of awareness. No matter how many times he looked away, whenever his eyes rested on her again he was as stunned as the first time he'd seen her.

Brigid placed the pot on the table with a thump. Tom quickly pulled it forward and began spooning the porridge into bowls.

"I'm sorry there isn't more," she said, taking the chair next to him. "There's been no boat to Dunquin for six weeks and we're running short of everything."

"There's plenty. I'm actually not too hungry."

She stared at him. "Are you joking me? It's ages since you've eaten anything."

"I've still too many pints of sea water sloshing around inside me. No room for much else."

Not fooled for a minute, Brigid dropped her gaze, cheeks flushed as he handed her a brimming bowl of porridge swimming in milk. She began to protest but he stopped her with a kiss.

"Eat your breakfast, love," he said softly.

When they'd finished, Brigid decided to tackle the project of changing her bed and cleaning the linens, which reminded Tom that he should check in with Isaac. He knew he couldn't impose on the doctor to remain on the island longer than he wanted to, but hoped he could negotiate at least a few more hours before their departure.

There was a slight breeze and a brisk autumn snap in the air, but the day was glorious. The sun was riding high in cloudless brilliance, as if trying to make it up to all of them for hiding itself for the better part of two months. Tom started along the path to the King's House, but along the way he spotted Isaac in the upper village. He was wearing his father's lucky sweater again – dry but a bit worse for wear – and seemed to be examining the village well. At Tom's approach, he came straight to the point without preamble.

"I wish they had as much food as they have water. These people aren't eating enough."

"I know," Tom said, not meeting his eyes. "I don't think anyone knew things were so desperate."

"Anyone? Who's anyone?" Isaac's sharp, intelligent

gaze skewered him. "Who the hell is looking after these people? Most of them are ancient! It's like a shipwrecked nursing home."

"I know," Tom repeated. Ashamed—of himself and of everyone else who had failed the islanders—he shifted on his feet, still looking at the ground. "Most of them will be leaving soon."

"Most of them will be dying soon." Isaac huffed an apologetic sigh and sat down on the wall next to the well. "Sorry, Tom. I'm just mortified by how much I ate of that poor woman's food before realizing it was probably half of what she had left. And I don't know why I'm yelling at you, because you're the one who did something. You performed a good and moral deed last night. In my community we call it a *mitzvah*. That little boy would be dead this morning if you hadn't acted."

"That's down to you, Isaac," Tom said, taking a seat next to him. "Liam owes his life to you."

"But I wouldn't be here if not for you. You shamed me into this crazy ride, and I'm glad you did. I'll never forget it." Isaac gave Tom a light poke with his elbow. "Beats the hell out of Ethel Merman's tonsils."

Tom laughed. "I'm hoping that means you're willing to stay a while longer. Maybe for two or three hours? I can have you back to Kruger's in time for tea."

"Actually, I'd prefer spending the night, here. I want to keep an eye on Liam for a good twenty-four hours. I see that idea appeals to you."

"It does." Tom blushed. "There's something I need to do before leaving, and I'm sort of waiting for the right moment."

"Sure. It's a delicate business, right? She's quite a woman.

Beauty, brains and heart. Killer combination." Isaac's wolfish grin softened into affection. "I don't think you need to worry much, Tom."

Tom nodded, grateful for the reassurance, which only made him realize how nervous he was.

～

"It was this very spot, Tom. Are you saying you don't believe me, now?"

Facing him, Brigid cocked her hands on her hips and tried to look fierce, but she couldn't help breaking into a smile. The autumn afternoon had turned out to be one of the finest she'd ever seen on the island. Too chilly for a picnic, but not for a walk. It was Tom who'd suggested a stroll along the White Strand, and who now seemed skeptical that they were standing on the exact spot where they'd met nearly eight months earlier.

He was so nervous, and it took no special powers of intuition to understand why. Brigid hated seeing the lines of anxiety in his forehead, but if she told him he needn't be worried it would only spoil it for both of them. She angled her head at him.

"So?"

"Oh, I believe you. Of course I do," Tom stuttered. "It's only I thought I'd walked closer to the boat slip."

"Maybe you're confused because you're still looking for the rock that wasn't one."

That brought a smile to his face at last. "Maybe."

Tom took her hand and seemed about to continue walking,

but then frowned and shook his head as if exasperated with himself. He took her other hand and they looked at each other for a long moment. Just when Brigid thought he was about to speak, he suddenly embraced her. Tom wrapped his arms around her waist and buried his face in her hair, as if holding onto something he was convinced was about to fly away from him.

Her heart ached for him then, realizing he had reason to be afraid that she would somehow slip from his grasp. She'd taught him to fear that very thing, hadn't she? Hadn't she always done it, with everyone? Nobody had ever known what she would do next. That was fine for a young girl on her own, flitting among ruins and coves, but not for a woman who wanted to join her life with the man she loved. Brigid swore she would settle down, and never give him cause to worry like this again.

He was down on his knees at last and she breathed a prayer of thanks. When he spoke, she could barely hear him above the sound of the waves.

"I love you with all my heart. Whatever beauty I've ever seen stands behind yours, and whatever hope I have for happiness in my life is already lost if you won't be in it. Say you'll be mine, Brigid O'Sullivan. Treasure of my heart. Say you'll marry me."

After so much worry and anxiety, the words were almost too beautiful for Brigid to bear. She could barely get the answer out of her mouth for the tears.

"Did I say I loved you after half an hour? I told a lie. I feel as though I've been walking towards you all my life, and I've loved you all that lonely time. I will marry you, Tom. I am ready to go with you."

They got no farther up the beach. The walk was abandoned, yielding to the pull of the powdery sand in the spot where they'd first laid eyes on each other. The afternoon sun was quickly disappearing behind them when they finally emerged from their sheltered cove. Tom was wearing his boots, but as they often were, Brigid's feet were bare and she rarely left the strand without dipping them into the water. He waited near the path while she ran across the sand, and was laughing when she returned.

"You'll be patient with me, Tom, I hope?" Brigid said, taking his hand. "I'll do my best to settle down and give up all these odd habits, but it may take a bit of time."

"Rubbish. The oddness is part of what I love." Tom laughed again, but then seemed to understand she hadn't been joking. He stopped and looked at her, his eyes serious. "I don't want you to settle down. You shouldn't give up any habits that make you who you are. Not for me. Not for anyone."

Brigid had thought she'd finished crying, but her eyes filled again. She pointed across the water at the mainland. "Are you not afraid of me wandering off to the hills over there, looking for stone circles and holy wells and high crosses?"

"Why should I be?" Tom looked genuinely puzzled, and then thoughtful. He turned her around to look at the ocean again. "Listen to me, now. My father said this to me once, though at the time he was talking about something else entirely. The tide comes in, and then it goes out again, because that's what it's meant to do. You can't pin the waves to the shore, but sure why would you want to? They always come back."

Tom smiled at her, brushing the tears from her cheeks. "You be the wave, and I'll be the shore. We'll both do what we're meant to. That will be all right, won't it?"

Brigid took a trembling breath and nodded. "That will be all right."

"Good." Tom grinned. "Please God every problem will be so easily settled." He kissed her forehead and wrapped his arms around her. "What will our children be like, I wonder? Will they be waves as well? Or a good, sturdy shore?"

"A little of both, I'm thinking," Brigid said, nuzzled against his shoulder. The question caught her off-guard and she was glad her face was hidden from him. Ever since Tom had arrived, she'd been tempted to tell him about her vision on the cliff the previous night, but had finally decided the risk was too great. The promise it offered was like the ocean mist surrounding it, tenuous and delicate, something that could easily disappear if grasped at or examined too closely.

Still, she would always remember the sense of wonder she'd felt in that joyful moment of recognition, and she would never forget the face of her son. Brigid knew she would see him again, and the next time it happened she wouldn't be alone.

The next time, they would see him together.

~

It was a difficult secret to hold in her heart, but Brigid McBride let her vision and its fragile promise remain there until one summer day when she left the house, crossed the back patio, and climbed up into the fields above Ventry Harbor. She found Tom working in the upper pasture, and on that afternoon—a brilliant one, the sky bluer than the Virgin's holy robe . . . she caught him by surprise.

Afterword

I first became familiar with the Blasket Islands during a trip to Ireland many years ago, when I visited the Blasket Centre in Dunquin and learned the achingly sad story of Sean Kearney's family, who watched helplessly as he died for lack of any means of communicating their need, or of getting medical assistance across the water through a fierce winter storm. The heartbreaking loss of one of the youngest men still living on the island is generally thought to be the event that finally broke the spirit of the islanders, even though many of them remained for several more years.

The official evacuation date given for the Great Blasket is November 17, 1953. The man in charge was indeed named Dan O'Brien from Tralee, and on that morning he and another man from the Irish Land Commission were transported to the island by a fishing trawler called the *St. Lawrence O'Toole*. The islanders were packed and ready to go, but when the boat reached the island the weather proved too rough to safely move everyone and their household goods. To the surprise of everyone, Dan insisted on going ashore in a naomhóg, to present the papers that would finalize their agreement and transfer ownership of several houses in Dunquin.

In the end, six islanders came over that day with whatever personal belongings they could carry, and the rest of the islanders left in a staggered fashion rather than in one large group.

Eventually a family called O'Sullivan (known as "the light-keepers" for being the last ones remaining on the island) left in November, 1954, and with their departure the island was well and truly deserted.

Although this novel contains a fictionalized "imagined" account of the island's story, I immersed myself in photographs, videos, memoirs and other resources in an attempt to produce an authentic flavor of the story of the community and the circumstances leading to its dissolution. I became so familiar with the faces that I started to recognize them from one photo to the next, matching the elderly men they became in Dunquin with their more youthful photos from the island.

Although a few names of my characters duplicate some that existed on the island, most are entirely fictional. I've mentioned Dan O'Brien as one notable exception. Another is Kruger Kavanaugh, whose character is largely based on what factual accounts I could find for him. Kruger's Guest House is still in operation in Dunquin.

There was a "Princess" of the island, but her name was Caít (Kate) and her sister Mary Pheats offered room and board to visitors. Also, in the early 1950s there really was one small (and adorable) child on the island named Gearoíd. His memoir is called *The Loneliest Boy in the World*, which was the title of an American newspaper article written about him, but his delightful recollections of life on the island make it abundantly clear that he was adored by all and anything but lonely.

As to what the others thought about their lives on the island and about evacuation, you could find as many opinions as there were islanders. Some expressed an eagerness to leave, others sorrow, and others a bitterness that more wasn't done to help them stay. To the news reporter who greeted the arrival of the *St. Lawrence O'Toole* with the question "Are you happy to be leaving the island?" one man's laconic reply (in Irish) was "Yes. We're a bit lonely."

I find myself most moved by the words of Eibhlís Ní Shúilleabháin in a 1942 letter to her friend George Chambers, as she prepared to move out to the mainland:

"...whatever happens on this island I have one gifted thing to tell you of it—I was always happy there."

Some Further Reading:
- *Hungry for Home: Leaving the Blaskets* by Cole Moreton
- *From the Great Blasket to America* by Michael Kearney (brother of Sean) and Gerald Hayes
- *The Last Blasket King* by Gerald Hayes with Eliza Kane
- *Blasket Spirit* by Anita Fennelly
- *Land of My Cradle Days*, by Martin Morrissey (charming memoir of 1950s Irish life)
- The Blasket Writers:
- *The Islandman* by Tomás O'Crohan
- *Twenty Years 'A Growing* by Maurice O'Sullivan
- *Peig: A Life* by Peig Sayers (if you dare!)
- *Letters from the Great Blasket* by Eibhlís Ní Shúilleabháin

Finally, a note to those who have read my other books, and are already familiar with Brigid McBride (and of course with the tall, dark-haired man who had a cameo role in this one!) This book is dedicated to those who expressed a fondness for her and a desire to hear more about her. Now you know how her story began. It would be technically accurate to say you also know how it ends, but I prefer to think of her as simply playing a more hidden role now.

As Conor himself would tell you, she'll never be far away.

Slán agus beannacht (Goodbye, God bless)

About the Author

Author of the award-winning Conor McBride Series, Kathryn Guare's character-driven novels are all somewhere on the spectrum between romance and suspense, and some are even perfectly balanced between the two. She has a passion for exploring diverse cultures and cuisine, Classical music and all things Celtic, and has a habit of mixing these into her stories along with other topics and enthusiasms that capture her interest. Formerly, as an executive with a global health advocacy organization, she traveled extensively throughout the world. Currently, as a native Vermonter, she hates to leave home during foliage season.

Also Available: The Conor McBride Series

Shop local! Order paperbacks from your favorite indie bookstore.
Or, order autographed paperbacks from the author:
https://squareup.com/market/kathryn-guare
eBooks available at Amazon.com

CPSIA information can be obtained
at www.ICGtesting.com
Printed in the USA
FFHW020637180319
51124357-56563FF